With or Wi

Nora flicked the flashlight on and off quickly, strobing the room so that she could see the activities in the darkness. My eyes took in images – flash! – a woman between two men. Flash! Three women together in a row, licking and kissing one another. Flash! A man pressing a woman up against the grey stone wall. All of these interactions were taking place without the aid of light. I saw that the floor was carpeted in a silky-looking rug. Thin pillows were scattered about, but no beds, nothing hazardous for people to trip over. At the flickering light, the lovers all looked our way.

Nora clicked off the flashlight and pushed me back up the stairs. She'd seen what she wanted. She'd made her own decisions. Now, she was ready to go home. I'd seen more than I'd bargained for. Images like artwork remained emblazoned in my mind. While Nora lost herself in mental plans of her future clubs, I walked back down those cold stone steps, over and over again, poised on the brink of action before turning back each and every time.

By the same author:

SWEET THING

STICKY FINGERS

RUMOURS

TIFFANY TWISTED

With or Without You

Alison Tyler

In real life, always practise safe sex.

First published in 2006 by
Cheek
Thames Wharf Studios
Rainville Road
London W6 9HA

Typeset by SetSystems Ltd, Saffron Walden, Essex

Printed and bound by Mackays of Chatham PLC

ISBN 0 352 34065 7
ISBN 9 780352 34065 8

*All characters in this publication are fictitious and any resemblance
to real persons, living or dead, is purely coincidental.*

Dedicated to SAM

'Life imitates art far more than art imitates life.'

Oscar Wilde

ThePinkFedora.blogspot.com

Hello my hat-wearing hotties,

This is Nora Hammond with some delicious news! Unfortunately, we have lost Vladimir Danielson, my right-hand man and chief bartender for the past six years. I can't say I'm not sad to see him go, yet Vlad is moving on to his own night-time talk show on the Bijoux Network. I wish him only the best of luck with his burgeoning career.

Of course, this means that his spot is open, and I'm hoping to have some fun with a new show of our own. The Pink Fedora will be hosting a stimulating new reality show. Twelve applicants start – one is left at the end. And this one lucky person, male or female, will embark on the wildest career I can imagine.

During Vlad's reign, he posed naked in two ladies' magazines, created his own romantic cocktails recipe book, and served as the honoured judge in several international mixologist competitions.

Do you have what it takes to step into Vlad's trademark scarlet eel-skin boots? If so, respond to our call for contestants. It's all happening at the Pink Fedora, the last Friday in October, and we'll be having a blast, with or without you. Check out the Call for Contestants below. Click here to print official invitation with details of time, date and address for the hottest event this Halloween.

Kisses,

Nora

Quote for the Day: As Janis Joplin said, 'I'm saving the bass player for Omaha.'

** Call for Contestants **

The Pink Fedora, the internationally hip nightclub known for non-stop naughtiness and raucous recreation, is currently searching for a new head bartender. Duties include running a nightly crew of twelve, creating an ever-changing bar menu and pampering Hollywood's exotic elite.

As the Pink Fedora isn't your average nightclub, the application process isn't your average job interview. In order for us to locate the perfect person for this position, we've joined the Bijoux Network to create a brand new reality show: You Can Leave Your Hat On.

Open-minded insomniacs are encouraged to apply. Applicants should prepare:

- *the recipe for your favourite sexy drink*
- *a creative bit of bar-house banter*
- *and your favourite happy hour story to share.*

Email headshot and résumé to pinkfedora@blogspot.com

All who enter must be at least 21 years of age. But you were all smart enough to figure that out already, weren't you?

Posted @ 21:59 (6 comments)

JLK said: What do contestants wear?
Nora Hammond said: If you have to ask, you shouldn't come.
Marvellous Marguerite said: What's the pay?
Nora Hammond said: Money, fame and love. Not necessarily in that order.
EleanorJRomano said: Are you serious, Nora? A *reality* show –
Nora Hammond said: Would I lie to you, Eli?

Prologue

'Sweet,' Byron whispered in a low voice, his lips pressed against the side of my neck. 'You're so damn sweet.'

He moved slowly, kissing his way to my mouth, then holding me tightly in a firm embrace, so that I could feel his muscular chest and, lower, his hips against mine. I looked up at him and, although I wasn't the slightest bit cold, a shiver worked throughout my body. We kept the apartment deliciously warm now, at the start of fall. Yes, California generally boasts mild autumn weather. But Byron had undoubtedly turned the heat on when he'd gotten home, preparing for this, our weekly tryst.

Still holding me in his arms, he kissed me again, first gently, then with a slowly increasing passion. His lips pressed against my own, and once more I trembled at his touch. Even after four years together, he knew how to make me dissolve into pleasure. My body responded beat for beat with the motions of his fingertips, as his strong hands ran up and down my back. Up and down, stroking and caressing.

All week long, I'd been thinking of this night. When Thursday morning finally arrived, I'd put extra care into my outfit, choosing my favourite pair of black panties from the dark sea of ebony lingerie in my underwear drawer. Black on black. My best friend Nora couldn't stand my underwear drawer. 'Why don't you have any crimson? Any chartreuse? You adore art so much. You love colour.'

I do appreciate colour, but on canvases, not myself. Besides, black panty sets are part of my standard attire.

I've always been a slave to routine, if nothing else. Part of me hated the fact that Thursday had become our evening to make love, but part of me relished the regularity. So what if we were paint-by-the-numbers when it came to sex? The satisfaction was as intense as it had been the first time we'd ever been together.

With our living room lights turned off, the exotic glow to the room came solely from the sunset. Pinks, reds and golds shimmered across the sky, thick bands of colour that disappeared into the horizon.

'God, you feel good.'

I looked into Byron's grey eyes and, as always, I thought of storm skies, or silver-tipped clouds moving across a pale twilight backdrop, thought of the paintings by Gerhard Richter, one grey monochrome after another. Grey taking on a deeper beauty than an entire rainbow of hues. I was down to my simple panties and bra, feeling sexy and in control, when he flipped me around, so that now I was facing out of our windows, looking down at the ocean eighteen floors below.

The ocean mesmerised me as I watched the waves fold over on each other. Foam met the sand and slid back into the sea. It was calming. Something predictable. Something I could count on.

Quickly, Byron got on his knees in front of me. I gazed down at him, wondering what was going on. My mouth was open to ask, but he shook his head and put one finger to his lips, letting me know that he had a plan, that I should trust him. When he slid my panties aside and brought his mouth to the split of my body, I gasped. *This* wasn't part of our normal routine. Generally, after work on Thursdays, we met in the living room and had sex. Always on Thursday evenings at the same time. Always in the living room, exactly the same way. Just like that 1960s Batman television cartoon – 'Same bat time, same bat channel.'

But tonight Byron was behaving in a far more ravenous manner. His tongue slid in slow erotic circles, exactly where I craved, and I placed my hands securely against the plate-glass window and sighed. The pleasure was intense, so much so that my legs started to tremble. Sure, we had engaged in oral sex every once in awhile, but not often enough for me to grow accustomed to how it felt, and never with me standing and Byron on his knees like this. I gave myself over to the sensation, my palms flat on the window, Byron's own hands around my waist, pulling me forcefully against him.

I could come like this, I thought, and the concept startled me. I usually climaxed with Byron, but only if he stroked my clit while he took me, the combination of being filled and being touched working to push me over the edge. And then there were my fantasies, visions I'd never confess to Byron, stories I told myself while we were fucking to take me over the edge.

This was different. Everything about this situation worked to thrust me off balance. Every motion of his mouth made me feel as if I might actually liquefy, melt away into nothing. But I didn't complain. I didn't say a word. I felt almost as if I were lost in a dream. If I made an unexpected sound, or an unplanned movement, the whole scenario might disappear, fold over itself like the foam of the waves, leaving me all alone. So I did my best to remain entirely still, concentrating every nerve of my body on the novel feeling of Byron's tongue slipping against me.

Around and around his tongue went, those overlapping circles making my heart race. The pleasure radiated outwards, and I thought of the artwork of Kandinsky – *Circles in a Circle* – exploding circles of different colours. Overlapping. Bursting.

In every aspect of my life I possess a corresponding image of art.

When the climax rushed through me, I would have lost my balance if Byron hadn't been supporting me with his hands. I closed my eyes tightly for a moment, wracked with pleasure, barely aware of when Byron stood up. My eyelids flickered and I had one glimpse of his mouth, glossy with my own shiny juices, before he moved behind me and slipped his cock inside me.

He took me like that, with his body hard behind mine, his hands gripping on to my slim waist. I felt the heat of his breath on the back of my neck, and I moaned softly – one of the first sounds I'd made all evening. Byron rocked back and forth, moving to the rhythm of the music on the stereo – U2 tonight, U2 as always on the nights that I chose. His hands roamed over my small breasts, his thumbs brushing against my nipples.

The sun had started to sink into the ocean only moments before, and now the sky was turning purple. There were people down below, walking, rollerblading and biking on the concrete path that snakes along the crescent of the beach. I wondered how many of them had just made love. How many more would go home to lovers tonight, partners waiting to give them pleasure like Byron was giving me? I liked the thought. In a city as large as Los Angeles, at any given moment, there must be scores of other people doing exactly the same thing that we were doing ourselves.

Some might find that intrusive or disturbing. I found comfort in the thought.

I couldn't have admitted it to Byron, but the concept of what other people do in the privacy of their own homes has never failed to turn me on. I suppose that makes me a bit of a voyeur. And the fact that we were making love in a floor-to-ceiling window made me a bit of an exhibitionist, as well. Even if nobody could see. Even if those tiny people down below would only receive the final crimson glare of the sunset mirrored back were they to look up at us.

I wondered what Byron was thinking about. We'd never spent much time discussing fantasies. But I suppose he had his own little visions in his mind, because as he came, thrusting hard, breathing harder, he said, 'I love you.'

'I love you, too,' I murmured. Just like I did every other Thursday night.

'I love you so much.' His body pumped, hips arched. 'Oh, God, Gwen, so fucking much.'

Nice thought, that.

Except for the fact that my name is Eleanor.

Chapter One

Words are my life. I write, translate, edit, revise. In my world, words have a heartbeat. They live and breathe. I strongly believe that once a word is said aloud, it can never be taken back. For this reason, I am generally in complete control of my words, and this is why it was so fucking awkward when Byron left me speechless.

After the unceremonious ending to our lovemaking, I locked Byron out of the bathroom while I cleaned myself, refusing to talk to him, to listen to his explanations shouted through the bathroom door. I took the longest shower of my life, even standing under the spray when the water finally faded from scalding to lukewarm to chilly. Then, showered and dressed, I sat in the very centre of our sofa smelling of soap and talcum powder. But still, I felt dirty. It would take more than a Silkwood shower to make me feel clean.

Byron stood before me in his long navy-blue silk robe, a present I'd given him the previous Christmas. The robe boasted a Superman logo on the back, as if the wearer were some sort of comic book hero, rather than the bastard he'd just revealed himself to be. Byron was doing his best to explain that calling me by his boss's name had simply been an innocent slip of the tongue.

Slip of the tongue.

As soon he said the words, he winced, understanding that his tongue had been slipping up and over my clit only an hour before. That perhaps this particular turn of phrase wasn't the most thoughtful.

I felt my eyes glaze over as he continued with his monologue. Although he wasn't cheating on me, it *was* true that he wanted to break up with me. Tonight's after-work romp had been his way of saying goodbye. I stared at him, feeling something akin to revulsion. Unfortunately, he seemed to take my silence as an indication that he should continue to talk, when, in reality, all I wanted him to do was shut up.

Byron spoke broadly, motioning with outstretched arms to nothing in particular, as if inviting our sofa, or fireplace, or framed art prints to join in the conversation. A lawyer, Byron's given to theatrical gestures, and I watched as he kept track of his movements in the gold-framed mirror above the mantle. Did he always need to look at himself in the mirror? His well-manicured hands reached beseechingly forwards, in a manner that he often employed when approaching a jury. Addressing me now, he used a voice vibrating with tender feeling. 'It's not that I don't love you, Eleanor.'

I clenched my bottom lip between my teeth, sensing what was coming, but not being able to fully believe he would actually say the words. I found myself dreading the very sound of his modulated breathing as he prepared to speak.

'It's just that I'm not *in* love with you any more.'

I despise clichés. At any other moment, I would have wished for a red Sharpie pen to strike through that line. But as he spoke, this cliché took on a personal meaning, and words – which I have always trusted more than any human being – failed me.

Silent, I stared past Byron and out of the window to the ocean. I found it somehow easier if I didn't have to look directly at him. From our eighteenth-floor apartment, the waves glittered in the moonlight, turning to silver as the foam broke over the sand. I wished desperately that I were down there on the beach, feeling the water on my bare feet, no matter how cold. Perhaps the cold would wake me up. This had to be a nightmare.

When Byron finally paused, I took a deep breath, let it out, and finally whispered, 'But you *do* love Gwen?' Even as the question escaped my lips, a small voice in my head asked: Do you really want to know? He's leaving you. Why he's leaving doesn't matter, does it?

'You must have sensed the end was coming. You must have known that something was wrong between us.'

I tilted my head to the side, aware that I was mimicking the look our canary gives me at feeding time. Was he actually calling me a fool for missing the signs? *What* signs? This evening his mouth had been pressed between my spread thighs. His tongue had made those delicious circles up and around, leaving me shaking. How could he possibly have thought that one last time together would somehow soften the blow?

The buzzer sounded and Byron, who had now begun pacing nervously from the fireplace to the kidney-shaped glass coffee table, perked up visibly at the chance to leave the room. I remained seated, aware of the soft velvet sofa cushions beneath me, the loud ticking of the grandfather clock in the hall. The sense of impending doom made me feel as if I were a part of a soap opera, one that I could not escape from by simply changing the channel.

Byron called out from the hallway, 'For you, Eleanor. This guy needs your signature.'

I stood slowly and walked down the cream-coloured carpet to the front door. A man in an all-brown uniform stood outside, saying, 'Package, lady, and boy is this bitch ever heavy.' He had a gruff, not unkind face, and I wondered fleetingly if he could see the tears in the corners of my eyes. But no, the man handed over a clipboard and turned towards Byron to discuss the recent respite from La Niña. I felt suddenly exhausted as I printed my name neatly on one line and signed just as neatly below. Eleanor Jane Romano. *Romano.* It would never be Eleanor Jane Millman. I would never be Byron's wife.

The deliveryman, expanding waist neatly encased in a thick leather support belt, grunted as he lifted the box.

Byron pointed to the small table in the front hallway, and the man lugged in the package and set it down heavily. He paused in front of me for a moment, looking down at the clipboard and reading my signature. 'Have a good evening, Ms Ramiro.' Then he slammed his way out of the door before I could correct him. Ramiro. Romano. What did it matter, anyway?

I waited in silence. The package held little appeal, but continuing the conversation with Byron held even less. I had to go to the kitchen for something with which to open the box. Tweety chirped happily as I rummaged through the junk drawer until I found the utility scissors. Back in the hall, I cut through the thick twine that wrapped the box and then through several layers of heavy butcher paper. Even when the cardboard itself was exposed, I had to jam the blade of the scissors through multiple layers of heavily veined packing tape. Byron stood to the side, watching me intently. Apparently, he had no fear of being near me and a sharp object at this point, although I seethed with a quiet rage.

I felt oddly ineffective as I dug through the packaging materials, letting the Styrofoam peanuts spill out of the box and onto the floor. Finally, with what seemed like Herculean effort, I had the box half-emptied. Inside was a pot. I could see it through the last thin layer of packing plastic. Once I cut through the final skin of bubble wrap, I exposed the large earthenware urn with painted designs around the rim, now faded with age. The top of the pot was covered and tightly sealed with some heavy-duty substance. I touched the surface to discover more clay, layers and layers of clay, followed by a thick coating of glaze. There were no cracks in the pot or in the covering. I let my fingers wander over the clay, feeling the smoothness of the glaze, broken by indents where designs had been inlaid.

With even more effort, I pulled the urn entirely out of the box and set it on the table, knocking the cardboard box to the floor. Then, momentarily forgetting Byron even existed, I took a step back to look at it and realised where I'd seen pots like this before: at ARTSI, the Art, Research, Translation, Science Institute where I work. Although the museum portion of our institute is smaller than places like the Getty or the LA County Museum of Art, our private funding has provided us with several lovely pieces from antiquity.

Byron stood at my side, amidst the abundance of tiny white Styrofoam packing peanuts. 'Who's it from?' he asked curiously.

I bent down and dug my hand inside the box, feeling around for a letter. Byron took a step forwards and flipped over the top of the box. There, imbedded beneath more layers of clear packing tape, was a packing slip. I picked up the stainless steel scissors again and cut through the surface, then pulled out a folded piece of paper.

While Byron watched, I stared at the letter through squinted eyes, not wanting to go in search of my reading glasses. 'It's from my great-aunt,' I said, softly. 'She willed it to me.'

'But what *is* it?' Byron insisted.

All the letter said was that the pot was mine, willed to me by my great-aunt Rose. The lawyer's letter was carefully typed, and attached to it, with a paper clip, was a faded handwritten note. I brought the note closer and tried to decipher my aunt's barely legible scrawl. Byron continued to investigate the pot, touching it, stroking it. I wanted to tell him to keep his hands to himself, but I just didn't have the energy. Not until he said, 'Shit, Nellie, it looks like a port-a-potty. Something you'd bring with you when you go out camping.'

'It's an urn,' I said, my voice hostile. 'My aunt knows – I mean, knew – I studied things like this, that I would never be able to have something like this for myself.'

Actually, no one really has things like this for themselves. Not any more. All ancient artefacts of this quality are in museums. It's always been a cause for some heated arguments in my family. My great-aunt was an avid traveller and collector, an adventurous archaeologist who funded her own excavations and occasionally kept the best treasures for herself. When family members urged her to give up her prized loot that lay scattered around her cavernous mansion, she said, in a voice roughened by years of smoking, 'Nonsense. Everything is stolen. The Elgin Marbles. The Rosetta Stone. Some of the most beautiful artwork in the world was taken by thieves in the night. Why should I give my art to museums? Should the museums give back all of their stolen art? And give it back to whom? The creators are long dead. Wouldn't they want the person who would most appreciate their artwork to keep it safe?'

I was still reading the letter when Byron's cellphone rang. He slid it out of his briefcase and checked the ID, then quickly tucked the phone away again, unable to hide the guilty look on his face as he did so. I knew without thinking that the call was from Gwen. I knew without understanding exactly how that the whole monologue he'd given me for the past half-hour had been a fantasy.

Without looking at Byron, I turned on my heel and headed down the hallway.

It was time to start packing.

Byron didn't seem to expect that. I don't know why – I don't know what he thought I'd do after he told me we were through. He watched me the way people watch accidents here in LA. Not offering any help, simply gazing as I grabbed a few different belongings and shoved them into my suitcase.

I stalked to the dresser and filled my small embroidered jewellery box with the few scattered gold earrings, antique brooches and delicate golden bracelets that lay on the glass top. I left behind any gift he had ever given me, taking only those items that were of family value or given to me by friends. Byron meant nothing. History meant everything.

'Listen –' he started.

I wheeled on him again, tossing the jewellery box into the bag and fastening the suitcase shut. 'I don't want to know what you did, or why you did it. I just want you to get out of my way.'

'Look,' Byron said next, and I had to physically push him away as I moved down the hall, glancing into our home office but deciding not to stop for the books. I could have them sent later, or have movers come and pack them for me. I paused only to pick up my laptop. I carefully zipped the machine into its sleek red case – a gift from my ultra-hip best friend Nora – then slipped the bag over my shoulder and hefted up my suitcase again. I took both bags to the front of the apartment. Byron continued to trail after me, sputtering gibberish.

'You can't just walk out of here. Talk to me. We need to make a plan. Who gets what. Who moves out. We need to discuss the situation, like adults.'

I whirled around on him. 'Discuss it? Discuss what? *You* are breaking up with *me*.'

He hesitated, looking at me in alarm. But once I started, I found myself unable to stop.

'Why are you freaking out now? Because *I'm* angry? Did you need to control the whole situation, Byron? Couldn't you have at least let me experience it in my own fucking way?'

I'd never sworn at him before. After working for so many years in a museum – before college, during college and after – I have hardly ever raised my voice from that hushed tone reserved for keeping other people quiet. A library voice. It suits me. Now, I found great pleasure in raising the volume.

'But where will you go?' he asked as I pushed past him.

'Don't,' I told him. 'Just don't. Don't pretend you care.'

I still felt ill at the fact that he'd been on me hours before. Knowing the whole time that we were through, he'd still wanted one last fuck – I shook my head. I couldn't even bear to think about it. I had my suitcase and my laptop, and now I needed to leave.

'You tell Gwen when she calls again that you're all hers.'

'Gwen,' he said, still trying to pretend that there was nothing there. 'Come on, Eleanor –'

'Stop,' I said, a coldness building inside of me.

He did. That guilty look I'd seen before flickered across his face once more. In a flash, I remembered all the different times she'd called. Work, he'd always say. But hadn't I wondered? Hadn't I told myself not to go down that route, not to worry? Even when I'd heard gossip at his office, people talking when I walked past, hadn't I pushed that out of my head, as well? Late nights at the office. Calls he'd go outside to take. It all made sense now.

I turned to leave, and then spun back around to face him, unable to keep myself from adding a parting shot, 'And, let me tell you, Byron, from what I know about Gwen, this little fling you're having will be over within the week.'

He didn't deny it this time. He simply stared at me. For the first time, I looked into his grey eyes and saw nothing. Not storm clouds. Not silver skies. Not paintings by an abstract artist. Instead, I saw an empty hollow. A cement sidewalk. Then, I continued, my voice steady but loud. I could feel my back molars clenched together and I relished the thought of chewing up each word and spitting it out at him. Words can hurt. I've always known that. I've never doubted their power. 'I've seen people like her in action, Byron. They like danger. They like creating chaos. Think about it. What did she talk about when she fucked you? Did she whisper about how dangerous your liaison was? About what might happen if the two of you got caught? She's a calculating, conniving cunt.'

I saw in his washed-out grey eyes that I'd hurt him. It gave me a spark of pleasure that was an entirely new sensation. Joy at someone else's pain. Who would ever have thought this sort of thing would give me happiness. Bitter happiness, perhaps. But an evil glee, nonetheless. Byron came a step closer, dullness falling away as his own anger was revealed. What did he have to be angry about? The fact that I was right? He caught me by the shoulder and held on.

'You're wrong.'

I shrugged him away and moved down the hall. 'Gwen likes the unattainable. Fucking you while you were mine gave her what she needed. Come on, Byron. You're a second-rate lawyer who's come pretty far without a lot of talent. You dress nicely and you have great hair. Really you do. But what else have you got?'

I'd hit him where it hurt, and I could tell.

Bravo, I said to myself.

'Bitch!' Byron yelled, grabbing at me again. He missed and came forwards, his open hand swinging, catching hard on the side of my head. Had he meant to hit me? I don't know. I'll never know for sure. But I stumbled from the blow and turned on him, hissing, 'I always thought deep down that you were nice. That's the one thing I always thought.' It's why I'd stayed. I was nice, and he was nice, and that little fantasy was gone like smoke. I was at him, now too, dropping the suitcase, my hands not outstretched and clawlike, but balled into fists. If I were going to fight him, then I meant to do it for real.

Byron stepped back, grabbing my wrists to hold them away from his body. Adrenaline coursed through me. With almost no effort at all, I got free and picked up my suitcase, but it was too heavy. I swung my computer bag instead, aiming for his head. In a movie, I'd have connected – I knew exactly how that would have felt, the satisfaction that the impact would have given me. In real life, I missed, and in the after-swing knocked the urn from the hallway table. The pot should have hit the thick creamy carpet and bounced, rolling gently to a stop against the wall.

It didn't.

Nothing was going right. My computer case, heavy with the PowerBook inside, swung the pot hard enough so that it slammed directly into the wall. And shattered.

Chapter Two

I don't know how I got to Nora's house. I have no memory of the drive, zero recall whatsoever. Somehow I managed to climb into my little red Toyota Prius, to place my suitcase and laptop on the passenger seat and back out of the tight parking space without hitting any nearby parked cars, a feat that's not so easy even when one is in total control. Apparently, in my dreamy state, I was able to pause at the mandatory stoplights decorating Ocean Boulevard, to weave my way through the congested evening traffic, a bumper-to-bumper carpet with everyone jostling to get home at once. I'm probably lucky to be alive, although 'lucky' wasn't a correct description of how I felt. People on the verge of breakdowns should not be allowed near motor vehicles. There ought to be some sort of test, like the blood/alcohol exam. If you are 1.98 per cent upset, you should have a designated driver.

Honestly, I don't even remember leaving the apartment. Once the ancient urn broke, my memory seemed to have gone with it. All I know is that I sort of 'came to' outside Nora's pink stucco Spanish-style Venice Beach bungalow, and that I found myself pounding hard on the window of her bedroom, knowing full well that Nora generally wakes up long after the sun goes down.

In order to gain access, I'd have to compete with her high-end headset and whatever newly fashionable band was playing on her NanoPod. Nora knows what's hot. She always has. It's why she's often invited to guest write a Top Ten List for our local alternative weekly, why she was profiled in one of my favourite women's magazines, why her hair colour changes as frequently as her mood. Upbeat? She might be sporting violet or fuchsia spikes. Pensive? She'll go for dark forest green. In love – or, more likely – lust? Crimson, as you might guess. At this point, I don't think she even knows what her true colour is any more.

I pounded harder on the window, praying that she was there by herself and not in bed with some drummer who'd stopped by to jam at her club the previous evening and ended up going home with her for a midnight snack. I knew that she'd be shocked to find me standing there in the plum-coloured dark, rumpled, angry, broken. I looked down to discover that in my haste to leave the apartment, I had managed to put on two different shoes – one flat, one with a slight heel, both sensible but mismatched nonetheless – and then I cupped my hands against the glass and peered hard inside.

Yes, she was in there – but as I stared into the dimly lit room, my heart sank. I wasn't competing with her headset alone. As I'd feared, she was on the bed in a clinch with a musician I recognised as one of her favourite playmates. There, on her low Japanese-style bed, were two specimens of sexual beauty: Nora and her man, a rumpled rose-hued sheet doing nothing to hide his fine muscular ass and strong back. He had several scrawling tattoos decorating his arms, and next to the bed was a battered guitar case, stickered all over with decals of skulls, roses, devils and angry messages.

So she hadn't fucked the drummer. She was fucking the bass player.

In true Nora style, the pair had on matching headsets, which was why she hadn't heard my pounding. A different sort of pounding took over now – the sound of my own heartbeat in my ears. Unable to look away, I watched as my friend moved sinuously beneath her most recent conquest. Was she moving to the beat of the music? Or to the pulsing rhythm of her own libido?

Why couldn't I look away?

Dean pushed up with his powerful arms, and I stared,

transfixed, as he thrust his hips forwards, his unbelievable ass looking like an advertisement for some new workout device. I could see now why Nora opened her bedroom door to him. God, they were sexy. At any other time, I would have turned my head, hurried off to lick my wounds in some dark corner. But I wasn't myself at all now, and I simply stood and stared, witnessing what I knew was a deeply private act, yet one I found myself drawn to view.

Was this art in motion? In my opinion it was.

Dean moved like a machine, up and down, and then he swivelled his hips and the sheet fell the rest of the way onto the floor. I now saw that Nora wasn't entirely naked. She had on a pair of fishnets the colour of a dark-red wine. The stockings made her legs look endless and, when she suddenly wrapped her legs around Dean's waist, I noted the high-heeled patent-leather shoes she was wearing. I recognised the pair – had been with her when she'd bought them, marvelling at the way she strode around the store in the four-inch heels. Had she put them on for this moment, playing a sexy dress-up game for her man, or had the two been so desperate to connect that she hadn't had time to take them off?

I'd never done a striptease for Byron, didn't own a pair of fancy stockings. Was that why I was standing out here, looking in? If I'd been more adventurous, would we still be together? Did Gwen like to play dress-up games? I worked hard to shut the door on those mental queries. I couldn't deal with those thoughts at a time like this.

Dean rotated his hips again, and I could almost feel him move against me, as if I'd magically taken Nora's place on the mattress beneath him. He was strikingly handsome, with his long rock 'n' roll hair loose down his back, his jaw like rock. I couldn't see his eyes, but I knew that they were almost black, as dark as his hair. He and Nora moved together, and I imagined that they were listening to the same band on their headsets. Wouldn't be a group I would choose, I was sure. They weren't listening to Sting, were they? No, something about the way they were moving told me that they'd be tuned into Nine Inch Nails or Nickleback. A hard sound to match the intensity of their motions.

As Dean pounded forwards, I sucked in my breath, wishing I were the one on the mattress beneath him. Wishing I were as free as Nora with my sexual whims. But could I ever be in such an erotic scenario without feeling as if I were playing a role? Nora likes to share her sexual stories with me – but this was different. I was watching for myself, seeing her throw her head back, seeing her headset come off with the motion, then seeing her large eyes open as she met my own gaze and shrieked.

Oh, damn, I thought, ducking back down.

Only moments before, I'd wanted her to see me, but now everything had changed. What to do? Nora had just caught me staring at her while she made love, and I had no excuse as to why I was there. My mind raced as Nora hurled herself across the room and raised the window with a 'What the fuck is wrong with you?' howl that died when she saw me standing there like some pitiful alley cat. The only thing missing at this point was a sudden rainstorm. Then I'd be truly bedraggled.

'Sorry,' I said, knowing I sounded like an idiot.

'Oh, Christ, Eleanor. I didn't realise it was you. I just saw a shadow against the glass and thought there was a peeping Tom out there.'

Even in my haze, I registered the thought that Nora had decided to confront a peeping Tom rather than call the cops. That's her style.

'You OK?' she continued, asking the question before she could stop herself. At no other time in our friendship had I banged on her bedroom window. If I were OK, I would not have been standing in her side yard. We both knew that. Still, I shook my head.

'Of course, you're not.' She could tell that from where she stood, peering out at me, beautiful as always in spite of her shock, confident in spite of being more than halfway naked. Concern showed fully in her face. In my everyday life, I'm as predictable as one might imagine. To find me breaking any sort of social rule meant something had gone wildly wrong in my world.

'Come in,' she said. 'You have to come in.'

I nodded this time and, for a split second, I imagined climbing in through her bedroom window and collapsing on her mattress, curling myself into a fetal position and letting every bit of sorrow pour from me. I saw myself crying until my eyes were as pink as Nora's stucco bungalow and my shirt was wet from my tears. Pulling myself into the window would have been a reverse of what Nora had done to escape her bedroom back in high school. She loves to tell the story of the time she got locked out and had to sleep under the window box, praying that she'd be able to sneak in undiscovered once her mother had brought in the morning paper.

As Nora motioned for me to go around to the front of the house, I saw Dean slipping his headset back on and leaning back against the mattress. He didn't seem put out at all by the shift in events. But maybe that's because he'd already come.

Chapter Three

'What happened?' Nora asked, pouring herself a cup of turbo coffee and me a shot of undeniably excellent whisky. With Nora, everything is the best, from her 400-thread count Egyptian sheets to her imported Viennese espresso beans. She had on a turquoise robe now, one that looked to be silk and was most likely more expensive than most of my best dresses.

'We're through,' I said.

'For real?'

I nodded.

'You're definitely not going back?' she demanded. As if on cue, my cellphone rang, punctuating her words. We both stared at my red computer bag, and when I didn't make a reach for it, Nora did. She held up the phone in front of me, as if this were a test, letting me see the call coming in was from Byron.

'No,' I told her forcefully, pushing the phone away. 'Never. We're done.'

'Good, I always hated the fucker.' She thrust the phone unanswered back into my case.

I couldn't help but laugh at the malice in her words. I knew that she and Byron didn't get along, but I wouldn't have guessed at the intensity of her feeling. Now, I understood that she meant every word.

'But what happened? What made you leave tonight?'

'Gwen.' I only had to say the name, and Nora instantly grimaced. Gwen is a casting director's dream lawyer. Meaning, she looks like a lawyer the way that Heather Locklear looks like your average advertising executive or Penelope Cruz resembles any doctor you may ever have had the luck to meet. She boasts classic blonde hair, bronze skin, almond-shaped eyes and a starlet's body. Put her on a beach in a red string bikini, and you've got an extra for *Baywatch*.

'Really?' she asked, wrinkling her nose in surprise. 'I thought he was only rambling on his blog about her. I never thought he meant anything by it.'

'You what?'

'Don't you read his blog, Eli? He's been talking about Gwen since she joined the firm last spring.'

I shrugged. 'I read it sometimes,' I told her, which was the truth. I didn't want to admit that I only read Nora's blog occasionally as well. The Pink Fedora blog chronicles a behind-the-scenes look at the clubs she owns. I joined in with other people who posted in responses every once in awhile. I'd teased her recently about her upcoming reality show, posting to her blog rather than coming right out and saying that I thought the idea was surreal. Nora's actually signed a deal in which contestants will vie for a spot as head bartender at her club. I couldn't help myself but join in on the comments.

But in general, reading other people's blogs seems far too invasive. Sure, this is coming from someone who just witnessed her best friend making love, but that's not my normal style. My favourite story about blogs came from the Talking Heads' lead singer David Byrne. *Esquire* magazine awarded him an ESKY for best blog, and he related a tale about a friend of his who had run into another blogger. When the friend asked how the person was doing, she indignantly replied, 'Don't you read my blog?' Byrne said that if he ever got to that point, *Esquire* should feel free to rescind the ESKY.

I love that philosophy.

Unfortunately, I'm one of the last people in LA *not* to have a blog. My hairdresser has one. The guy who runs the Roach Coach that parks outside ARTSI at lunch everyday has one. The last valet attendant who parked my car actually left a business card tucked into my never-used ashtray that featured information about *his* blog. But friends' blogs are the worst, because friends can find out if you don't keep up with the drama of their daily lives.

Maybe I don't want to know when Nora's jonesing for a hot session with her Adonis-like bouncer, he of the chiselled jaw and iron pecs. Maybe I was never overly impressed by Byron's play by play of every case he ever won. Or his bitch fests in regards to the few cases he lost. Or his weekend discussions about his tennis matches in which he analysed every single shot.

'Seriously,' Nora said. 'He would just wax poetic about her. Her eyes. Her clothes. Her style.'

'You're kidding me.'

This actually *was* news. How had I missed it? I didn't read all of his entries, but shouldn't I have at least picked up a clue or two about this sort of thing? Did I live in a fantasy world, surrounded by antiques all day, able to understand items from thousands of years ago but not to see the plain truth when it was right in front of my eyes?

Nora seemed to think so.

She shot me a look and then reached for her laptop. When she opened the computer up on the coffee table, I saw that she was already online. I gave her a quizzical stare, and she shook her head at me. 'Airport, of course,' she explained with a sigh.

I nodded. That's right. Nora's online anywhere in the house. She also has a version of airport at the club, so that people can check their email or surf the internet wherever they are. With a few simple keystrokes, she'd pulled up Byron's blog, ingeniously titled 'Byronsblog', and then she scrolled down the entries until she found the following:

With a fierce look in her bright blue eyes, Gwen Roberts paced before the stand. Her body language let the jurors know that she meant business. And believe me she did.

'He fancies himself to be another John Grisham or Scott Turow,' Nora said with a cynical smile. 'But he's just one more in a long line of legal hacks, huh?'

I didn't respond. I couldn't believe I'd missed this.

Gwen, outstanding in a form-fitting suit of pale cream, refused to back down from her fierce line of questioning.

'See? He's got a rep on the word "fierce."' Nora knows how I feel about word repetitions. 'Don't look so down, Eli. You have to really read it to get that he was fantasising about her, because those sorts of descriptions are all embedded in information about court trials.' She glanced at the screen with a scowl before flicking her computer shut with a resounding click. Then she looked at me, her gaze fully sympathetic. I could tell that she was ready to listen, but I didn't know where to start.

Finally, I found my voice. 'What on earth were you doing reading Byron's blog?' There had to be a million other blogs in Southern California alone that were more interesting than the one penned by my recent ex. Even the one by the valet attendant – which I had skimmed, myself, and which was like a verbal orgasm about the makes of the different cars he parked – would have been time better spent in my opinion.

Nora shrugged. 'You know me. Insomnia. I read everything in the wee hours of the morning, when the club's closed and there aren't any cute boys to play with.' She was being self-deprecating. As the owner of the Pink Fedora, on the outskirts of the Hollywood Hills, Nora has access to many cute boys. Her club is an ultra-hip A-list-only nightspot where people like me would have no hope of getting in if we weren't put on the guest list. 'Plus, I'm nosy,' she continued. 'I like to know what's going on with my friends. And since you don't have your own blog ...' She gave me a look of total incredulity, but I just shrugged. What on earth would I write about? Immersing myself in yet another phone-book-sized tome on ancient artefacts? Aside from me, and maybe four other intellectual snobs on the planet, who would want to read about that?

There was a grunt from Nora's bedroom, and she got up and quietly closed the violet-shellacked door to the hall. 'Dean and I were up far too late,' she explained. 'Or far too early.' She gave me a little half-smile that managed to look slightly guilty and devilish at the same time. 'We'll just let him sleep in before turning him loose.' She spoke as if he were some wild animal she had taken in and fed. And then I remembered meeting Dean at the club one night and seeing him play in his band One Plus None, and I realised that description suited him. On stage, he *was* an animal – and I'd seen for myself that he was also one in bed.

'I'm sorry about that,' I said, gesturing to the hall, letting her know how awkward I felt for having watched her.

'Don't worry about it. I'd never have heard the front door bell.'

I nodded. I knew that. I'd tried that first.

'Still,' I said, thinking I should at least attempt an explanation, but Nora held up her hand. She didn't need any more from me. I could tell from the look in her eyes as she stared at me, running a hand through her short electric blue-tipped hair as she did.

'So what are you going to do?' Her voice was kind, her jade eyes sad.

I gazed down again at my mismatched shoes, then polished off the glass of whisky. Yes, this was the good stuff. So smooth I could hardly imagine the type of hangover the amber liquid would leave behind as a memory.

'I mean, aside from moving in with me.'

'No, I can't.'

'Of course you can,' she insisted. Another grunt came from down the hall. 'Besides, where else are you going to find all the excess men you'll need to sleep with in order to erase the very existence of Byron from your mind forever?'

I smiled at her. Nora always knows the right thing to say.

'You think I'm kidding.'

'Nora,' I started, 'you know me.'

'I *do* know you. I know that you've been wasting yourself on an unappreciative numbskull for four years. The man wasn't even worth a second date, Eleanor. I don't know why it took you so long to see that. He was jealous of you, hated when you succeeded.'

I started to try to explain, to defend myself but Nora interrupted.

'And I also know that the best way to get over heart-break is to fuck the pain away.'

She was quoting one of her favourite songs, and I knew it. But still I was unprepared for her taking me by the hand and leading me towards the hallway door.

'Come on, Nora,' I told her, starting to feel nervous. 'I can't.'

'You don't have to do anything,' she said. 'You just have to relax. And trust me.'

As she spoke the words, she led me down the hall to her bedroom. Dean was still sprawled on the mattress, but his headset was off and he looked at us expectantly as we entered the room. His hungry look made me think that he was expecting some sort of room service, arriving right on time to bring him breakfast.

'You remember Eleanor,' Nora said in a perky playful voice, as if she were steering me around at a cocktail party rather than introducing me to the man I'd just watched poised over her in bed. 'She just broke up with her steady,' Nora continued, handing me my glass of whisky – I hadn't even seen her bring it, or refill it – and motioning for me to drink up. 'And she's at a bit of a loose end.'

Dean nodded and gave me a knowing smile, as if he

could read my thoughts. I hoped he couldn't, because at the words 'loose end' I'd just had an unexpectedly sexy vision, one that involved Nora's recently discarded wine-hued stockings and my own willing wrists. Christ, where were these images coming from? Unplanned, unbidden, I saw myself starring in an X-rated movie – co-starring, actually – with my best friend and her favourite bed-mate. One of her favourites, anyway.

'I don't have to be at the club for a few more hours,' Nora said, gazing at the clock on her dresser. 'So, I thought we might all get to know each other a little better.'

This was all she needed to say. Dean moved over on the mattress, making room for me and, as if in a dream, I felt myself step forwards. 'You thought,' he prompted, and he gave me a look that was so utterly sexy I wanted to throw myself at him. I wondered whether he'd been sleeping while Nora and I had talked in the other room. Or had he possibly been listening? Did Nora ever talk to him about me? Did he know how long Nora and I had been best friends, and what I did for a living, and what my boyfriend was like – or did none of that really matter to him at all – the mere prospect of bedding two ladies at once enough information for him?

Because clearly, that's what Nora was planning.

Dean looked me up and down, and I was once again aware of how hurriedly I'd thrown on my clothes, aware of the fact that my shoes didn't match, that my hair was captured in its normal staid ponytail, that I was as plainly dressed as Nora was wildly decked out in her turquoise silk robe and multi-hued hair. But from the way Dean grinned at me, I could tell that none of this bothered him. He tilted his head from Nora to me to Nora again, as if waiting for one of us to give him the go-ahead. Nora did so willingly.

'Look,' she said, 'Eleanor's a little shy.'

Dean reached up to snag the whisky glass from my

trembling hand and took a sip. 'So am I,' he said, and I started laughing. He'd definitely managed to break the mood.

'Yeah, right,' I said, suddenly finding the nerve to take one more step closer to the bed. '*You're* shy.' The handsome man in front of me was entirely naked, hardly even bothering to hide under a sheet. Besides that, he knew for a fact that I'd watched him making love to Nora earlier in the evening, and he didn't seem to mind at all. As far as I could tell, there was not one shy thing about him.

'Really,' he said, beaming at me. 'It's all I can do not to trip over myself when I walk up on stage.'

'Come on,' I protested, not believing a word.

'I'm dead serious. My eyes are always on my feet, looking straight down. If I make a mistake and glance out there and see all the people, I feel as if I'm going to pass out. The very first time I was up on stage, I actually did – ask Nora.'

'That's a fact,' she told me. 'It was at Faux Pas. We had to pour water on him.'

I looked down at Dean, wondering if they really were telling me the truth, or if all of this was a ruse to make me feel comfortable enough to take off my clothes. Either way, the trick was working. Here I was in Nora's dimly lit bedroom, being charmed by a man I'd watched in motion less than an hour before – and I had no desire to flee. The thought of climbing onto the bed with the two of them was making me feel more than a little bit sexy. But did that truly mean I was ready to embark on a three-way? Something I'd never done before. Something I'd hardly dared to fantasise about.

Perhaps . . .

My mind grasped recklessly, uselessly, for some image of art that would help me. Art always holds the answers to my dilemmas. The swirls of colour on a canvas echo my emotions. The smooth lines on a sculpture soothe my soul. But for once I came up empty. There was no masterpiece that could let me know if I should participate in a ménage à trios. What I needed for that was a Magic 8 Ball.

'Eleanor,' Nora whispered, her body behind mine, gently urging me forwards. I closed my eyes, trying to figure out what I should do. I wanted to sit down on the mattress, wanted to feel Dean embrace me in his muscular arms. As soon as I'd caught sight of the two lovers through the window, I'd had the desire to be on the bed with them. And now I had the chance.

Still, it was difficult for me to believe that I was experiencing these feelings. I'd left my boyfriend mere hours before. Byron. The thought of what he'd say about this situation made me cringe. He'd ramble on about Nora's bad influence on me. But he'd be flat-out wrong. Nora's never pushed me to do something I haven't wanted to, haven't been ready for. Sure, when I've been single in the past, I've never been the type to rush headlong into sexual relationships. I leave that particular type of excitement up to Nora, who at this precise moment seemed poised to help me take the plunge.

'I've seen you,' I finally said to Dean, disbelieving. 'You're not shy at all.' I owned an image of him, fingers flying over the strings, head bowed in concentration as he strummed his guitar, every woman in the crowd wishing he were playing her instead.

'Not once we start playing,' he agreed with a nod. 'But before. You've never been backstage with me. Nora has. She can vouch – if you need her to.' He gave me another one of his winning smiles, and I felt my heart start to race, but I understood what he was talking about.

That's where I was right now. *Before.*

'It's OK, Eli,' Nora murmured, sitting so close to me. 'Trust me. I was right about the whisky, wasn't I?' I looked at her, saw her grinning. 'This is *exactly* what you need, and you know it.' As she spoke, she started to help me out of my clothes, her hands on my cardigan sweater, pulling, tugging. She didn't care at all that her robe had come open, revealing her naked skin. She seemed as comfortable in her lack of clothing as Dean was. I knew that even when I was nude, I wouldn't be the same as them. I'd want that sheet over my body. I'd want the lights down even lower.

I took a deep breath, still feeling as if this wasn't fully happening, as if I'd fallen into an X-rated version of Alice's rabbit hole. But I allowed myself to be undressed, to be pushed down on the bed, to be adored. Dean helped, and I thought I might swoon when I felt his fingers on my skin, as he unbuttoned my shirt and pulled aside the thin fabric, revealing my bra, my flat stomach, the waist-band of my skirt. If only I'd had on a pair of bright lipstick-red panties. Or a fancy frilly demi-cup bra. As might have been expected, I was wearing one of my standard sets, simple black. First thing this weekend, I would go out and buy a rainbow of coloured lingerie. But tonight, it didn't really matter what my bra looked like, because Dean undid the clasp and effortlessly pulled the little bit of fabric away in one easy motion, and then he moved me into the centre of the bed and went to work on the side zip of my skirt.

The sound of the zipper brought me back into myself. I leaned my head on Nora's wondrously soft pillows and I lifted my hips, wriggling to lose the skirt from my body. Dean's warm hands caressed my legs, and then he fitted himself between my thighs and bent forwards.

In a flash, I remembered the very first time I had sex. I chose an experienced lover, didn't want my initiation into the adult world to be lost in high school fumblings. Nora was impressed by the fact that I wound up with my art history TA, a man who turned out to know as much about bedding co-eds as he did about ancient Egyptian artefacts. We dated for two years, and I spent that time learning all I could about lovemaking.

After him, I dated a student my own age, and then there was Byron. But never had I played the way Nora does. Never had I been with another girl, just to see what it was like, or visited a sex party, or tried bondage. After spending four years with the same man, doing the same things every Thursday night, I felt rusty.

Dean's hands stroked me, and when I looked up at him, he gave me a wink. 'It doesn't have be so serious,' he murmured. 'You can have fun, you know.'

I wished for Nora's grace. I wished for her confidence. And then, Dean leaned in and kissed the hollow of my neck.

Fun, I thought. I can have fun. But this all seemed desperately serious to me. An initiation. A rite of passage. I closed my eyes as Dean moved slowly up until he kissed my lips. I could feel Nora watching, sense her drinking us in. I was the centre of attention, and I basked in the sensation. But when Dean started to kiss lower down my body, I felt a wave of fear crash over me. I turned my head to look at Nora, begging her silently, and she understood.

'Let me,' Nora said, pushing Dean down onto the bed and moving to the other side.

'Let you what?' he teased her.

'Let me show Eli what you like.'

Dean crossed his arms under his head and shot her a look that was more of a dare than anything else. Nora immediately went to work, bobbing her head on him, her lips locked around the head of his cock. She worked expertly, her fist around the shaft, pumping. I stared, in awe, as my best friend pleased her man, and then I found an urge building within me to take over. I put one hand out, touching the silk of her open robe and pushing her aside. It was now or never. That's how I felt. Nora licked her lips and moved out of the way, and then I was taking her place, my mouth on Dean's hardness, swallowing him up.

He put one hand down on my hair, stroking me as I pleased him. A warm beat of excitement pounded through me as Nora and I took turns – she'd kiss him, and then I would echo her movements. She'd suckle from him, and then I would follow. By the time I climbed astride Dean's powerful body, I was so wet I could hardly stand it. And for once, I led. It was me who took the first ride, while Dean put his hands on my waist and helped me, letting me buck against him, letting me . . .

I realised that I understood what he meant about being shy.

The music was playing. I was up on stage. Fear faded away.

Chapter Four

Nora was the only person in the world who could have talked me into going out that evening. But she did it. With only a few mild threats, and another glass and a half-glass of Glenfiddich, she dressed me in one of her more subdued numbers: a tasteful black cashmere sweater, a pair of sleek black pants sporting a lizard pattern embossed in velvet and footwear that actually matched.

'I don't wanna,' I'd told her as she laced up the boots for me. I kept running my hands over the velvety pants, finding tactile comfort in the raised pattern. Nora and I have always been about the same size, but we don't share clothes. It showed what my current state of mind was that I let her pour me into her favoured attire. 'Really, Nora, I don't want to go.'

'I don't care,' she replied, sounding an awful lot like Tommy Lee Jones in *The Fugitive*. I didn't have a precipice to jump off of, like Harrison Ford had. I was forced to give in to Nora's whims, and go along with what she claimed was the very best medicine for me. At least, she didn't expect me to drive. As Dean headed off towards a gig, Nora and I climbed into her lemon-yellow Mercedes. I watched the scenery blur by, thinking about the act we'd just engaged in, thinking about what it means to be Nora's best friend.

We've been nearly inseparable for ten years. Ever since we met in Santa Barbara as college freshmen and decided together that the sorority system sucked. (That was her term.) We both felt that there *had* to be a better way to meet people, one that didn't involve any type of hazing or being fondled by drunken frat boys. Nora was sporting a rebellious punk look even then, and I was all buttoned up as only a librarian-in-training can be.

Nora and I weren't actually buddies right away. In fact, I didn't know who she was until the middle of my first semester. I only discovered that there was someone who resembled me on campus, because one afternoon a popular boy in my 1960s art class kept looking at me strangely. Whenever I turned towards him, I caught him staring at me. I didn't have enough male admirers so as to be accustomed to this sort of undivided attention. After class, he approached me and said, 'You know, you look totally different today.'

'Different than what?' I asked. Did he mean that I looked different than I usually looked? He couldn't, because that wasn't true. I *always* dressed like this, a rather refined preppy. It was my concept of how college students ought to dress. Of course, most of them didn't. Most looked as if they'd tumbled out of bed after having slept in their clothes. But I couldn't help that; I could only take care of myself.

'Different than you did at the Sinuosity concert.'

I hadn't gone to the Sinuosity concert, and I told him so. I hadn't actually heard of the band Sinuosity. My listening tastes veered from the innocent to the mundane. Steely Dan. The Beatles. Paul Simon. Dire Straits. The Rolling Stones were about as edgy as I got. I thought 'Under My Thumb' was deviously delightful.

'Yeah, you did,' he said, not in the least bit convinced by my denial. He spoke as if trying to remind me of an event that must have slipped my mind. 'You were wearing a little sparkly top as a dress and all that purple eyeliner like Siouxsie.'

'Who's Susie?'

He pointed to a sticker on his binder, and I saw that he was referring to someone who spelled her name 'Siouxsie' and who played with a group called 'the Banshees'. 'And you were dancing up on stage,' he continued, as if that settled the matter. His attention to detail let me know that he'd liked what he'd seen, but I couldn't take credit for the fashionista he was describing.

'Not me,' I insisted, thinking: Purple eyeliner? I stuck with brown or olive. And a top as a dress? Perhaps, the man was on drugs. That wouldn't have surprised me. Many of my fellow art history students appeared to be high most of the time. Quite a few envisioned themselves to be the artists of the future, and most seemed to believe that an artist's temperament depended on altered substances. While that's true for some artists, you need talent to start with before you can take off for the stratosphere.

This student gave me a confused frown, as if he thought I were lying to him, and unsure why I would be that cruel. As he walked away, he continued to shoot me hurt puppy dog looks over his shoulder. He must have believed that I was trying to shake him off. I wouldn't have done that. I had very little experience with boys so far, but this one was good looking in a punk-rock sort of way: shredded jeans, ragged T-shirt, khaki backpack with anti-establishment buttons studding the rough fabric. I would have loved to continue to talk with him, but my mind didn't work like that. I could have filled hours discussing the floor plans of churches that had long ago disintegrated into dust, or compared ancient Greek iconography to the type found in Gaul, or even expounded on the different styles of Monet and Manet. But talking to boys was beyond me.

I decided that *he* was the crazy one, and put the incident out of my mind. At least, I did until a similar episode occurred at James Grounds, the best coffee bar on campus. A tall student in a Lichtenstein T-shirt that said 'Oh, Brad!' walked by and asked what I was in costume for.

'What do you mean?'

'You're not wearing that for real, are you?' he asked, in obvious disbelief.

I had on a cashmere argyle cardigan sweater done in various shades of pink, a tweed pencil skirt and shiny maroon penny loafers with bright silver dimes tucked into the cut-out slots. I felt ever so clever for putting dimes in my loafers rather than pennies, as if this were a wicked bit of wit. Yes, I was a bit more dressed up than usual, but I'd just come from an interview to do volunteer work at the campus outdoor sculpture gallery. I'd done my best to look professional, yet from his expression, I could tell this wasn't what he meant.

'I mean, come on, what's up with the freakin' glasses?'

My hand went immediately to the bridge of my nose, self-consciously pushing up my shiny black frames. I've always worn reading glasses, and I thought these ones made me look more adult. Sitting in the café, studying before my next class, I had actually thought I looked good until this man came along.

'And how'd you change your hair so quickly? It's got to be a wig.' He looked as if he might actually grip into my hair to test, and I flinched away from him.

'Come on, Nora.' But then he took a step closer to me and lifted his shades. And then, as reality set in, he murmured, 'You're *not* Nora, are you?'

'Elea*nor*,' I told him.

'And that's your hair for real?' He didn't say this as if it were a compliment.

I nodded, wondering what on earth he was going on about.

'You have a doppelgänger,' he told me. When I continued to give him a blank stare, he explained further, 'A double. But your eyes are different. And her hair is green right now. That's what I couldn't understand. I just saw her last night. There was no way she could have done such a complete reversal in a matter of hours.' He gave me another look. 'But it's eerie. On first sight, you could be her twin. Now, that I look at you closer, you're more like a little sister.'

A double. That made sense. It explained why I

occasionally felt as if people were looking at me strangely, why students that I didn't know waved to me every once in awhile. And it explained the two boys and their insistence that I was someone who I wasn't. I felt oddly excited. Somewhere out there on campus was a student who lived a life I had no concept of. A green-haired girl who had many friends of the male persuasion.

I made it my mission to find this girl, the one who danced on stage, who dyed her hair daily, who wore sparkly dresses and purple eyeliner. A girl who would never choose outfits like those nestled in my own closet. A student whose friends thought that *my* clothes looked like costumes. Turns out, when I found her, she was looking for me. Her buddies kept reporting seeing her in an altogether too preppy look. They hadn't understood, thinking she was engaging in some sort of subversive performance-art piece, dressing like a normal person for extended periods of time and refusing to sit with them when they waved her over at the cafeteria.

When I finally saw her, I immediately understood the confusion. At first glance, we do look quite similar: same height, same build, same heart-shaped face. We both have slim bodies, small breasts, large wide-set eyes, full lips. I played my lips down with nude gloss. She played hers up with dark red or bubble-gum pink or shimmering blue.

'You,' she said when we finally met. '*You're* the one.'

And I stopped and gazed at her, realising the same thing. She didn't have green hair any more. She'd changed it to snow white with a pink frost on the tips. Her make-up was comical to me, like theatre make-up. I had been taught to use cosmetics to enhance my features. To wear make-up so that it looked as if I didn't have any on at all. Nora used make-up for effect. She had on tangerine-hued eye shadow, lip gloss with fancy silver sparkles and streaks of peony blush to emphasise the sharpness of her cheekbones. Her face was a canvas gone mad, a painting made by one of the Pop artists from the

50s and 60s. Warhol would have swooned for her. He would have made her his queen.

The most interesting thing to me about seeing her was realising what someone else might do with my body. I'd always sort of wondered. If another person had the chance, how would they dress me, how would they fix my hair? Nora's was super short and spiky. Her clothes were form-fitting, thrift-store snagged purchases. A red-and-black plaid schoolgirl skirt safety pinned at the waist, a Ramones T-shirt with the short sleeves intentionally shredded, a pair of holey black fishnets and lizard-green slouchy suede boots. She didn't wear a backpack like most of the campus drones. Instead, she carried her books in a leather messenger bag, slung around her neck and off one shoulder. The bag looked positively ancient, and this added to her charm.

I wouldn't even have dressed like her on Halloween, but I could see that she was pretty, and since it had only been boys who had approached me so far, I knew that she won her fair share of masculine attention. Who wouldn't notice someone with hair like hers?

Nora took in my own clothes with a sad little shake of her head. I wondered if her thoughts mirrored mine – that here was what someone else would do with *her* body. She was intrigued that I had true-to-life hair colour, a light-caramel brown that streaked blonde naturally in the summertime, and she was shocked that my lips were glossed in a natural tone – why would I waste bee-stung lips with something beige and boring? Mostly, she appeared completely flabbergasted by my penny loafers. It was as if she'd never seen average, everyday shoes before. She viewed me like some specimen in a science experiment, and appeared to be mildly revolted by the results.

'Man,' she said as we walked, 'I couldn't believe the stories people were saying to me. That I was wearing argyle. That I got an A plus on an art history paper.'

We headed towards the coffee shop together, comparing notes. When we made it to the front of the line to order, she rummaged into her bag, but came up empty-handed. 'Can you buy?' she asked. 'I promise to pay you back.'

I nodded, handing over a crisp five, watching as she carefully noted the amount of her small debt in a surprisingly neat ring notebook.

'People kept stopping me,' she continued as we found ourselves seats in the corner, 'asking how I could change my hair so quickly. Really, I choose a new hue every week or so, but they couldn't understand how it could get so long so fast. They were sure I had on a wig. Which wouldn't have been beyond me. But wigs are really expensive, and they're not the sort of thing one wants to buy used.'

'Guys kept telling me about places I haven't ever been,' I told her.

'Like where?'

'The Shadow Box. One guy told me he'd seen me up on stage, but I've never even been to the club.'

'You don't go dancing?'

I shook my head quickly.

'Are you, like, Amish, or something?'

I gave her a look, but then saw she wasn't kidding. Here was an actual reason that would have made sense to her. It would have explained why I didn't dance, why I dressed so simply, why I never dyed my hair. 'I don't have religious beliefs that prevent me from engaging in motion to music,' I told her, but she seemed to be waiting for a longer explanation. 'Look, I just don't know how to dance.'

'You don't know how to dance.' She repeated the words softly, but she didn't ask them as a question. It was almost as if she believed *everyone* knew how to dance, but I was trying to pull a fast one on her. I shrugged helplessly. I had never liked dances. I didn't feel as if I had any sense of rhythm, and I tended to get lost in my own embarrassment. All through school, I was a wallflower, ultimately choosing to spend dance nights at the library rather than suffer the humiliation of going and not engaging.

'You have to just *dance*,' she said, as if that made sense, as if her words of wisdom would clear everything up for me from now on. 'You *feel* the music.' They were playing James Brown, which is what they always played at this coffee shop, a pun on the shop's name. The song was 'Papa's Got a Brand New Bag', and Nora started to move to the beat. I didn't actually *hear* the beat, but I could see, staring at her, how sexy she was. And people thought I was Nora. Did that make me sexy, as well? Or did it give me the potential to become sexy?

'What are you studying?' I asked, trying to woo her back to earth.

'Everything.' She was still moving her slender shoulders to the sounds of James Brown.

'What does that mean?'

'I don't have a major yet,' she admitted, still grooving to the music, shifting her hips seductively in her chair. 'I know I have to declare one at some point, but I can't decide. I like anthropology, but what does that do for you? I'm not going to live in the wilds studying monkeys. Where would I get the dye for my hair? Crushed berries? And afterwards, what can you do with that sort of degree? Become a teacher? They'd never let me in front of a class of students. Imagine what I would do to impressionable youngsters. How about you?' She spoke in a rush, so many words at once, that I had a difficult time following her. When she stared at me, I realised she was waiting for an answer.

'Art history.'

'So you're going to be a teacher?' She laughed and shook her head, as if she'd said exactly the wrong thing.

'No. I want to work in a museum.' This was my big dream, even back as a freshman. I've always been focused on my future.

'Then why do you dress like that?'

'What do you mean?' I asked.

'I'd have thought someone who liked art would be more –' she hesitated, but Nora has never been anything but blunt '– more artsy.'

'I let the art be artsy,' I said lamely, 'and the artists. I only know about the sculptures and paintings. I don't make any sort of art myself.' Perhaps because I'm not artistic myself, I admire those who are. I revere them. And I don't mean only the classicists. Some of my all-time favorite artists are the ones who push boundaries, the ones that other people cannot understand. Keith Haring. Claus Oldenburg. Julian Schnabel. Basquiat.

'Sometimes I want to be an artist,' Nora said vaguely, her eyes focused on one of the pathetic student-done canvases on the wall. This was a rip on Jackson Pollack. Or an homage. I knew that instantly. And I also knew the theory behind it. Splash stuff on a blank canvas. Call it a form of expression. But it had already been done, and done so much better.

'What sort of art do you like?' I asked. Here was a conversation I felt much more comfortable with than the one about dancing.

'Myself.'

Inwardly, I cringed. 'A performance artist?' I could imagine her smothering herself on stage with hot fudge sauce, or standing in one place for hours at a time, not moving a muscle.

She nodded gleefully. But my fears weren't realised. She didn't want to be an artist on stage. She wanted to be an artist in *life*. Everyday life. Nora named her individual looks, believing that she was a painter of hair colour and make-up. She might be Ziggy Stardust one day and a Spider from Mars the next. She kept Polaroids of each outfit, never replicating the same look twice. She might wear the bottle-green stretch pants emblazoned with black skulls for two different outfits, but the rest of the look would be entirely unique. I'd never wear stretch pants, or skull-emblazoned anything. Back then, I had no idea who Ziggy Stardust was, and the thought of basing an outfit on something called 'Spiders from Mars' made my head hurt.

But I liked Nora.

I couldn't explain the attraction to her, other than she was different from all the other people I knew in school. I wasn't a total loser. I did have friends. But *my* friends were the type who would have shushed *her* friends in the library, had her friends ever gone to the library. Just like her crowd, my gang tended to stay up late – but we went out studying not dancing. The group I hung out with actually had the gall to correct teachers in class. They prided themselves on knowing all there was to know about artists who had been dead for hundreds of years. One of my classmates actually carried a set of home-made flashcards of church floor plans with her at all times. Whenever Gina had a free moment, she'd test herself. I tried to imagine what Nora would think of a person like that, someone who considered viewing a series of tiny black dots on an index card a good time.

Nora and her crowd were alive in a much more vibrant way. They missed classes, and didn't seem to care. They stayed up all night long, staring at the ceiling, talking for hours about things they didn't know anything about. Nora was the best of them, and they seemed to realise that, coming in tight around her, as if trying to make a little bit of her power rub off on them.

I didn't want to be like those members of her group. I didn't want her to think I was a hanger-on. But I realised fairly quickly that she liked me back. She appreciated my sense of purpose, organisation and dark humour. I'd never tell other people the jokes that I told her, but when I was by her side, I could give in to the wicked observations that I made mentally on a daily basis.

What I learned from being friends with Nora was that sometimes opposites do more than attract. Sometimes opposites perfectly balance each other, keeping each other sane and safe. Nora and I were able to provide each other with the type of flat-out honesty that you can't always get from a lover, that you can't even expect from your family. We were there for each other, to extremes that boyfriends and girlfriends hardly ever reach.

Nora created her first club while we were still in college, transforming her dorm room into a members-only environment. Waxe Wod (or WW) was an anti-sorority/anti-fraternity environment to which both male and female students could retreat, like an officers' club. The words Waxe Wod were from a poem circa 1200. She didn't take the poetry class. *I* did. She read the piece in my book one evening when she was bored, coming upon this poem:

Fowles in the frith
The fisshes in the flod,
And I mon waxe wod,
Much sorwe I walke with,
For beste of boon and blood.

(Translation: The birds are in the wood and the fishes in the flood, surely I go mad, all the grief I've had, for best of bone and blood.)

Nora decided that 'waxe wod' stood for 'surely I go mad'. And she liked that.

Most of the patrons at WW were punk and goth, art-house friends of Nora's who dressed like her. Well, perhaps not *quite* like her. I have never met anyone else who actually named their outfits – and I've hung out with my fair share of artist types. But these were the students who I should have looked more like. We shared classes together on art history – ancient and modern. We sat in the sculpture gardens together, cramming before tests from coffee-table-sized tomes. Yet I was the most out of place physically, never having the nerve to dye my hair the colour of a ripe plum or pierce my eyebrows, tongue, nose or any other body part. But Nora always made me feel welcome.

Even if I am conservative in my own dress style, I've never judged Nora. And even if she is more adventurous in her lovemaking, more adventurous in every part of her life, she would never judge me.

There were times back in school when Nora would hide out in my room to get away from the circus she'd created at Waxe Wod. She'd slip away, unseen by the masses who'd come to pay their respects to her, ducking under the clouds of clove cigarette smoke, manoeuvring around the velvet pillows spread all over the floor. I'd hear her knocking and, when I'd open my door, would find her standing there, similar to the way she found me at her place this very evening. Not bedraggled, exactly, but insecure. Nora exudes confidence. She is a bright flame. But every so often she has moments of self-doubt. On nights like these, she would climb onto my twin bed and lay her head on my pillow, wondering when the people in her room would notice her absence. But almost as soon as the curious clouds would come, they would lift, and she would be Nora again. Filled with animation. Fully sure of her choices.

I watched her the way I viewed art. She taught me to take myself more loosely, not to be so uptight about an A− or a B+. I went to concerts with her, and I learned to appreciate the colourful array of life that was displayed around me. Nora has never felt the need to look for art in a museum. She sees it everywhere she goes. Graffiti on a building – art. A fabulously decadent hairstyle – art. A pair of the most perfectly worn-in holey jeans – art.

I could spend all day talking to Nora, could spend my whole life talking to her, and never run out of things to say. I could listen to her forever, and still want to hear more.

Of course, Byron hated her on sight. He didn't let me know his true feelings about her right away, because that would have been a deal breaker. At first, I think he might actually have thought there was a chance that he'd get the two of us into bed. When I took him to the club to meet Nora, he danced with her, and then with me – I've gotten to the point under Nora's instruction that I don't make a total fool of myself on the dance floor. But once that fantasy wore off, he claimed she was pretentious. 'If there was nobody watching her, would she even exist?' he asked. I said he simply didn't understand her, and we left it at that. Nora never has had a long-term relationship with a man, so I've not had to compete with her love life for attention.

Thank God. I don't think I'd be up to it. Not after joining her and Dean in that unexpected ménage à trois. Things like that are commonplace in Nora's world. But not in mine.

Once we reached Nora's club, she set me up in the best booth in the room, a semicircle in the far corner upholstered in a dark-fuchsia vinyl and trimmed with multicoloured marabou feathers. The booths on the edges of the dance floor were all done in different shades of shiny material and different types of fringe: glass beads, silver bells, tiny twinkling Christmas lights. This was the best one because it had the clearest view of the rest of the club.

After making sure I was comfortable, Nora ordered our drinks. And then she spent all her time with me, as if I were as important as the celebrities who continually stopped by the table to pay their respects to her, the doyenne of the club, the queen of the hour.

'Nora, I didn't even tell you the rest. The thing that happened after Byron and I broke up. The best thing.'

'I was there,' she teased.

'I don't mean with Dean.' I flushed. 'I mean, while I was still at the apartment.'

My best friend sipped her cobalt-tinted drink and waited, tapping her berry-hued nails against the base of the glass in rhythm to the music. Actually, her nails weren't totally berry coulored. Every other nail was – the ones in between were painted a glossy black. In the lights of the club, this was difficult to discern, but when Nora held up her Martini glass, the candlelight played over her hands, and I could see. With Nora, things are never exactly normal. It's probably one of the main reasons why I like her so much. She doesn't follow other people's rules. Or, rather, she only marches to the beat of the drummers she wants to fuck.

'So tell me,' she insisted. 'What's the best part of getting rid of that loser? I mean, aside from getting rid of that loser?'

'He wasn't really –' I started, but she held up her hand.

'He actually said another woman's name while he was inside of you.'

I winced and looked down at the découpaged table. The pictures under the clear coating were all of Bettie Page. I stared down at the bondage maven and realised that Nora was right. Why the hell was I trying to defend him? Because I didn't want to think I'd been dating a villain for four years. Didn't want to admit that I'd been with someone so low. If I looked at our relationship too closely, and still couldn't see the signs, then what sort of moron did that make me?

'Has that ever happened to you?' I asked.

Nora shrugged. 'Sure,' she said. I opened my eyes wide at her, surprised until she continued, 'At least, when I've been playing some sort of fantasy game. I've been called Marilyn and Madonna and Brad.'

'You're joking.'

She raised her arched eyebrows at me, and I realised that she wasn't. And why should she have been? Nora has the ability to transform herself on a daily basis. Why shouldn't she use this ability when in bed? She is definitely the type to wear a white dress and stand over a grate, to put on armfuls of rubber bangles and a bustier as a top, to purchase and wear a harness and a strap-on if this sort of thing would work for a lover.

'But back to it,' Nora insisted, her hand squeezing

mine. 'I don't think you two were engaged in role-playing activities at the time, were you?'

'No.'

'Were you ever?' she asked, curious.

I shook my head. Should we have been? If I'd become Marilyn or Madonna or *Brad* would he have stayed with me? Were any of those people the type to please Byron? I didn't think so.

'So don't let him off the hook for it, kiddo. Just tell me what was good about your departure.'

'I broke this antique,' I began, closing my eyes as I recreated the scene in my head. 'This ancient Greek urn that my great-aunt willed to me. I have no idea how much the thing must have been worth.'

'Rose died?' Nora asked, looking shocked.

'Well, she didn't die so much as disappear. But her immediate family has waited the prerequisite amount of time. The will has gone into play.'

Nora held out her glass reverently. 'To Rose,' she said. She'd never met my great-aunt, but she'd heard the stories. She knew that Rose was worth millions of dollars, and that she loved me.

'You can see that the urn was priceless –' I paused '– and I broke it.' I sighed, still in semi-shock at what I'd done.

'You didn't mean to,' Nora said matter-of-factly, as if that made things better.

'Course not. But that doesn't change the fact that I destroyed the thing. Still, when it broke, I went on my knees to pick up the pieces. Even *one* of those shards of pottery would have been worth money to a museum, and I had some fleeting thought of crazy-gluing it together. Crazy all right. There's no way.' I sighed. 'And even with Byron standing there, screaming down at me, I was thinking of the museum. That's when I saw it.'

'It?'

'This ... This sheath of papers. This manuscript in the

rubble. I don't even know if Byron saw the thing at first, he was so out of his head at the thought that Gwen might not really be in love with him.'

Nora made a gagging noise, like a cat fighting with a hairball.

I lowered my head in my hands, wanting to clear the memory, wanting to think about the positive rather than Byron. After a moment, I looked back at Nora, ready to continue. 'I scraped the bits of the urn into my suitcase, and picked up the papers – they were practically crumbling at my touch – and I wrapped them in some of the brown paper the box had come in, stuffed them in the bag and left.'

'Where are the papers now?'

I motioned to my sleek red computer carrier. I hadn't wanted to leave the bag in my car, hadn't wanted to leave it at Nora's. I wouldn't feel truly secure about the manuscript until it found a home at ARTSI.

'What are they?'

'I don't know. I saw the writing as I put the pages in the case. They're in Greek. Or some form of Greek. Scrawling writing. I can't read Greek – Latin, but not Greek – but I can recognise it, after having seen so much of it in the museum. Think of the concept, Nora. These papers must be thousands of years old. The only reason they survived this long is because that urn was airtight, sealed completely, and then broken by me in a heated fight with an imbecile.'

'What will you do with them?' Nora was obviously entranced at the thought. This was fanciful, the stuff of fairy tales. Exactly the sort of story she could appreciate. Her large green eyes looked lit from within.

'Bring them to the museum, I guess. Show them to Marcia –' I paused again '– or Anthony.'

Nora grinned. 'Anthony,' she murmured. She took another sip of her drink and then gave me a wink. Her mascara-drenched eyelashes fluttered becomingly. They were tipped in glittering eggplant that went well with her green eyes. 'I remember Anthony,' she continued dreamily. Nora has a good memory for men, and Anthony isn't a man *anyone* would quickly forget.

'Come on, don't tease me. I can't even think about this whole thing clearly.'

'Nobody could think clearly once Anthony enters the picture.'

I looked down at my green apple martini. 'And even less clearly after one of these.'

Nora ignored me, and began to list Anthony's attributes, counting each one off on her fingers. 'He's the James Bond of ancient literature, Eleanor. Profiled in the *LA Times*. Written up in *GQ*. The man has it all: brains, brawn and a killer accent.'

'I broke up with my boyfriend *today*,' I emphatically reminded her, not wanting to admit that she was right. 'Just hours ago.'

My best friend gave me a look that said, 'Come clean.' Her looks are like mental polygraph tests. She can always tell when someone's lying to her. Besides, she had just personally escorted me back into the sea of sexual pleasure. Why was I trying to hide from her?

I took a deep breath. At this moment, a famous, and handsome movie actor slid by our booth, blowing an air-kiss to Nora. She winked back at him, and I found myself as awestruck as ever. Had she been with this man? I hadn't heard about it if she had.

'Did you –' I started.

'You really *don't* read my blog, do you?'

I flushed, and then took a quick sip.

'Don't worry,' she teased me. 'Let's get back to your man.'

'He's not my man,' I insisted.

'He will be. He wants you, Eleanor. You've said so yourself. Every time the two of you have worked together, he's been more than attentive.'

'Crush on Anthony Ginsburg aside,' I told her in a serious voice, 'it was very odd. As soon as I saw the papers I found myself less angry at Byron. I thought: look at us. We're totally insignificant. We destroyed – or, rather, *I* destroyed – an ancient artefact. Something that existed buried in the dirt, undisturbed and unharmed, for centuries. Here's a manuscript that someone wrote thousands of years ago, half a world away. I started to feel very small. When I looked at Byron, his cheeks all red, smoke nearly pouring out of his ears, I thought that he looked awfully small, too.'

'*Was* he small?' Nora asked. This was a topic she could sink her teeth into. 'I mean, he had fairly big hands.'

'You can't tell anything from a guy's hands.' Even I, with my little experience, knew that.

'I know,' she said, 'but I'm always curious. He looked like a, you know, European cucumber to me, but in those handmade suits, I never could tell. Was he more of an Armenian cuke? They tend to curve at the end. Or was he built like an Oriental cucumber? They're long and skinny.' Nora likes things large. And she has absolutely no problem discussing this particular fixation. The fact that she uses cucumbers as size gauges wasn't new to me. She's been doing this ever since she dated one of the darling chefs in the city, a man who took her to farmer's markets, who pointed out the differences in flavours from one cucumber to the next. (*He* was the size of an American pickling cuke, if I remember correctly. Not that long, yet plenty thick.) But I didn't feel a need to describe my ex's member, using vegetable terminology or anything else. In fact, I wanted to forget what Byron looked and felt like as quickly as possible. It's why I had taken the marathon shower, why I kept wanting to spray myself with perfume. Anything I could do to erase him.

Nora eyed me expectantly, but I shrugged off the question, getting back to what I really wanted to talk about. I stared out at the dance floor and then at the movie showing silently on the wall. It looked like an X-rated film, but I knew what it really was. Nora has several private rooms in her club. One features images from the web that customers can call up at will. Basically, the walls are large screens that show exactly what anyone is surfing for. You might see porn or music videos or even blogs, such as Nora's own, ThePinkFedora.blogspot.com. Another room is called Would I Lie to You? This room features all black walls with a do-it-yourself polygraph machine on a small wooden table. Nora understands how obsessed people are with this sort of gimmick. She thinks it's amusing to send a couple back there to learn each other's secrets. There's a room in the rear called Body Graffiti, outfitted with edible body paints and a shower – for after; there's another called Friction; and one called Smile, with Polaroids and video cameras.

But the room at the end of the hall is the most popular: Cinéma Vérité. Anyone can go into it, knowing ahead of time that they will be filmed, and that their antics will be projected onto the wall of the dance floor. Although I've never been in that room myself, I've always liked it best. Every time I go to Nora's club, I pretend to be watching dancers on the floor, but I stare at the amateur porn stars, getting into the mood in that small mirrored room. There's a part of me that wants to be as free as the customers who head to that private paradise.

Right now, an enchantingly pretty Asian girl with long blonde dreadlocks was entering the room. I watched, mesmerised, as two attractive men followed her in – one dark, the other light. The dark one had on leather pants and a tight-fitting red T-shirt. The other was dressed down in jeans and a button-up white Oxford shirt. As I watched, the two men began to kiss the girl – kiss her face, her neck, her breasts. It was as if the threesome had been plucked from some other world, where people did this sort of thing on a routine basis.

Nora reached out and touched my hand. When I looked at her, she let me know she was going to order us more drinks. 'And check on my bartenders,' she added. 'It looks as if one of them is getting ready to fuck one of the patrons.' From the way she said the words, I couldn't tell if she was pleased about this or not. Would that be a no-no in Nora's club, or the sort of thing to get you a bonus? Then, with a nod towards the screen, she indicated that I should keep watching.

I gazed back at the screen, focusing once again on the vision above the dance floor and the music playing in the background. I knew the song, because I'd heard it so many times at Nora's: 'Stuff Me Up'. Peaches and someone named Taylor Savvy. It was a perfect soundtrack for this sexual scenario, Nora's favourite by the singer aside from 'Fuck the Pain Away'. I think she likes that one simply because she enjoys saying the words, like the way her patrons adore ordering sexually charged drinks at the clubs: 'Give me an Orgasm,' 'I want Sex on the Beach,' 'I'd like to order a Blow Job.'

Had the trio in the not-so-private room been ordering drinks like this? Something had definitely gotten them in the mood. It was as if Nora's DJ were paying attention to the needs of the people in the Cinéma Vérité room. And most likely, she was. When I gazed over at the DJ – the always stunning Miss Take – I saw that she was following the antics of the trio as willingly as were the rest of the club's patrons.

The music in the club suddenly reached a crescendo, and the threesome reacted with even more outrageous behaviour. I stopped thinking about the soundtrack and started paying attention fully to the lovers. There was something about the way that they moved, kissing one another so passionately, hands overlapping, bodies pressed together, that fully captivated my attention.

God, they were pretty.

The girl was especially luscious, her mouth painted the dangerous dark black-red of a ripe cherry. Her golden skin gleamed with some sparkling silver fairy dust. She had those long blonde dreads that made absolutely no sense with her features, but somehow added powerfully to her allure.

The two men were focused entirely on the pleasure of their female partner. They took turns kissing her mouth, first one, then the other, until all three were wearing the remnants of her dark lipstick. The boys looked so sexy with the red stains on their lips, and the girl looked positively in heaven, her eyelids fluttering as she kissed first one, then the other.

I stared, unmoving, until my cellphone rang. I felt the phone rather than heard it. The smooth vibrations worked through my computer bag against my thigh, and I reached into my bag and lifted out the small device. It was Byron. Big fucking surprise. Undoubtedly, he wanted to continue our argument. The one thing that Byron hates most in the world is losing a fight. I slid the phone back into my bag without answering the call, and then looked up at the screen once more.

I watched as she continued kissing one man and then the other, and I shifted my hips against the vinyl of the booth, unable to help myself. The vision was more of a turn-on than I would have known. I always see the unexpected at Nora's clubs. Sometimes you'll read in the gossip magazines about starlets who dance on bar tops, or slip off their bras and pin them to the ceiling of a local watering hole. There isn't much left for people to do to shock the A-listers. But Nora always manages to draw in an interesting crowd: drag kings and drag queens, customers whose clothes are literally painted onto their skin, people who come to the club solely to have sex where others can see them.

That's apparently what this trio had in mind.

The girl kissed her blond partner in a way that let me see that they both had pierced tongues. The tiny silver barbells gleamed in the light as the lovely minx just barely touched the tip of her tongue to his. I wondered what it would feel like to kiss someone with metal in their mouth. I could ask Nora. I'm sure she knows. I watched as the girl then backed away from her partners and nodded, giving a silent instruction.

Instantly, the two men started making out with each other. I caught my breath. It was fantastical, watching the way they embraced, as if under the command of the female member of their party. Even though she was small, she was clearly in charge. There was no doubt about that. She could have been dressed in head-to-toe leather, holding a whip in one hand, and she would have looked divine. But she didn't need faux dom attire. Her power emanated from within her very person – tiny though she was. I recognised that ability from seeing Nora in action.

Watching men kiss wasn't something brand new to me. Art students are by definition liberal. You can't view naked bodies on a day-to-day basis without being at least somewhat open minded. Still, this sultry threesome was eye-catching, if only for the sheer beauty of the players. I wondered: Was this something they'd agreed upon before heading to the club, or were they strangers, having come together only moments before on the club dance floor?

Which concept did I find more erotic? The possibility that this was an organic experience – as well as an orgasmic one. Just as Nora, Dean and I had come together unexpectedly, I liked the idea that these players had simply hooked up while dancing, not even knowing one another's name. But the more I watched, the more certain I felt that this was a fantasy come true for this team of three. That they'd talked it over, planning every move ahead of time, taking the time to discuss their every desire. This concept was sexy, too. Maybe they'd gone out to dinner at one of the better restaurants: Ivy on Robertson, Shecago on Main. Over lobster or sushi or something expensive, they might have talked about what each person hoped to win from the evening.

Regardless of how the players came together, they were hypnotic.

I stared, mesmerised, as the two men continued to kiss. They looked so hungry, the way the dark-haired man cradled his blond beau's face in his hands. The brunette was the top of the two, I could tell, moving his partner to suit his own satisfaction. I hadn't known I'd find an image like this so sexy. Sure, I liked *My Beautiful Launderette*, *Another Country* and *My Own Private Idaho*. But what did that say about me? That I enjoyed art-house films?

This was real life, with the men devouring one another, kissing as if they'd never stop. I watched, spell-bound, as they made out. They both had their eyes closed, lost in the total pleasure of the moment, and then the girl joined in, parting them like the sexual choreographer she was, getting in between them. Awestruck, I suddenly realised that I was the only one so intently focused on the room. Yes, the dancers on the floor were watching, but they were also still dancing. I wouldn't have been able to move from the booth. I was wildly turned on, shifting again in the booth as I sensed how aroused the scenario had made me.

And then things got sexier still.

Chapter Five

The door to the Cinéma Vérité room opened and I realised with a sudden shocked intake of breath that Nora had just entered the tiny space. As if needing to verify the vision on the screen, I looked over at the bar, surprised that she'd been able to pass by the booth without my noticing. But I'd been lost in my thoughts, trying to pen them in, make sense of them. Now, I stared as Nora pushed the two men aside and kissed the girl. A raucous wave of approval from the dance floor greeted this new erotic antic. Customers were definitely paying attention now, focused as Nora made her way down the girl's body, following the zipper on the girl's vinyl dress with her own berry-glossed lips.

The blonde closed her eyes and leaned back against the mirrored wall as Nora started to kiss her. I wondered how far my best friend would go. I've always known that she likes to divide her attention between men and women. And I've witnessed scenarios in the past that let me know she's fine with more than a bit of exhibitionism. But was she actually going to have sex in that room, right now, with the whole club as her witness?

Nora's universe is so alien from mine. Even after ten years as friends, I am still in awe of her ability to captivate those around her. This skill was what made Waxe Wod so popular back in college. Nora sells a bit of herself with each club that she owns. She doesn't hide behind the scenes, she steps right up to the front of the stage and MCs them.

I suppose that I shouldn't have been surprised by her actions. Had I been paying more attention, I would have realised she was planning on playing in public this evening. Nora had worn her white mink fedora to the club. She has a code – she's described to me in the past – a hat code the way that some gay men and women have hankie codes: bondage top (grey), wants oral sex (light blue), dildo user (light pink). Of course, Nora explained, it also matters which pocket the hankies were worn in.

'But what if you didn't mean it?' I'd asked her. 'What if you just had a cold or something and you tucked a hankie into your pocket and someone –'

'What? Fucked you against the bar? There's always a discussion first, silly. It's not like you don't still have a will of your own. It's just a way of letting people know what you're into. It cuts to the chase.'

With a hat, there was only one choice of how to wear it – no right pocket, or left pocket – and very few people know the codes to Nora's desires. Only me and a few select bed partners. Still, Nora owns a breathtaking assortment of fedoras. Some are rhinestone studded, others made of mohair. Each one signifies a different desire.

What might I have if I were to choose a similar code system? A book – that would do it for me. If I had a black book with me, that would mean I wanted ... wanted what? Wanted a fantasy life like Nora's? Wanted Anthony? I didn't need a book to know that, and apparently Nora had understood what I'd thought were my hidden longings only too well.

On screen, Nora was now pressed up against the blonde vixen, her hands on the girl's breasts, her lips still moving over the woman's slender body. The men stood on either side of the Asian girl, and they were kissing her as well, working their mouths along her neck, down to her breasts, touching and kissing her all over. The girl looked as if she might swoon from the pleasure, as if she would melt away if not for the support of her friends. Nora had her mouth now against the vinyl fabric covering the space between the girl's thighs. The vinyl looked wet under the bright lights, and I was sure that it was wet for real under Nora's ministrations, wet on the inside.

The camera in the room didn't move. It was set firmly on its pedestal, able to catch only the motions that were within the eye of the viewfinder. So when Nora disappeared out of the screen, the customers on the dance floor had to use their imaginations. Was she moving her way down the pretty blonde's thighs? And if so, what was she doing down there? We all knew. Of course, we did. But wondering made the concept that much more sexy. I could imagine what Nora was doing. I'd seen her work Dean. I knew that she had well-developed oral skills.

I stared back at the dance floor, pondering this thought, and I would have stared on longer, but Nora suddenly poked me. I started, as shocked to see her in person as I had been to see her up on the screen, still believing that she was up on screen, off in that room.

'Where were we?' Nora asked, passing a fresh drink to me.

I couldn't believe her. She actually wanted me to get back to my story. Apparently, she'd slipped out of the room stealthily, leaving the trio to their own erotic endeavours, satisfied with playing her role as the match that sparked the flame of lust. Not that they'd really needed her assistance, but they'd definitely enjoyed the help.

'You really want me to keep going?' I asked her. I saw that her lipstick was slightly smeared, but she still looked plenty put together. The Cinéma Vérité room was still up on the screen, the men now with their shirts off, sandwiching the Asian girl between them.

'Of course,' she said. 'I was only giving the crowd a little thrill.'

'A *big* thrill.'

'People expect something special when they come here,' she said, unconcerned by my shock. I have been at the Pink Fedora often enough to know that she was telling the truth. She makes the gossip rags on a regular basis. Celebrities feel free to let their wild sides show. Nora has a loyal staff. She hasn't caught anyone selling stories to the grocery-store magazines. But that doesn't mean she doesn't spill a few choice secrets herself every once in a while – how else to stay at the top of her game?

'Go on,' she said now, pulling a lip gloss out of her purse and retouching her make-up. 'You were describing how you felt when you found those papers.'

I watched as she redid her lips without the help of a mirror. She was using her favourite brand of gloss other than her own, one called Delux Beauty, which is known for naming their lip glosses after men. One of the reasons Nora has so many cosmetics is that she is the head of her own Pink Fedora make-up line. She considers buying cosmetics part of her job. She keeps an antique goblet filled with the different mini-lip glosses at home, each one featuring a different man's name. Nora has told me in the past how much she likes the concept of having an assortment of her favourite men in her pocket: Edgar, Rowan, Riley, Melvin, Jasper, Marshall, Gus, Antoine. I suddenly wondered if there was a Byron. If there was, she'd have to throw that gloss out.

'Eli,' she said, pulling me back to Earth. 'Tell me.'

How Nora could stay on track like that was amazing. I suppose this ability is also why she can run three clubs at once. She's eerie in the way she's able to compartmentalise her different emotions. I'm organised in my work, but disorganised in my feelings. I hesitated one more moment, doing my best to gather up my thoughts. My cellphone throbbed again, and I took the time to see who it was. Nora grabbed it from me.

'Byron,' she said.

'I know.'

'Why don't you go in that room and join the lovers? I'll take a photo of you and send it to him on the phone, so he can see what you're up to.'

'No thanks.'

'We know you're not so shy,' she pressed on.

'What we did back at your house is different from barging in on a threesome of people I don't know.'

'I'll introduce you,' Nora teased. 'The girl is one of my bartenders. This is her night off.'

I shook my head.

'Then why don't you go into the ladies' room and take a shot of your ass? You can send *that* to him. You know, with some text message that says: "Kiss this!"'

'And then what? He'll email it to all his friends?'

She sighed. The things that Nora would do and the things that I am willing to do are often polar opposites. 'I could send him a picture of *my* ass,' she suggested.

I started laughing. I couldn't help myself. She would do it, too. If I asked her. If I handed over my phone and told her to email a picture of her derrière to Byron, she would do it in a heartbeat. 'That's what friends are for,' I told her and, when Nora grinned at me and sipped her drink, I could tell that she was pleased by my response.

'Go on, Eli,' she said, 'tell me the rest. You've been dying to. And then I'll tell you my big news.'

It was difficult, but I gathered my thoughts, and then I explained the sensation in the very best way I could. 'It's like when you go outside, out in the desert or up in the hills. You can see all the sky, and you think that people have looked up at those stars for thousands of years. It makes you feel tiny, totally insignificant.'

'You speak well after a few drinks, don't you? You're positively poetic.' She wasn't buying any of this.

'No, it's not that.' I flushed. 'Well, yes, it's probably that, but also it's why I work in a museum. You always tease me about becoming as obsolete and unused as the ancient objects I categorise and write about. But I love it. All day long, I'm surrounded by terribly old pieces of art, and I can daydream and think about how long they've survived. The fact that they were here thousands of years before us and that they'll be here, barring other human errors like my fight with Byron, thousands of years from now. After we've been reduced to dust.'

'Lovely,' Nora said sarcastically. '*Every* day you think that? No wonder you're always wearing those stiff black suits and mundane dresses. You're fashioning yourself after a mortician. What a morbid way to spend your time.' She sniffed, disgusted.

'Not morbid,' I corrected her. 'It's not. It's peaceful.'

'How many papers are there?' Nora asked, dismissing what I'd just said with an impatient shrug. 'There must be only a couple to be able to fit into the case with your computer.'

'I left the computer there. I put it on the table and put the papers into the case.'

'You *what*?' She looked at me with narrowed eyes, and I could tell that she was trying to guess whether or not I was kidding.

'The computer was totally thrashed. I hit the urn hard enough with the computer bag to shatter the top of the PowerBook.' I stared at her. 'Fuck the computer, the papers were more important.'

'Your book,' Nora said, then caught herself, obviously realising that maybe this wasn't the most tactful concept to bring up. For the past four years I've been writing a book about art versus artefact. I'm not sure if my studies will interest anyone else, but the work lets me think in English instead of Latin, and that has to be good for my psyche.

'On CD, of course,' I told her. 'I was out of my head, but not insane. I have the CD in the case,' I explained. 'But that doesn't matter either. *This* matters. Finding out what's in them. I don't know why, but it does.' I put my hand protectively on the computer bag, then looked at my friend. I can trust Nora with every feeling I have. She'll never let me down. Now I said, 'I know you're thinking that I'm simply transferring my anger into something else, right? But that's not it. I can't explain it any better.'

I looked at Nora and my eyes must have pleaded. And Nora, who has been my best friend for a decade, who knows me better than anyone in the world, was kind enough to say, 'All right. I understand.' Seeing those imminent tears in my eyes, she added, 'It's OK, Eli –' using that pet name once more, a nickname that only she can get away with '– Don't worry. It's OK.'

The Pink Fedora closes at two. Officially, anyway. Best friends can stay on longer. Besides, where else would I go? Not to Nora's without her. Not home, because the beachfront apartment wasn't my home any more. Had it ever been my home? Byron had decorated it to look like the living space of a TV lawyer. I'd never liked anything in it other than the prints on the walls, and I'd never had the guts to voice my opinion.

I hung around while Nora did all the little after-hours housekeeping she likes to engage in. Just because the club is shut for the night, doesn't mean it's time for her to rest. She tends to be wired for hours after closing, and I know that she gets a thrill in being in this space that she's created herself.

Nora has confessed to me that she doesn't have to put nearly as much effort into the club now as she did when she first started. But that doesn't mean she's slacked off. She likes control. More than that – she revels in it.

While I watched, Nora flicked on the overhead lights from a hidden panel by the rear door, instantly bathing the room in a glow that felt far too bright. This was a place both destined and designed for the dark. Seeing the tables so well lit was disconcerting, like learning the trick behind the magic show. Who really wants to know that the magician's hat has a faux bottom? Doesn't everyone, down deep inside, hope that the glossy white rabbit appeared there by magic?

Travis helped her put things back in order. They didn't bother with the glasses or the litter on the tables. Those would be picked up later by the cleaning crew. Instead, the two worked to blow out the candles. To snag any left-behind jackets, scarves and cellphones and bring these to their Lucite lost-and-found box behind the bar.

I watched them through tired eyes and then finally I set my head on my crossed arms, my vision fading away to darkness.

In my dreams, I was making love to Byron, pressed against the window once more, my body chilled by the cold plate glass, my eyes focused on the faded denim-blue of the ocean below. In my dreams, I was moving with him, our bodies joined. Music played in the background, softly. 'With or Without You' on endless loop.

'You give up your power so easily.' That was Nora speaking. Was she in the room with us? No, the scene had changed in that watery way of dreams. We were all in the Cinéma Vérité room. Nora, Byron and me. I was the one clad in vinyl. Nora had on a pinstriped suit with a matching fedora. She looked like a gangster. What did a pinstriped fedora mean in 'Nora code'? I couldn't remember.

'You hand it over,' she said, watching as Byron slid my form-fitting dress up my body and began to fuck me from behind. 'Don't do that. What do you really think? That you can't live – with or without him? That's imbecilic. Of course, you can. You can live plenty well. Better than that. Better than with him. That's for sure. Didn't you learn anything from being with Dean?'

I looked in the mirror and suddenly saw not my reflection, but Nora's. My hair was short like hers, and frosted blue at the tips. My eyes were her ever-changing shade of green, not the normal hazel I see when I look in the bathroom mirror. Was she fucking Byron? Was she fucking me?

In a flash, Byron disintegrated into a cloud of dust, a pile of broken shards of clay, decorating the floor around my feet. But there were still three of us in the room: Nora and Dean were on either side of me, Dean moving his body against mine, Nora watching. It had been sexy, hadn't it? The three of us entwined. Nora had shown me what Dean liked best, and we'd taken turns pleasuring him, suckling from him until he collapsed back against the pillows, one of his hands on each of our backs, his body wracked with spasms of pleasure.

And the dream changed again. Dean was gone and Gwen stood in his place. Nora was still there, commenting, critiquing. 'So what do you think?' she was asking Gwen. 'Armenian or Oriental? You can tell me. I promise I won't tell anyone else.'

I opened my eyes and looked up at the wall behind the dance floor. There were Nora and blond-haired Travis, in a clinch. He had his hands supporting her, and she had wrapped her long lean legs around his body. It took me a moment to realise that *this* was reality. That Nora was capable of having sex with Dean solo, then engaging in two ménages à trois before hooking up with another man all in a matter of hours. I kept my head resting on my arms, but I knew they couldn't see me. They were back there in the movie room, making their own sexual cinema.

Music was playing, but it wasn't U2.

It was Def Leppard's 'Pour Some Sugar on Me'.

And my dream was over.

Chapter Six

After college, Nora and I decided to travel abroad together. It was my belief that this would be the last time in our lives to do something on a whim. Of course, I was wrong. Maybe the trip was like that for me. But Nora continues to live her life whim by whim, fantasy to fantasy. And I never really have done anything on a whim, before college, or after. Even this trip was planned meticulously.

We travelled the old-fashioned way, moving through the different countries on our agenda by overnight train. This was my choice. I think Nora would have preferred to have rented a bright-scarlet sports car and venture at a hundred miles per hour along the circuitous highways. But I had always dreamed of taking a train throughout Europe. It seemed to me the way people were meant to see Europe, out of the windows of a swiftly moving train. Since I was paying for the trip, and Nora was bunking for free, the mode of transportation was my choice. I'd been saving for this trip for years. Nora swore she would pay me back – but it didn't matter to me. I would have gotten a sleeping car whether I was with her or by myself.

I'm lying.

I can't imagine having gone on the trip without her.

All through Europe, we shared a sleeping car, and even though the space was tiny, we never got on each other's nerves. At least, we shared the car whenever Nora hadn't found someone else she wanted to sleep with. Then I had the sleeping car to myself, and Nora disappeared with her conquest for the evening, always returning to me in the morning with stories of romance that were as exciting as any of the steamy paperbacks I'd taken with me to help pass the time. Nora loved to divulge her sexy secrets over coffee in the café car, licking her lips seductively if her most recent lover happened to pass us by.

While Nora was out in the real world, I'd be snuggled in the tiny berth, reading late into the night about people who were just like Nora. Free spirits. Embracers of lust. The irony wasn't lost on me, yet I didn't have the ability to change the scene, didn't have any idea of how to become a heroine in a novel of my own.

But nobody really behaves like those pulp novel characters, do they?

No one but Nora.

In the month that we travelled, she bedded an Italian conductor, a French physicist and a Spanish soldier. She met two graduate students from Australia and slept between them for two nights in a row. 'I was like the Vegemite,' she joked afterwards, the coffee cup warming her hands as she spoke. 'You know, like in that Men at Work song? I was the Vegemite in a Vegemite sandwich.'

'What's Vegemite?' I asked, curious.

'No idea,' she said, grinning, 'but I think it's some sort of a spread.'

When we did alight at various stops, she'd stage a 'hostel takeover', creating the same sort of ambience in whichever youth hostel we chose that she had maintained in her dorm room. Nora has always been the life of every party. That's the one constant about her.

I hate to admit that I often fantasised about taking her place, of slipping into her shoes, or her battered black leather motorcycle jacket with the white stripes on the back and down the sleeves, or her ripped red T-shirt with the word SWALLOWS written across the chest, flanked by two little blue birds. I dreamed about having the confidence to respond when some man paid me a compliment. Nora and I do occasionally pass for twins, we can look so much alike. But our resemblance is solely on the surface. And even after being her friend for so many years, I still am unable to channel even a tenth of the confidence that Nora possesses.

What I would have given to experience a railroad romance, like she did. But my mild flirtations never went further than a bat of my eyelashes, didn't lead me to another passenger's berth or a sojourn into anyone else's sleeping car.

I told myself not to worry. That love would eventually find me even if excitement eluded me. Besides, the purpose of the trip for me wasn't to have a summer romance. It was to visit all the artwork I'd studied over the past four years. The purpose for Nora was to gather information about the underground clubs she'd heard of. She was on a mission to visit as many as she could, to discover what made them popular. There were dozens out there, more than I would have thought. Nora listened to gossip in other languages, and she had an uncanny ability to find the right people who would give us a password that would enter us into worlds of debauchery.

By day, we went to the museums, using our soon-to-expire student IDs to get in cheaply. As students this was our last hurrah. All day long we spent viewing the ancient art and artefacts that made my world whole. We blended in with the other tourists: I looked like any other future historian; Nora resembled the gaggles of students who didn't really want to be there, the ones who had a much better time in the cafeterias, or sprawled out in front of the museums, sunning themselves and sharing sodas.

By night, we went to the clubs, Nora falling into them, the way I fell into my favourite paintings. I've been known to get lost in a piece of artwork, to be able to stare at a picture for hours, hardly moving, barely even remembering to breathe. I have friends who speed-walk through museums, wanting to get their money's worth, which means to them that they need to see every single piece a museum has to offer. I know other people who only wish to see the most famous works on display. Show them the *Mona Lisa*, and they're finished. Point them towards Monet's *Waterlilies* and they can call it a day.

I have never had any such desires. If I can find one painting that speaks to me, I am satisfied. It doesn't need to be the most famous. It doesn't even need to be well known. If a work lingers with me, in my thoughts, desires or dreams, then I feel fulfilled.

Nora's the same way – with nightclubs rather than artwork. After hours, in tiny clubs, she comes to life. The place doesn't have to be the coolest, the hippest, the one that's written about in every gossip magazine from *Hello!* to *OK*. The environment simply has to sing to Nora. Some part of the atmosphere must call out to her, touch her in a way that's unexpected.

Even after college, she continued to be a piece of work in progress, creating her looks carefully, naming and chronicling them. At night, during our journey, she became herself when dancing in the darkness. She lit up, her eyes aglow. I held back, as might have been expected, viewing from the sidelines, never judging because that's not my style, only watching.

How funny that we worked together like that. Nora keeping me company from art show to art show, museum to museum, never complaining that her feet hurt, that we'd viewed too many sculptures to keep track of, that once you'd seen one Monet you'd seen them all. Then, to repay her, there I was as her date, her constant companion, entering worlds of sin I'd never even imagined existed.

In college, I'd focused every bit of myself on learning all about the art of the world. Nora had spent those same four years focused on learning about people. What they wanted. What they craved. She hadn't been a bad student, simply a vague one. The only subjects aside from anthropology that truly captured her interest were the languages she took: French, Italian, Spanish. And I think she really only learned those languages so that she could communicate with the exotic foreign students who came to Santa Barbara for their semesters abroad. She quizzed them about all sorts of things, learning about their favourite music, the types of dance clubs they frequented, the trends from their native lands. Her love of language paid off during our travels – as did her friendships with the various students. Wherever we went, Nora knew people to take us out, people to put us up, so that our nights not spent on trains or in hostels were spent jammed in tiny apartments with six or seven roommates, all more than happy to share their space with us – and more than happy to share their beds with Nora, if she'd have them.

The only place we paid for a really nice hotel was in Paris. Here, we splurged – or, *I* splurged – because this was the best world for both of us. Paris boasted my favourite art, and it contained Nora's favorite of all the clubs. We spent a week in the city, visiting the Louvre, the Pompidou, the Picasso Museum, the Musée D'Orsay and all of the tiny galleries lining the Seine.

Every evening, we headed to the student quarters, where we hung out at the open-air cafés, drinking glasses of dark-red wine and listening to the nearby patrons as they talked about where to buy the best hashish. Students are the same all over the world. They might have been speaking French, but they sounded exactly like the kids who hung out at Waxe Wod, trying to impress one another in spite of their total lack of knowledge.

Each night, Nora found us a different place to go dancing. She favoured the clubs that played synthetic dance music, heavy with techno beats. Nora liked to dance until her whole body ached, until the soles of her shoes gave out like the princesses in that famous fairy tale. But she wanted more. I could always tell when she was yearning for something new. She would have the same expectant look on her face that I get when I walk into an exhibition featuring an artist I've never heard of. My whole body attitude changes. I feel electrified, exhilarated.

In Paris, Nora decided that she wanted to go to a club that only allowed in couples.

'What are we going to do?' I asked her, betting on Nora to scrounge up two men for us to mate with. Or if not actually mate with, then dance with. Two men who would at first glance believe this was their lucky day – and for Nora's, it probably would be. For mine, the date would be a bit of a dud. Unless the fellow liked to discuss art.

With Nora, she could practically snap her fingers and men would appear out of thin air. She's magic that way. But for once, the idea of finding dates didn't appeal to her. If we brought along two guys, we'd have to interact with them, and on this night, Nora was only after information. So rather than go as two couples, we became one.

'What do you mean, we're going to *be* the couple?' I asked, as confused as if she'd started speaking to me in a foreign language.

'Trust me,' Nora insisted. She's always said that to me, and I do trust her. Sometimes, begrudgingly, but I do.

Nora dressed in drag, which was easy for her with her short hair, her slim build. She bound her breasts and wore a crisp white shirt and black blazer, black tuxedo pants with a black satin stripe down the side and men's Oxfords, all purchases from the flea market on the outskirts of Paris. With the help of her cosmetics, she added a rough five o'clock shadow to her cheeks. Her hair was blue-black and she fashioned it into a spiky rebel look. The end result was that she didn't appear entirely masculine – there was too much beauty in her face to hide the girl there. But she didn't look exactly feminine either. She possessed a totally androgynous look, which she understood would work for the night. If she paired herself with me, people would take it for granted that she was a man.

This wasn't the first time Nora had dressed in drag. During her various experiments in how far she could push the limits of fashion, she'd occasionally ventured out on campus wearing her male friends' clothing. She liked to see how many people she could fool, going as far as entering the men's room while clad in her costume. Nobody ever stopped her, but I don't know if that's because she actually managed to fool them – like the author of *Self-made Man*, a different Nora, Norah Vincent – or simply because she stared them down. Nora's known for her dead-eyed stare.

On this night in Paris, she pulled out all the tricks, including stuffing a rolled pair of nylons down the front of her slacks.

Was it wrong for me to think she was handsome? Was it wrong for me to want to fuck her?

I kept those feelings to myself, staying silent as she dressed me to look like her ultimate dream date, creating more cleavage than I actually own with the assistance of an under wire demi-cup, pulling a frilly red dress over my head – also purchased at the fabulous flea market that had taken an hour-long metro ride to get to – making me wear heels that I'd never have chosen on my own. One needs sensible shoes to log as many hours as I do walking through museums. Sensible isn't a word that Nora puts much faith in.

'I don't know,' I told her, staring at my reflection as if seeing myself for the first time. I couldn't believe how sexy I looked. How did she do it? I wondered silently. How did she make me look so pretty? When I am left to my own skills, I definitely know how to use a mascara wand. But I am never able to win the same results that Nora achieves. She's a magician with make-up. On this night, she outlined my eyes using a silvery pencil and suddenly they seemed as large and bright as her own.

She used a rose hue on my cheeks and coloured in my lips with a dark merlot.

'You look amazing,' she insisted, standing behind me, adjusting her package with the attitude of a pro. Immediately, she had adopted the swagger of a man. As one who studies people with the relentless scrutiny that Nora possesses, she didn't find it at all difficult to stand the way a guy would. To move like a man. To put an arm around my waist, the way a man would, holding me casually, but close.

'But will they buy it?' I asked, still unsure. I could see the maleness to her, but I could see her feminine side as well. Was it only because I knew there was a girl underneath those clothes that made me worry? Or would others stop for a second look when she passed by, wondering whether my date was a he or a she?

'Trust me,' she said. 'No one will have any clue.'

As usual, she was right. We got into the club without a problem, the hostess in her tiny racer-back black dress checking us off the reservation list without even a mild register of disbelief. Either we really looked like an honest-to-goodness hetero couple, or the woman didn't actually care. I felt my nerves start to build as we walked inside. To my great relief, Nora stayed by my side.

The club was located in a quiet out-of-the-way neighbourhood. If Nora hadn't known of its exact location, we never would have found the spot. Nora has used that information for her own clubs. You'll never find her setting up in storefronts out on Hollywood Boulevard or bellying up to Rodeo Drive. You have to know where Nora's clubs are located in order to gain entrance. Average Joes simply can't stumble into her heavenly headquarters.

The Two Muses was created with the same philosophy. Only those in the know were granted access – but once inside, all doors were open. The club featured three floors of frivolity. The ground floor was devoted to dining and dancing – no live band, DJ only, American music the darling of the hour. As we sipped our drinks and watched attractive couples grooving on the dance floor, we heard Aerosmith and Madonna, Prince and Bon Jovi. Couples were dressed quite like Nora and myself. That must have been why the hostesses hadn't spared us even a look of interest. Men were in black suits and white shirts, while women were clad in more colourful frocks. I'd always thought of nightclubs as places filled with leather. But heavy fabrics don't lend themselves to dancing. As the club became crowded, the room grew hotter. People peeled off any extraneous layers, revealing ever more skin as the evening passed.

'Dance?' Nora asked after we'd killed several cocktails.

'With you?'

She nodded as if that went without saying. Who else would I dance with? I eyed the couples around me. One of the perks of this club was the fact that it was couples only – no worries about lecherous lone-wolf males hoping to prey on the ladies – yet couples could easily divide and mix with one another, morphing into brand-new couples. In spite of my reservations, I was pleased that Nora wanted to dance with me, and I watched as she stood and helped me to my feet. I had a difficult time simply staying upright in the shoes, but with Nora's help, I found my balance. Since our very first conversation at school, she'd made it something of a challenge to get me comfortable on a dance floor. I'd never become the type to go up on stage. Not like my fearless friend. But I did have a better ability to hear a beat.

Under a glittering silver disco ball, Nora and I danced. I stared at her, focusing on the way she moved. She was dancing differently this night. She was actually dancing the way a man would. I couldn't believe how well she blended, able to pull off this charade as if she were a classically trained actor.

But suddenly I felt that other people were watching us, too.

'Do they know?' I asked, when she pulled me in tight for a slow dance.

'No, they just like us.'

'What do you mean?'

'This is a couples' only club for a reason,' Nora explained, her lips pressed against my ear so that I could make out her words over the beat of the music. Yet even though I heard what she was saying, I still didn't get it, didn't understand at all what she was talking about. 'Couples come here to play.'

'Play?' I echoed.

'You know,' she murmured, her breath tickling my neck, '*play*.'

At her words, I looked around the room, and now I saw that in some of the darker corners, people were making out. But they were doing more than kissing. One couple was necking passionately while another couple stroked them, fingers running all over their bodies. The foursome seemed not to notice that others were watching, yet I could tell from the way that they moved that they relished the thought of an audience. One of the women – the one kissing her partner – had her eyes shut. I watched her shift her hips, then spread her thighs wider apart, so that I could see the sliver of her pale pink panties beneath her short dark skirt. The sight made me grip onto Nora more tightly. I did not want her to leave my side.

Finally, Nora decided she wanted to explore the lower level. 'If my information is correct,' she said, 'the next floor down is for fucking.'

'Excuse me?'

'You heard me,' she said as she took my hand in hers.

She was right, I had. I only didn't quite believe what she'd said. 'What do you mean, though?' I asked. 'What do you mean "for fucking"?'

She couldn't be totally serious, could she? We'd been to several risqué clubs during our travels, but most simply encouraged naked dancing. Or featured pretty girls in cages suspended over the dance floor. Every once in awhile, we'd caught sight of a sexual encounter, often in the hallways near the restrooms, but there hadn't been an actual location where people were encouraged to get together.

Nora didn't respond to my query. She didn't need to. All became clear as we made our way down the stairs, coming to land in a world of beds. Beds made up in velvet and satin. Round beds. Low beds. Beds halfway hidden by long heavy curtains. The walls all around us were lit with sconces. Purple and gold draperies hung along the walls, shielding the lovers from the chill of being thrust below street level. This underground level echoed the same coldness in the air as the catacombs had, which we'd visited the day before at Nora's insistence. But with the glow of the lamps and the heat from some unseen source, the floor was welcoming.

I must not have been the only one to think so. There were scores of people using the provided beds. Women and men dancing to a different beat. Those who wanted to watch, rather than join, leaned against the walls or perched on the edges of the mattresses for a closer view.

So Nora's information had been true. The lower-ground floor of the Two Muses *was* for fucking. And the basement was . . .

'A dungeon,' she said in her matter-of-fact style.

'A what?' Once again, I'd heard her, but I didn't like the sound of the word. Did she mean a *dungeon*-dungeon? Could she possibly? Besides, even though she'd scared me with the new concept, my mind was still on the second floor.

'That's why we're really here, Eli. It's a dungeon, a stone room down below. That's what it's called anyway.'

Instantly, I envisioned chains and whips, men in leather masks, *The Story of O* come to life. Yes, I knew all about O. I'd read the story at Nora's recommendation. She's always had the desire to broaden my sense of the world. Now, Nora did little to shake my image.

'You have to walk down the winding staircase that takes you below sea level. The lady at the top gives you a flashlight to help guide your way, but on the lowest level there are no lights allowed at all.'

I was shocked by the thought. Truthfully, I'd already been shocked by the sight of lovers entwined on the lower-ground level. Here, couples were willingly exposing themselves to others, stripping off any false pretences as well as their clothing.

Yes, most of the clubs we'd visited so far had been slightly more adventurous than I'd expected. You might catch a girl taking her top off, or win a glimpse of naked flesh when someone spun quickly in a dress, revealing a decadent lack of underclothing. But the concept of strangers fucking in total darkness floored me.

Nora, of course, took the whole notion in stride. She might not have been planning on offering a similar arena back at home, but she still wanted to see how it was all done. Even when we were this young, she hoped one day to have clubs of this sort in LA. The trip was research to her. It speaks of my endless trust for her that I headed down those steps to the basement level. Nora promised me nothing untowards would happen to me. I took her at her word.

In the darkness, I saw nothing, as might have been expected. My eyes wouldn't focus. This wasn't like being out at night, where stars or streetlights would offer some safe glow. This was total blackness, reminding me of *Murmurous Moto, Maestro*, by John Chamberlain, the painted and chromium-plated steel sculpture that's blacker than anything I can imagine.

When my hand left the railing and met the flesh of a stranger's back, I immediately recoiled and turned to head back up the stairs.

'Wait,' Nora whispered, her hand on my wrist, holding me steady.

'No, I can't.'

'Just a second,' she murmured. She was enthralled. I

could tell. I'd heard that tone of voice before. But I wouldn't stay. This was too much to ask of me.

Nora flicked the flashlight on and off quickly, strobing the room so that she could see the activities in the darkness. My eyes took in images – flash! – a woman between two men. Flash! Three women together in a row, licking and kissing one another. Flash! A man pressing a woman up against the grey stone wall. All of these interactions were taking place without the aid of light. I saw that the floor was carpeted in a silky-looking rug. Thin pillows were scattered about, but no beds, nothing hazardous for people to trip over. At the flickering light, the lovers all looked our way.

But was lovers the right word? These were strangers, coming together in the darkness. Strangers, giving one another exactly what they desired.

Nora clicked off the flashlight and pushed me back up the stairs. She'd seen what she wanted. She'd made her own decisions. Now, she was ready to go home. I'd seen more than I'd bargained for. Images like artwork remained emblazoned in my mind. While Nora lost herself in mental plans of her future clubs, I walked back down those cold stone steps, over and over again, poised on the brink of action before turning back each and every time.

ThePinkFedora.blogspot.com

Don't worry, chicklets. You didn't miss anything.

You missed everything.

While you were sleeping, the Cinéma Vérité room got one hell of a full-body workout. This was late Thursday night, with two stellar runway models. (You're thinking women, aren't you, you sexist piglets? These were male *models!) The two lovelies created a pussycat sandwich around my favourite new female bartender. The show was taped. View playbacks this Sunday and Thursday evening. Or create your own movie fresh.*

Now, remember we're starting the countdown now to my new reality show. Keep coming back for the latest posts. We'll be putting some headshots up on our site to let you vote for your favourite contestants. And we'll be listing the drinks that they mix so that you really can 'try this at home'.

But don't stay home. Come join us at the Pink Fedora!

And don't forget to wear your hats. Anyone in a fedora gets in free.

A pink fedora wins a dance with me.

Kisses,

Nora Hammond

Quote for the Day: As Billy Idol said, 'Everybody got it wrong. I said I was into *porn* again, not born again.'

Chapter Seven

Nora drinks like a man. Like many men, really. A whole football team of men. She can pound shots without looking back, a talent which she considers part of her work ethic. Drinking is a skill she's honed over the years, building up her ability like an athlete in training. I've never had the stamina she possesses, and I was rusty, anyway. Byron and I weren't the club-going type of couple, even back at the very start of our relationship. We didn't think we were too highbrow. We were just too boring.

After returning from the Pink Fedora, I lay on Nora's sofa bed and gazed up at her ceiling. She has painted the walls of this room the perfect shade of red, what I'd call rose red and she'd call cocksucker red. But the ceiling is panelled in black and white tiles, like the floor of an old-fashioned kitchen. In the centre of the room hangs a chandelier – not your normal crystal, either. Nothing's normal in Nora's world. This chandelier is made from antique silver forks and spoons that dangle somewhat dangerously overhead.

I know that Nora designed the room herself, without the help of an interior decorator, and I wondered for the first time whether Nora was able to be so creative because she's never had a long-term partner. If she'd been married, or at least dating steadily, would she have been as free to decorate as she saw fit? That led me to questions I wasn't fully ready to answer: Had I become dull because I'd given over my life to Byron, or was I dull because I'd always been?

It was too late to ponder such thoughts, so I looked around the room instead.

Nora's house is an extension of the wildness of her clubs. One bathroom is done entirely in Kit-Kat clocks, their eyes swinging back and forth in time with the motion of their tails. She has the famous original clocks, black ones with simple white bow ties, as well as assorted colours: turquoise, lemon yellow, plum. Some have been decked out in rhinestones. All tick-tock like mad.

In her dining room, the only lighting is lava lamps. She's positioned them in rows around the room, hundreds of lava lamps. Dinner parties in this room are like acid dreams come true. You can't take your eyes off the colourful alienlike objects slithering up and down in the liquid.

As I looked at the forks and spoons over my head, I wondered when people decide that it's time to grow up. Nora never has. Is that why she's still able to stay out late, to fuck all night, to cruise through life on caffeine? When do most people decide the dance clubs are for the kids. Is it about the same time they start worrying about middle-aged spread and condo payments? Is it when they lose their lust for life or decide that no such thing exists?

Sure I've always tended to dress like a school marm, but hadn't I been more alive when I was younger? More vibrant, somehow? Was 28 going to be the end of the road for me? No, it couldn't be. Just look at me. I'd been in my first ever threesome this very night.

I gazed around the room, still lost in my thoughts. Nora's house is small for someone as wealthy as she is. I've read interviews in which people have asked her why she doesn't have one of the mansions in Holmby Hills or Bel Air. She claims that she prefers this small stucco house in Venice Beach. It's not shabby by any means, but Nora could upgrade, and she knows it. 'I like to be able to clean my house myself,' she told one interviewer. 'I don't want to have people I don't know underfoot.'

How different from Byron. His whole goal in life was

to move up. Move from the apartment we were currently renting to the penthouse at the top floor of our building. Trade up the Audi he owned for a BMW convertible. Trade in his girlfriend for a shiny new model. One with all the bells and whistles.

Was that the real reason why we broke up? Did he look to Gwen to put more excitement back into his life? Or had he simply traded up? I wondered whether Gwen would take Byron out for picnics at their lunch break, the way he and I had gone out when we first started dating. Did she rekindle some lost sense of fun for him? Or was it all about the sex?

Thoughts like those would have kept me up, if I hadn't been so drunk. At some point, my mind spun out, and I fell asleep. Hard.

In the morning, I could barely find my way out from under the comforter Nora had thrown over me the night before. Unfortunately, the world didn't become much less blurry when I stuck my head out from under the blanket. Why had I let Nora take me out? Because 'let' wasn't the correct word.

Nora had made me actually want to go out. By the time she'd had me dressed, I'd been looking forward to a night of not thinking. That's how it always is with Nora. Not only can she get you to do what she wants, she can make you think you want it, too. If that's not a skill, then I don't know what one is.

Sighing, I lay back against the plush cushions of my best friend's black sofa.

I didn't have to go to work today. I could call in sick – take a few personal days off – if ever there was a reason, right? Besides, my work isn't the life or death sort. I'm not a doctor in charge of a wing of patients who need my expertise in order to survive. I'm a researcher, focused on poring through antique tomes. My assignments stretch out for months, occasionally for years. And as one might expect, I'm intensely focused when it comes to projects, always ahead of schedule. Missing even a week or two would do nothing to put me off my routine.

But my mind suddenly turned to Anthony, and I imagined him looking over the manuscript I'd discovered. Quite honestly, I imagined him doing all sorts of other things as well. Things that only happened in places like Nora's club. Or in her bedroom, I corrected myself, thinking of playing with her and Dean the day before. How unlike me to do something like that. Was this the start of a new era for me? One in which I would find myself much more in tune to Nora's way of life.

I settled back into the sofa, lost in an instant daydream. Would Anthony go into that room with me, the Cinéma Vérité room? And if I could talk him into tripping down that hallway by my side, would he be the sort to baulk at public displays of affection, as Byron always had? Or would the concept turn him on?

I thought of the recent split between two A-list movie stars. One had immediately paired up with a dark-haired minx, a femme fatale who had once happily proclaimed that she and her then-husband had fucked on the way to the Oscars. This full-lipped beauty reminded me of Nora, and I appreciated her candour when it came to all things sexual. Would Anthony go for someone like that? Because I've always been the more reserved type. Not that I don't like sex – I do.

I simply got stuck in a rut. A rut called Byron. I thought that true love meant bending myself to fit his mould. I hadn't realised he was looking outside of the box until he came right out and said so. I lowered my head into my hands, feeling the scream of the hangover wail from ear to ear. Work would be good for me. I couldn't lie around all day thinking about Byron, hating him. Truth was that I felt conflicted. I was more upset at what *I'd* done to myself than anything he'd done to me.

I'd compromised. That was the feeling that came back over and over. I'd transformed into someone he wanted.

Someone I thought he wanted, anyway. And in doing so, I'd lost sight of what I wanted for myself.

Or had I ever really known?

Softly, I made my way down the hall to Nora's shower. I knew she'd be sleeping in – as she always does on nights she works at the club. I didn't want to disturb her as I got ready for work.

Still, as I was about to close the door to her apartment, I heard the unmistakable sounds of lovemaking coming from down the hall. So even though we'd driven home together, she hadn't stayed alone. Typical Nora. I shut the door with a click and headed to my car, wondering which boy she was greeting the day with – Dean or Travis?

Nora started her first official nightclub right after college. Well, right after she left college. She never actually graduated, never actually was able to declare a major. Too many subjects captivated her attention, although none held her interest long enough for her to pass many of her classes. She was too busy experiencing life to study a book – that's what she claimed, anyway.

She started club Phon-E on her twenty-first birthday. It was a perfect spot for hip Los Angelenos, down in the dark heart of Hollywood where everything is a façade, nothing what it seems.

Club Phon-E was decked out entirely in 1920s décor, nearly all of it snagged from local thrift stores and garage sales. Nora's always had an eye for style. She can enter a store filled with incredibly ugly furniture and find the one prize lurking within. I have the same ability at art auctions. I can always locate the treasure among the trash. Nora brought me along with her when she bought furnishings for her club, but she never bothered to ask my advice on anything. She had a vision, and she turned that vision into a reality. The low-ceilinged room was crowded with black leather club chairs and tiny round glass tables. On each table stood a heavy black lacquered phone outfitted with a number done in neon. Patrons could call each other up and talk. The club was an instant success.

Nora reinvents herself on a daily basis. She's never gotten over the concept of being an actual work in progress. I think she hopes someday to have her own art show, to blow up the daily Polaroids she takes of herself. To show the history of her different artistic looks. This chameleon-like ability assists her in the running of her clubs, as well. She likes to have different places to go to suit her moods. When she grew tired of hearing phones ringing all the time, she began to dream up club number two.

Faux Pas was Nora's second endeavour, even more successful than the first, with a narrow stage along one wall featuring live bands. Her concept was the belief that where there was live music, there were bound to be mistakes, and those were embraced at Faux Pas. Nora has always had a knack for finding local talent destined to explode. She opened her doors to bands nobody had ever heard of, and beamed as she watched her protégés make it big. I teased her that she only opened Faux Pas in order to maintain a steady line of musicians she wanted to fuck. She smirked in that classic way of hers but never told me I was wrong.

The Pink Fedora was her third club – more of an old-fashioned dance hall than anything else. Had disco still been in demand, the floor would have been lit up and a mirrored ball would have dangled from the ceiling. Instead, the club has a kaleidoscope theme, with floor-to-ceiling mirrors on the walls, and a dance floor that actually rotates. When the lights get going, multi-hued ribbons and swirls of colour flash over the crowd, reverberating in the mirrors into infinity.

Nora owns all three places, and she bounces from one to the other depending on who she's with or what she's in the mood for.

As I drove to work in the recently refurbished downtown LA, I thought about Nora, about her nearly endless supply of self-confidence. I wished she had been up this morning before I left. I needed her advice as I considered talking to Anthony. I wanted to approach him about the manuscript. And I wanted to do nothing of the sort. The two opposite urges kept running through my mind as I parked the car, and continued to frustrate me as the morning progressed.

It's amazing how much work you can get done when you're procrastinating from doing something else. I organised the top two drawers of my file cabinets. Truthfully, they were already fairly neat. But now I made sure that all of the file folders were the same colour – a vibrant chartreuse – and that the font on the little tabs matched precisely.

Once I completed my reorganisation of files A through Z, I turned my attention to my cellphone. It took only the push of a button to delete Byron from my electronic phone address book. He'd left me two additional voicemail messages since the night before, which I erased without listening to.

I'll admit that I didn't actually erase them right away. I stared at my phone, saw the phone number of the person who'd left the voicemail and felt torn. We'd been together four years. Shouldn't I at least listen to what he had to say? Then I envisioned what Nora would do in a similar situation. 'Look, Eli,' she'd snarl in her attempt to protect me, 'what could he possibly have to say that would interest you? That he and Gwen love each other? That you were wrong about that? Trust me, you've heard enough of that bullshit already.'

She was right. I didn't even need her in the room to know what I had to do. I deleted all messages, and then set the phone in my purse, where I wouldn't be bothered by the vibrations.

Finally, when I could amuse myself no longer, I took a deep breath and headed down the hall to Anthony Ginsburg's office. Nora and I still might look a lot like one another, but our shared resemblance is skin deep. I tried my very best to channel her charm as I held my manuscript and prepared to knock on my crush's office door. I remembered what Dean had said the day before. That his nervousness only lasted until he played the first note. I prayed this concept would work for me, as well.

The door to Anthony's office is emblazoned with train paraphernalia. Colour photographs of engines, ticket stubs and train stickers make up a collage dedicated to the railroad. It looks like the bedroom door of a five-year-old boy, rather than the office door of a forty-year-old man.

I'd passed by Anthony's office often enough, rarely having a reason to go inside, but peeking through his doorway whenever possible. I knew that there were awards hanging on his walls, that his desk was as messy as mine was clean, and that every so often he had one of our patrons in for a drink, pouring some amber liquid from a crystal decanter kept on his bookshelf.

This time, the door was shut, and I knocked as hard as I dared and then waited, shifting back and forth from one foot to another. I thought about how Nora had teased me the previous evening, naming off Anthony's many attributes. What was I doing here? Was I simply looking for a new boyfriend? Was this just a pipe dream I'd conjured up, this need to have the manuscript translated? Did all I really want was a new model, same as Byron?

I hoped not.

I'd been in one relationship after another for the past eight years. Maybe I wasn't able to be on my own for more than 24 hours. That was a sobering thought, and not one that I wanted to look at too deeply. At least, not now, with Anthony calling out to me in his crisp British accent: 'Enter!'

Inside, as I recalled from my peeks into his office, any resemblance to the world of a five-year old boy ended abruptly. There sat Anthony, behind his cluttered mahogany desk, reading something obviously mesmerising in a thick black book, his aristocratic fingers following along with a line of prose. His dark curly hair was pulled back into a ponytail that hung past the collar of his blue Oxford-cloth shirt. I gazed at his face, his stark cheekbones, strong chin. In a cartoon, I would have licked my lips. Instead, I continued to stare at him, knowing that I would have to look away quickly once he put down the book.

'One moment,' he said when I stepped into the doorway, not offering me even the merest courtesy of a curious glance. While he finished reading, I took in the tiny model trains along the edge of his desk, the 'genuine' train whistle carved from wood, the advertisement for a Lionel train set framed on the wall behind him. So there was a bit of the boy still in the room.

Finally, Anthony closed the book and looked at me. With a bit of surprise in his voice, he said, 'Eleanor, I'm so sorry.' His smooth accent caressed the words. There was something in the way Anthony simply said my name that made it difficult for me to breathe. 'If I had known it was you, I would have stopped sooner. But when I'm reading another language, it's always hard to pull myself out of it.' He grinned. 'You know how that is, I'm sure. I've seen you working on those illuminated manuscripts.' He paused again, looking me up and down. Immediately, I felt underdressed, and then just as swiftly wished I was actually *un*dressed, wished he was undressing me. 'Can I help you?'

'Oh, yes.' I wanted to say. 'You can most definitely help me. You can help me obliterate any thoughts or emotions I still have left for my ex-boyfriend.'

'How can I do that?' he would ask.

'Simple,' I would tell him with a sexy half-smile stolen directly from Nora. 'You can bend me over your beautiful messy desk and fuck the living daylights out of me. Touch me while you fuck me. Bring one hand between my legs and stroke my pussy for me, then pinch my clit hard. I'll cry out when I come, calling your name over and over, and that will take you to your own limits. People on other floors will hear us, and they'll come running to see what the problem is. But there won't be any problem. There will just be you and me, locked together, our clothes dishevelled, our bodies as one.'

Where in the hell had that come from? Had being part of a sexual sandwich with Nora and Dean turned me into a whole new person? Had seeing that threesome afterwards – and briefly a foursome once Nora had entered the party – done something to my brain?

Thank God, I had a mission. If I'd been without one, I would have stood there like a total moron, gazing at him the way a teenybopper would look at one of her idols in the flesh. Unable to think, or speak, or breathe. Yes, I'd worked with Anthony in the past, had been in his presence often enough to consider him a solid acquaintance if not an actual friend. But I rarely ever spoke to him one on one, and never with him looking at me like that.

With only a slight tremble to my voice, I told him what I wanted, handed him the papers, then waited for his answer. I forced myself to stare at him, and I stamped down on the urge to give myself over to another sexual fantasy. How easy it would be to lose myself in his eyes, daydreaming about what it might be like to be as sexually free spirited as Nora is.

'Honestly, I'm not all that good at ancient Greek,' Anthony said, still looking at me instead of the ancient pages. 'Give me a few tablets of cuneiform and I'll take you places you've never been, baby.' He gave me an unexpectedly lounge lizard-like look, and I nearly giggled. Where was my self-confidence? Where was my poise? Standing in front of his desk, I felt like as nervous as an intern, useless and unsure of myself.

Still, I was on a mission – my lovely, trusted mission – and I forced myself to explain to him what I needed. 'Serina told me you're a whiz at Greek.'

Serina works in our ancient art department, dating objects. When we receive something from an archaeological dig, she studies the piece until she can place it in the correct time period. I knew that she was a friend of Anthony's, and I had gone to her for help before walking down the hall and into this world of trains.

'I studied it, sure,' Anthony said, 'but I never got higher than a solid C.' He sounded as if he were teasing me, or lying to me, and I had no idea why.

'I don't have cuneiform,' I told him matter-of-factly, thankfully sounding much more like myself and less like a fawning fan. 'I don't have hieroglyphics. I don't have Sanskrit. I have this.' I stared at Anthony, challenging him – Serina had told me that Anthony likes a challenge – and he stared right back at me through those sexy glasses in heavy tortoiseshell frames. Mmm, I liked the way he looked in those. At Nora's insistence, I'd long ago traded my round frames for more chic European-style reading glasses. But on Anthony, the old-fashioned lenses made him look more appealing than ever.

'You're the only one here who can come close to translating this,' I insisted. 'And, besides –' now, I realised why he was playing with me '– you just won some sort of award for a Greek translation. It was written up in the ARTSI in-house newspaper. And you majored in ancient literatures at Oxford right?'

Anthony nodded, looking slightly embarrassed. I turned my head to check out the various diplomas on the walls. A plethora of awards and medals fought for room on the bookshelves. Anthony Ginsburg is a top-rate academic – modest, perhaps – but brilliant.

While I took in my surroundings, I heard Anthony breathe in deeply and then exhale, almost longingly. I faced him again and gave him a curious look, and he quickly stared down at his cluttered desk, at the papers spread before him in the one clear section. With me watching him, forcing him to do something, he opened his top desk drawer, removed a pair of thin rubber gloves and slid them on. Instantly, I was captivated by the movements of his hands, fingers interlaced evenly to secure the gloves before he gingerly lifted the first piece of paper from the sheath. He looked so intent as he worked that I almost felt as if I'd disappeared, vanished entirely from the scene. With his eyes so focused on the papers, I let myself fade into a brand-new fantasy. This was an unusual sort for me, but I didn't fight the vision, didn't stop myself, didn't say no.

As I watched him work, I envisioned his gloved fingers on me, touching me as carefully as he touched the pages. I saw myself spread out on top of his desk, as if I were a piece of artwork, something valuable that needed classifying.

The desk was different in my daydream. It was clean, for one thing, and covered with a red leather padding. Anthony spread me out and began probing and examining me.

'You're beautiful,' he said. 'A work of art.'

I easily imagined the feel of the chilled rubber against my skin, the sensation of his rubber-tipped fingers sliding into my willing open pussy. I was dripping wet, and he noticed. There would have been no way for him not to. He gave me a fierce look as he slid his fingers in ever deeper, and then he brought the evidence of my arousal in front of my eyes, waiting for me to acknowledge how turned on I was.

With my eyes lowered, I started to blush. Even in my fantasies, I'm shy.

'So wet,' he said, 'you're so fucking wet,' bringing me closer to him as he spoke, pressing me up against the length of his still-clothed member. He was hard and ready, and I revelled in the sensation of impending pleasure. What would it take for him to fuck me? What would I have to do? 'Do you see how wet you are?'

'Yes.'

'Why are you so wet, Eleanor?'

'Because ...' I stammered, unwilling, unable to continue.

'Because why?'

I was undone, my hair loose and falling in my face, my heart racing. Every uptight part of me vanished, and I was his to take, to mould, to do with as he desired, however he desired. I was like Nora for once. Someone willing to walk down an unknown road, or to chart a new path, discovering pleasure in untold ways.

Where had that fantasy come from? In all the years I lived with Byron, I'd never had a similar thought. In all the times I've been to a doctor, I'd never once dreamed up a fantasy like this. Now, in less than five minutes of standing before Anthony, I'd envisioned one of the dirtiest scenarios I could think of. Sure, I knew that in Nora's world a doctor/patient concept would be positively G-rated on the scale of naughty thoughts. For me, however, this was unique.

Anthony remained focused on the papers. I looked at him, and continued to fantasise. It felt deviously decadent, having sexual thoughts about him while he was so close. I could kiss him if I wanted to. I could lean forwards and brush all the papers off his desk – the old ones and the new ones – littering the floor of his office with a mess of manuscripts. I could put myself in front of him and make him notice me.

I pictured myself wearing an outfit much more suitable to Masquerade Night at the Pink Fedora than for a day of work at ARTSI – something tight and white, short enough to show the tops of a pair of garters, complete with fishnets and clear high-heeled stripper shoes. Something Nora would have in the front of her closet for a Wednesday or Thursday, not for any special reason at all. I'd have my hair up and wear chandelier earrings, so long that they'd brush my collarbone. When we fucked, I'd leave on the earrings and the shoes. Nothing else. Anthony would like me this way. I knew it. He would want me to leave on the shoes, to use them as we made love, to leave marks on the backs of his legs from where I dug in with those heels.

Christ, who did I think I was, having thoughts like this? What would Anthony say if he could read my mind the way he was reading the manuscript? What did I really want from him? Not for him to decipher this sheaf of ancient Greek papers, but to decipher me.

I felt a world-class blush work from my jaw up to bloom in my cheeks.

'It looks like Greek,' Anthony said, 'but how did *you* know that's what it was?'

Grateful that he was still looking at the pages instead of looking at me, I cleared my throat and explained, 'The clay pot.' I didn't take offence at the question. There was no reason why I would have been able to tell it was Greek. It's not my field. 'I brought in several of the fragments to Serina this morning and she placed it for me. She says Athens, most likely, based on the types of designs. She couldn't immediately give me a date, but she's still working on it. Just from the few pieces I brought her, and from the quality of the workmanship, she thinks it's about three hundred BC.'

Anthony whistled appreciatively and then began sliding each page into a separate clear plastic envelope and sealing the tops firmly. 'Trying to protect it from the elements,' he explained, although I knew what he was doing. 'I think the pages are made of papyrus. That's what it feels like, anyway. Must have been doing some trading with the Egyptians. But whatever it is, it's older than old. Who are you going to give the manuscript to?'

He continued to house the pages in safe surroundings, but he looked up at me when I didn't immediately answer. I stared back at him, totally disregarding his question and fixating instead on the colour of his eyes. Even through the thick glasses, they were hypnotising. Anthony has bottle-green eyes, and they seemed to gleam beneath the fluorescent lights. His eyes are a different colour to Nora's, darker and deeper, like still water in a lake. Nora's change colour with her moods, turning a light blue, a pale grey, a soft minty green. Anthony's didn't look as if they would go any colour but darker. I wondered if I'd have the chance to experiment, to find out how they'd look when he was happy, how they'd look when he was intent and how they'd look when he was lost in the midst of a climax, with me astride him.

I could practically feel it, the way my body would fit on top of his. He'd look up at me, his glasses off, his eyes so dark they were almost black. He would reach one hand up and trace the outline of my lips, then slide two fingers into my mouth and let me suck on them.

Oh, Lord. I really was turning into Nora. A sex queen. Would I have a billboard out on Sunset of my own one day, like Nora in her pink fedora?

'I mean, which museum?' Anthony asked when I remained silent. I willed the dirty thoughts to leave my head. Maybe instead of asking him to be my private translator, I should have just gotten it over with and asked him to fuck me. Would he turn me down? Or would he tell me to lock the door, push me up against the back of it, slide one hand up under my skirt until the fabric rippled at the waist. 'Will you try to keep them here?' he asked next, prompting me.

'I'm not sure,' I said, finally, my voice unbelievably steady in relation to what I was actually thinking about. 'I want to know what the papers say first.' I knew this wasn't rational, knew that I sounded like a child, but I couldn't help myself. It was true.

'You can't keep them for yourself,' Anthony insisted, as if I were insane. 'They belong in a museum. Or a library. There will probably be a fight for them between Greece and Los Angeles, if I know anything about how the museums work these days.' He indicated a newspaper clipping posted on his bulletin board. 'You're following the fight for the art stolen by Nazis, aren't you?

The descendants want it back. The European museums say that it's been theirs for so long, they now own it. Does time really create ownership? If someone stole a car, but kept it hidden for twenty years, would the car then be owned by the thief or should it go back to the original purchaser?'

'Then we won't tell anyone right away,' I said, my voice dipping into a conspiratorial tone, which wasn't like me at all. 'You do what you can with them. I'm going to cruise the Net to see if I can locate any other ancient Greek historians.'

'I may have just turned forty, but I'm not all that ancient,' Anthony said quickly, 'except, I suppose, by LA standards.'

He was smiling at me now. I watched as he pushed a lock of wayward hair away from his glasses and, for an instant, I could see what he must have looked like as a kid. Then, with an impatient gesture, he took off the thick frames, set them on his desk, and ran one hand over the bridge of his nose. With glasses on, Anthony looks like what he is: a studious translator of ancient literature. With the glasses off and face tilted upwards towards me, the seriousness faded away. He looked a bit like Superman, or like Clark Kent, still in the 'before' role: *before* the crises started, *before* the glasses were tossed in a corner as he prepared to go off and save the world. I suddenly understood why Nora had called Anthony the James Bond of the museum.

They shouldn't allow smart people to be so sexy, I thought. It simply isn't fair.

Every time I looked into his eyes I forgot what I was about to say. It took me a few seconds to regain my composure, then I said, trying to joke with him, 'You're not ancient at all, just terribly knowledgeable.' I found myself stroking Anthony's ego without thinking, used to wheedling Byron in this same way, manoeuvring in a slightly underhanded fashion to get what I wanted. It didn't seem to have much effect on Anthony. At least, not until I added, 'And if you can translate at least a page for me by dinner time, I'll take you out to eat. You name the place.'

That got his attention, and he slid his glasses back on and made a dismissive gesture with his hand, one I had seen him use often with other museum workers who were bothering him.

The gesture meant that he had already started working and would like to be left in peace. I was quick to oblige. As I closed the door behind me, Anthony called out, 'I'll have something for you by five, Eleanor.' A pause, then, 'Don't be late.'

ThePinkFedora.blogspot.com

It's the day. The DAY. THE DAY!

Or the night, rather.

Come join the fun as we whittle down the contestants for the new reality show to be filmed entirely at the Pink Fedora. Fifty contestants will be trying their hand Cocktail-*style behind the bar, hoping to be one of the lucky twelve who will appear on the Bijoux Network's soon-to-be-run-away hit:* You Can Leave Your Hat On.

Come judge for yourself as the beaux and belles of the bar mix drinks, tell tall tales, and light the night on fire. (At least, if their pouring any Flaming Mimis. Don't worry, Fire Chief, we've got our extinguishers at the ready.)

Wear a leopard-print fedora for a free first drink.

Wear all leopard print (and I mean all, *from head to toe, knickers included, and you know I'll be checking) and you get in on me.*

Blog, baby, blog.

Kisses,

Nora

Quote for the Day: As Grace Slick said, 'Reporting I'm drunk is like saying there was a Tuesday last week.'

Chapter Eight

I couldn't work. This had nothing to do with my slowly dissipating hangover and everything to do with my wickedly thriving sex drive.

'Shake out of it,' I told myself. 'You've got papers to read.'

But my body rebelled. All I wanted to do was kick back in my chair, put my feet up on my desk, and fantasise about Anthony, handsome Anthony, pushing me up against the wall of his office. Anthony telling me what he was going to do to me a second before he actually did it. 'Unbutton your pants and unzip the fly, I'm going to take them off you, Eleanor. And then I'm going to slide your panties down your legs, and you're going to step out of them.' I could practically feel the rich black fabric slipping down my thighs. 'Oh, God, you're wet. What a bad girl. Did you get this wet just thinking about us fucking? Or have you been engaging in naughty thoughts all morning when you should have been working?' Once again, I told myself to stop it. 'Control yourself, Eleanor,' I whispered. 'He's only translating. This isn't going to be a date.'

With a false show of enthusiasm that I didn't actually feel, I spread out all of the research I'd done so far for the newest ARTSI show, then stacked the resources I still had yet to peruse. I made neat piles, and then reshuffled the pages, making sure that the edges lined up, losing myself in unnecessary tasks rather than forcing myself to focus.

Usually, I would be excited to see all the work that lay before me. My job electrifies me, even after all these years. The thought of learning something new, of discovering information about the art world, invigorates me – it opens me up.

Now, I felt nothing. I took a large sip of coffee, and realised that was not entirely true. I felt exhausted. Every part of me felt tired at the thought of skimming through all of those pages. I have never lost my quest for learning about art in the most minute detail. But today, my mind remained consumed by two concepts: what Anthony would discover about the text I'd given him, and what Anthony might be like at dinner.

I paced around my office until my feet started to hurt, and then I sat back down at my desk and stared into my now-empty coffee cup. Had I imbibed too much caffeine this morning, or not quite enough?

The pious angel on one of my resource books held an expression that seemed to mock me. I pushed that heavy heavenly tome aside, only to be greeted with another image, this one featuring several angels, all with their halos outlined in shimmering gilded foil. I flipped the book face down, as if that would somehow shield me from their grace. But there was no hiding the fact – my own halo was askew.

The new ARTSI show focused on angels featured in sculpture, paintings, illuminated manuscripts and Bibles. The installation was called 'Everywhere, Angel!' For several weeks, the project had consumed all of my work time and energy. I nudged the top book open and was instantly greeted by a celestial army of angels, all with golden hair, like Gwen's. I felt myself grow cold. Had Byron taken advantage of my preoccupation with religious iconography in order to spend more time with Gwen? And why did I even care? I didn't want Byron. I didn't want to answer his phone calls, return his text messages or spend even one more second thinking about him.

Refocused, I grabbed one of my folders and flipped it open.

My assignment on the show was to research early

writings about angels – in song, poetry, and text. I would have enjoyed writing about angels in paintings, but one of my fellow co-workers had snagged that choice job.

On my desk were printouts of the internet research I'd done thus far. I had spent hours reading about the way people have described angels in text throughout the centuries, learning when halos were first introduced and discovering the rationale behind choosing that symbol to equal heavenly purity. I'd been surprised to discover that the halo appeared in both Christian and Buddhist traditions. All my mental images were of Christian paintings. I paged through one of my folders, flipping to the different items that I'd flagged to include in the brochure accompanying the show. The halo first appeared in ancient Greek and Roman art, but was incorporated into Christian art by the fourth century. There are assorted types of halos and each one has a different meaning – kind of like Nora's fedora code.

The show was to cross the ages – from ancient to modern. As a nod to the present culture, there would be music playing on the headsets in between a vocal reading of the history. I was thrilled that I'd been allowed to hand-select the music. At first, I'd thought of only playing angel-themed music: 'Calling All Angels' by Train; Roxy Music's 'Angel Eyes'. But then, in a wave of inspiration, I'd gotten the idea to play devil-themed music instead. Nora liked the concept, once I'd explained it to her. She'd been so supportive that she'd even taught me how to use iTunes.

Instead of pouring through the books I'd borrowed from our research department's voluminous library, I wound up spending the entire day listening to different music on iTunes and thinking about Anthony. The fact that I was searching for devil-themed music set the mood for how I felt. I selected the Stones' 'Sympathy for the Devil' and Nick Cave's 'Up Jumped the Devil', INXS's 'Devil Inside', 'Devil with a Blue Dress On' by Mitch Ryder, Elvis' '(You're the) Devil in Disguise' (which also features angels), and Dave Matthews' 'Some Devil'. I also chose the Squirrel Nut Zippers' 'Hell' to end the show.

Our permissions department would have to contact the correct companies to secure the rights to use the songs during the show, but that wasn't my concern. At the moment, I was able to lose myself in the music and my thoughts about Anthony.

We had collaborated on projects several times before. My favourite had been for an installation called 'FREE!' The artist, Nina Morgan, had created an entire household using only items that she had found by the side of the road, objects mysteriously left behind by their owners. Some items had been cast-offs or giveaways, with hand-lettered signs stating FREE to let people know that the pieces were available for the taking. Others were things the artist had found in the trash or at the dump. In my opinion, the best part of the installation was the row of shoes beneath the bed in the bedroom. Who hasn't seen shoes by the side of the road and wondered where the owners were and how the owners had gotten home? Barefoot?

'FREE!' had been written up in several big newspapers. Most of the critics focused on the fact that at the end of the installation, all of the items were actually free to the audience. Anyone could take the raspberry-red couch, the Kenmore washing machine, the coffee table. The artist had refurbished all of the items in the show, so that they were truly in good-working condition. Some of the pieces were amazing. There was an old-fashioned record player with a stack of vinyl albums by its side and a mirror surrounded by gilded golden lilies. The art on the walls was excellent – Miss Morgan had haunted the alleys behind several studios in town, plucking cast-off canvases, half-finished works that had, for some reason, won displeasure of the artist.

The attention to minute detail in this installation was impressive. On the bedside table stood a water-filled carafe. On the nightstand was a hairbrush, a paperback novel, a framed photograph and a pair of reading glasses. The dining table was set with mismatched dishes. Half-burned candles stood in ornate holders. Magazines stood neatly in a rack by the sofa – a copy of *Playboy* magazine actually peeked out from beneath the mattress in the bedroom.

Anthony had worked on that show with me, translating the text I wrote for the brochure into four different languages. His words, and mine, were recorded and played on headsets that could be worn throughout the show. I'd told Nora about Anthony back then, had talked so much about him that she'd figured out I was nursing a crush. Guilt had made me fearful of being myself around him. I'd played the role of the uptight researcher – something that comes naturally to me – while Nora coached me to relax, coached to no avail.

Things are never truly what they seem, I realised now. How could I be so fiercely angry at Byron, when I'd had fantasies myself? Because Byron had acted on his and I'd stamped mine down to dust. Are all relationships so precariously built? An ever-changing teeter-totter of power, of reigning in one's true desires. I'd thought that safety and companionship were the ultimate trade-in for lust and excitement.

But although Anthony and I had occasionally collaborated, I'd never allowed there to be a time when there'd just been the two of us together, we were always part of a larger group. Plus, being a good girl, I had worked hard not to let my true feelings colour the relationship. I had never let myself do more than fantasise about him, except for one simple kiss beneath the mistletoe at the museum Christmas party the previous December. Or maybe it hadn't been quite so simple.

'Harmless,' I'd lied to Nora afterwards. 'Totally and completely harmless.'

Nora, who had been my guest at the party, a twelfth-hour fill-in for Byron who had decided at the last minute to attend his own Christmas party at

Hawthorne, Fox, and Hawthorne, had seen the kiss and called it for what it was: 'Unbelievably sexy,' she'd countered. 'You should have seen yourself, you should have demanded an out-of-body experience so you could have watched the way he held you, his hand at the small of your back, his eyes open, your eyes closed.'

'Why did he have his eyes open?' I asked, even though Nora would have no real way of answering the query.

'Because he wanted to look at you.'

I felt myself grow warm all over at the thought, but I didn't want to admit that to her. Instead, I turned the discussion around, 'Who would have guessed someone as cut-throat as you could be such a romantic?'

But Nora wouldn't let it go. 'Are the security cameras on? We could go upstairs and ask them to give you a playback. Then you can see for real what I'm talking about!'

'Don't you think that might raise some eyebrows?' I asked, not wanting to admit that the idea held some appeal. 'The security guard calls my boss and tells him that I want to, what – playback a kiss?'

I couldn't even finish out the scenario, but I'd enjoyed hearing about the kiss as seen by Nora, because it had happened too fast to dissect. It was like taking a ride on one of the old wooden roller coasters at the Santa Cruz boardwalk. I'd known I had loved it, but couldn't remember all of the individual details. All the twists and turns, the dips and rises. When I pictured the kiss, trying my best to remember every part, I instantly thought of champagne, the smell of Anthony's spicy cologne, the jingling noises of the band playing speeded-up jazz versions of Christmas carols. All blurred together.

I also thought of the way that one of his hands had swept casually down my back, to give me a light little spank on the rear. Hardly a spank, but just enough somehow to let me know that where sex was concerned, Anthony would take the upper hand. My legs had felt weak at the thought.

I'd wanted to melt into him at that kiss – and now, alone in my office, painfully aware of how many hours I had until five o'clock, I played out the kiss in my mind as Nora had described it. I painted a mental vision with as much detail as possible, recalling the outfit Anthony had worn. At work, he dresses in a style I would consider casual hip, meaning that most of the time he looks something like a college professor during office hours. And on Christmas Eve he hadn't given into the desire of many men in our department to dust off a rarely worn suit and tie. Instead, Anthony had worn faded khakis, engineer boots and a tan suede jacket over a pale-green shirt. I'd felt the soft suede with my fingertips as I'd leaned forwards for the kiss.

Back up, I admonished myself. Don't kiss him yet. Smell him, first.

He was wearing a musky scent, something familiar made of spices combined with notes of sandalwood and, when he'd bent to kiss me, I had felt his cheek brush against mine. His skin was smooth, cool. His lips were warmer, soft against my mouth . . .

Back up, I told myself again. Slowly, slowly. Make it last.

I recalled every detail that Nora had shared, and in my head I now added my own figure into the scene, as if I truly were watching, a witness from outside, another partier in the room, one who had nothing to lose. There I was, in a red silk dress that was more than slightly provocative compared to my normal attire. I had my hair swept up into a French twist, and this gave me a look of simple elegance compared with my normal everyday ponytail. I had dressed with Nora – the dress was, in fact, one of Nora's. I had even allowed Nora to do my make-up for me for once, although I'd refused to let her dye my hair for the occasion. I didn't listen when she said red and green streaks would look festive, or that I should consider bleaching my light-brown hair birch white for a snowy effect, and I even brushed her away when she asked to put silver glitter in my fringe.

'Killjoy,' she'd said with a frown.

'You can look like Santa's naughty helper if you want,' I told her. 'But this is a business event for me. I can't show up with different-coloured hair. And sparkles would make me look like a teenager.'

Nora shot me a hurt look. She has no plans to ever outgrow sparkles.

'Then wear the red dress,' she finally countered. I'd been planning on black. Black as usual. Black as always. 'You're going to a party, Eleanor, not a funeral.' She'd won out on this fight. But I didn't own any dresses that weren't black. I stand by my desire to let the art around me shine. I have no need to compete with it. But Nora had come through with a dress that was tasteful for her and only mildly trashy to me.

In the twinkling lights of the museum's main lobby – and in the twinkling lights of my own memory – I looked as fanciful, as attractive, as the women depicted in the tapestries on the walls of the lobby. The queens and princesses and rich ladies dressed for parties held centuries before, glittering with jewels, spilling over with creamy white cleavage, their eyes sparkling as they gazed down upon us.

Wearing heels much higher than normal, I had worked on simply standing up and walking without trotting. 'Heel, toe,' I'd whispered to myself, 'heel, toe.' Until Anthony, who had also apparently been watching me, grabbed my elbow and whispered, 'Look up.' A strand of mistletoe dangled directly above our heads.

'You know what that means,' he'd murmured.

'I know entirely too well,' I'd said, because I had been the one to write the invitation to the party, this office party mixed with an ARTSI fund-raiser. For weeks, I had lost myself in the research, learning about the history behind the tradition of kissing under mistletoe. I had started to tell Anthony, despite Nora's frantic headshaking, saying, 'Mistletoe is the common name for both the *Loranthaceae* and the *Viscaceae* families of chiefly –' only to be silenced by his lips on mine.

Warm lips.

'I read the brochure,' Anthony said when we parted. 'I wasn't interested in the history of the plant, only in what it would be like to kiss you, what it would be like to . . .'

I yearned to know what he was going to say next – I could hear the words in my head: What it would be like to fuck you. To spank you. To – But then, like some childish Cinderella, I had thought of Byron. Had I always been such a good girl? That was easy to answer: yes. I gave in to my fantasies, gave in to them shamefully, knowing that fantasies are free. Aside from that one Christmas kiss, I never went any further than that.

Now I realised Byron had probably been in the arms of the sultry bombshell Gwen. My guilty complex had made me push Anthony away. Nora, sulking at what she considered my obscenely moral behaviour, had joined me beneath the doorway, and some of my more immature co-workers hooted and howled, showing their champagne. I suppose they were expecting, or hoping, that we might also kiss each other, that they might actually get to see two women kissing. People can be so incredibly juvenile, even academics, once the champagne has been flowing for several hours. Of course, if we'd been at one of Nora's clubs, rather than at ARTSI, a kiss would have been the mildest thing that they'd seen.

Nora had dragged me into the ladies' room and pulled all of the details out of me. Thinking back, I wondered exactly what else Anthony had wanted to say.

My therapist – ex-therapist since I hadn't gone in over a year now – would explain that I was transferring. That Anthony was an instant rebound relationship being used to diffuse my anger towards Byron. But when I *paused* – a trick that this same therapist had explained: pause in your thoughts to see where your emotions are truly coming from – I didn't feel angry at Byron. I felt nothing at the thought of Byron, everything at the thought of Anthony. My therapist had liked to talk about co-dependency, about what I did for Byron and what he didn't do for me. 'It's not an even relationship,' the woman had said once. I'd disagreed, insisting that although we were different, we were good together. Maybe my therapist had been right.

Now, not having a therapist to discuss the situation with, I called Nora for advice. Nora is always more fun to talk to, anyway, plus she doesn't charge $175 an hour.

'Are you up?' I asked.

She made some soft noise in response. Not a yes, but not a no, either. The mere fact that she'd answered the phone let me know that she was at least willing to listen to a conversation, even if she weren't all the way ready to join in.

'Are you alone?'

'Not really.'

'What does that mean?' This was Nora speak for the fact that she had male company.

'But don't worry.' I heard the sound of a door closing. She was moving down the hallway. 'Dean stopped by again.'

'Twice in one week? For you that's practically a relationship.'

'*This* is why you woke me up? To give me a play by play of who I'm fucking? Should I tell you how many orgasms he gave me? Or let you know whether he's better or worse in bed than Travis?'

'No,' I said, speaking fast, in case she got truly upset by my minor wisecrack and hung up on me. 'I'm going out with Anthony tonight.'

'Anthony,' she repeated, and I could tell that she was smiling. I could hear the familiar sounds of Nora making coffee in the background. 'That was quick, wasn't it?'

'What do you mean?' I felt my defences rise. Nora claims that I am a serial monogamist. Since our summer abroad together, I have rarely been unpartnered. If my relationships haven't exactly overlapped, as Byron and Gwen's did, they have definitely come close.

'He's already asked you out on a date? A *date*-date?' She emphasised the first "date."'

'It's not a date,' I insisted, as if wanting to convince her as much as myself. 'As a favour, he's translating the pages I found in the pot. I'm repaying him with dinner.' Even to me, that didn't sound entirely plausible. Why would I have to take him to dinner in order for him to do this for me? Shouldn't co-workers be able to ask one another for a hand without having to reward them?

'Who's idea was that?'

I hesitated. 'Mine.'

Nora snorted again. She sounded like a displeased filly. 'I told you what you need,' she said.

'You told me Anthony was going to be my next man.'

'Yeah, after you fuck some sense into your head by doing one of my bartenders, and a drummer or two, and maybe one of the DJs, and Dean when you feel like it. He said you were a doll.'

'Nora, I'm not the type to behave like that. And you know it.'

She didn't want to hear this. 'I saw you last night, Eli.'

'I was out of my head last night,' I countered.

'You can't go out tonight anyway,' she declared.

'And why is that? Have you taken over my social schedule?'

'I would if you let me.'

'Why can't I go out with Anthony tonight?'

'Does *You Can Leave Your Hat On* have any meaning to you?'

That stopped me in my thoughts. 'Oh, God,' I said softly. 'Your show.'

'That's right, my show.'

I made a face, but Nora couldn't see me. The concept for her reality show had been in motion for several months, and try-outs were tonight. Nora had been blogging the hell out of it. Called *You Can Leave Your Hat On*, the network was going to be filming at the club. Twelve bartender hopefuls would start out together and each week one would be rejected and ejected. Nora had worked hard to think of the way the person would be cut. She knew about *The Bachelor* and the striking red roses. She knew Heidi Klum's '*Auf Wiedersehen*' at the end of each episode of *Project Runway*, when she said goodbye to one of the designer hopefuls. Nora had decided that she would take the losing person's hat off to let them know they'd been cut.

'But that means they have to wear hats, right?'

'Pink fedoras, of course.'

'Are you serious?'

'Dead serious. And you have to be there tonight. With me. To help. That's what I meant by saying you could have a bartender. I'm sure I'm going to be flooded with eligible men – and women, too – who would do anything to stay in the running.'

'Nora,' I said softly, repeating my words from before, 'you know I'm not like that.'

'I know.' She sighed as if once again disappointed by my morals, and I could hear her sipping her coffee. 'Anyway, back to Anthony. Yes, I think he's perfect for you. I just thought you might actually take the time to get on your feet again, you know, move your belongings out of Byron's apartment before shacking up with a brand-new beau.'

'But Serina told me to do it. She said that Anthony works better with incentive.'

'And you're the carrot on the end of the stick?' Nora sucked in her breath. 'It definitely sounds like a date.'

'It's not,' I said. Maybe if I said the statement enough times, I'd believe the words. 'And the place *wasn't* Byron's apartment. Both of our names are on the lease. It's ours together.'

'You think that makes things better?'

'No. More confusing than ever.'

'What are you wearing?' Nora asked, switching topics so fast that I felt thrown off balance.

'What?'

'It's not a difficult question, Eli. What are you wearing?'

'You know,' I said.

I realised that Nora hadn't seen me leave in the morning, but she had seen for herself that I'd only brought one suitcase to her home when I'd left Byron, knew that it undoubtedly wouldn't contain more than a few of my normal, well-made, slightly boring suits. Since college, I've expanded my wardrobe slightly, choosing more expensive outfits than I wore as a student. But my tastes have ultimately remained the same. I stand by my desire not to compete with the canvases I write about. My favourite designer is Calvin Klein for his elegant sophistication.

Nora, on the other hand, has changed massively since college. That's not to say she isn't as flamboyant as ever, because she is. But she can buy the top designer looks now, doesn't need to shop at thrift stores. She once bought two pairs of $500 shoes that were exactly the same except that one was fuchsia and the other was cobalt. She wore the right from one set and the left from another – just as I'd worn two mismatched shoes the night before. But I'd dressed that way in my haste to leave Byron. Nora chose two different coloured shoes on purpose.

'What are you wearing?' Nora asked again.

'One of my suits,' I confessed. 'And I'm not going back to change before dinner. We're leaving form here. Together.'

'How's your hair?' she asked next.

'In a ponytail down my back, like it usually is at work.'

Nora and I are true opposites. If I could, I'd dress exactly the same every day, and I know just what I'd wear, too. A pair of chic black slacks, my favourite patent-leather black penny loafers, a black T-shirt, black cashmere cardigan and my hair in a ponytail. In fact, I *do* dress like this everyday. Or a variation of it. I think it's unique that I have euros in the slots of my shoes rather than actual pennies, but that's about as edgy as I get.

Black helps me fade into the background. But black also means that I don't have to think – black blends with black.

'Do you have time to get your hair done?'

'Don't you think he'd find that odd? He's already seen me today. He knows how I looked when I arrived at work.' I raised my eyebrows, staring at my reflection in one of the framed pieces of artwork on the opposite wall. 'Wouldn't he find it strange if at five o'clock I suddenly looked totally different?' But, of course, as soon as Nora suggested the idea, I found myself considering it. How would I look with my hair in loose curls framing my face or up in pretty plaited braids? What might Anthony find sexy? I tried to remember the various gossip I'd heard about him over the years. I knew that he's been with some of the artists whose work has appeared in the avant-garde galleries. Did that mean he would rather be with someone like Nora?

'It would be a surprise,' Nora said, as if that might be a good thing, 'but forget that. You'd never get into a good salon this late in the day. Let's move onto bigger issues.' Her voice took on a crafty tone. 'I don't recommend that you sleep with him tonight. I know *I* work that quickly, but Anthony is worthy of a long-term relationship. Plus, you should never do the things that I do. Unless I invite you to,' she said, reminding me once again of our previous evening. Now, she paused for emphasis. 'You *don't* want to hop in the sack with him on a first date.' Nora is very good at choreographing the dance steps during the early part of the dating/mating ritual. She could have written a book on the subject of how to get a man to want you. It's the staying power that she doesn't fully grasp.

'It's not a date,' I insisted over the phone, repeating, 'I'm taking him to dinner to thank him for doing some work for me.'

'How are your toenails?' Nora asked.

'What are you talking about?' None of her questions were making sense to me. What did the state of my toenails have to do with my dinner with Anthony?

'I never sleep with a boy if I have chipped toenail polish. Ever. I think it's something about my attitude towards grooming habits. I'd feel all dirty if my nails weren't properly pedicured. Dirty in a *bad* way,' she explained, knowing that I am fully aware that she usually thinks 'dirty' is good. I tried to remember what Nora's toenails looked like, and then got a picture of them in the gingham sandals she'd worn the night before. Yes, they'd been perfect, painted as ripe and red as shiny cherries. Now Nora lowered her voice as she gave out her trade secrets. 'This is my surefire way for making certain I don't give into temptation on a first date, even if the guy is totally hot. *Especially* if the guy is totally hot.'

'Don't the guys usually give in to you?' I asked, slyly, but before she could answer I said, 'Nora, I got a pedicure on Saturday, but it doesn't matter. He's not going to see my toes because I'm not going to sleep with him. This isn't a date.' I was starting to sound like a scratched CD, repeating those same words over and over.

'Did you shave this morning?' Nora asked next.

'Shave what?'

'Legs, under your arms, your . . . you know?'

'My . . .' I was stunned. This was a question only Nora would dream up. And I could only think about answering it because Nora was the one asking.

'Do you need a bikini wax? I didn't really look last night.'

I hesitated. 'I don't know.' This was too much to think about. 'I don't shave every day, anyway. I'm really light.'

'People with naturally light hair have all the luck,' Nora said, wistfully. Yes, Nora and I do look a lot alike, but our hair colour is dramatically different. Since Nora dyes hers all the time, nobody would really know that. But I have light-brown hair and her natural shade is much closer to black. 'With your peach fuzz fur, it almost doesn't matter. But it still matters. Not shaving is even more of a turn off. If I absolutely, positively, no-doubt-in-my-mind want to keep myself from sleeping with a guy too soon, *even* if I have chipped toenail polish, I don't shave. Just to make sure. There's nothing less attractive than scraggly hair down there. Especially when it's black, like mine. I've only made exceptions twice, and one of those times was for a guy who was just into the idea of lathering me up and shaving me bare. He actually insisted that I abstain from shaving for a week before our date ...' Nora trailed off, lost in the world of her memories. I remembered that guy. Nora had dated him for almost a month, which was nearly a record for her.

'I'm not sleeping with him,' I said again, bringing the conversation back around to me and Anthony. 'This isn't a date.' I paused, considering. 'Besides, we really *are* going straight from work. When could I possibly shave? In the bathroom here? Using the liquid soap in the canisters by the sink?' I had a vision of myself with my pants down, spreading the rose-pink bubbles all over my nether regions, trying to explain my actions to any of the other women in the bathroom who might be primping or using the facilities. It wasn't a pretty picture.

'I said "don't",' Nora repeated. 'Unless you do want to sleep with him. If that's the case, Eli, you can just go to Paradise Salon on your lunch hour and get a wax. It's right around the corner from you, and Natasha does a fabulous job on bikini areas. It hurts like hell, but she won't miss a hair.' Nora paused, obviously checking the clock. 'That will give you plenty of time for the redness to fade before tonight.' She paused again. 'So the big question, Eli, the look-deep-inside-yourself question is this: do you, or don't you, want to fuck him?'

'I don't know what I want,' I lied.

'I'd better make you an appointment,' Nora said, deciding for me.

Chapter Nine

Nora's words set my fantasies in motion. Not that I needed much assistance at this point. I wondered what it would be like to fuck Anthony. For some reason, I kept using that word when I thought about the action. *Fuck.* Hearing the word in my head turned me on. Maybe this was because to me Anthony didn't look the type to make love. He had a powerful presence about him, as if he might back a girl up against a wall, hold her wrists over her head, slam his body against hers.

Or was that simply what I *wanted* him to do?

I could see every single frame, the way his eyes would stay open, holding me in place with his expression alone. I envisioned him moving slowly, undressing me piece by piece. For once, the fact that I wore layers was a good thing. He would have to take off my sweater, my blouse, my bra, my shiny black loafers, my slim-fitting slacks, my panties – so many items before I would be naked. There would be a puddle of black clothing on the floor when he was finished, and I would stand in the centre of it, nude, one hand covering my pussy, the other across my breasts. With my hair down, and my body so revealed, I'd resemble the goddess in that famous Boticelli painting *The Birth of Venus* – but I'd be standing in a pool of black clothing rather than in an open shell.

Anthony would still be dressed, and this worked to arouse me even more. For once, I wouldn't be hiding myself, wouldn't be avoiding notice. I would be like a work of art, for Anthony to admire. But I would be living art, something for Anthony to rotate, to manoeuvre, to use however he desired.

I fantasised about him fucking me right here, in my office. In all the years that Byron and I were together, we never had sex at either of our places of work. Why was that? Wouldn't you have thought that at least once, during some extra-long lunch break, or after one of our work events, we would have thought to try it on a desk?

I suppose he had tried it on his desk with Gwen, and I did everything I could to replace that image with one of me and Anthony. I wasn't only fantasising about Anthony as a way to get over Byron, though, was I?

No, because in the few years that I'd known Anthony, he had definitely featured in my sexual daydreams. I wondered what he would do right now if he knew I was daydreaming about him, about him stripping me. Would he come to my office if I called? Would he make each one of my fantasies come true?

Nora had said to surprise him. To wear my hair differently. To dress up or dress down. In my flirtatious fantasies, I put her words into action. I suddenly saw myself not naked, but wearing an outfit much more appropriate to Nora's world than to mine. Something sexy and skintight. Something you might see on a starlet strolling down the red carpet. But that wasn't me. Not for real.

If I could recreate myself, how would I do so? I wouldn't be punk – never punk. I couldn't imagine myself with spiky hair like Nora's, or a rainbow of hues to match my moods. But I could see myself in a more rock 'n' roll creation. Slim-fitting black leather pants. A lipstick-red T-shirt that featured an image of one of Nora's favourite girl singers, Joan Jett, with the message below it: WWJJD – What Would Joan Jett Do?

My hair is generally off my face in a no-nonsense ponytail. I don't put any effort into styling and, unfortunately, it shows. When I'm bent over a book reading, a ponytail is the easiest way to keep my hair out of my eyes. In my daydream, I wore my hair down and flat-ironed, glossy in the light. Anthony gripped onto it as he pulled me in for a kiss, working me much more roughly than I've ever been taken in the past. Telling me without words that I was his. *That's* what I was so sure of. I don't know why. But I knew, just knew, that fucking Anthony would be a powerful ride.

Should I sneak out of the office and redress myself? The thought didn't seem as crazy as it had when Nora first suggested it. I could claim that I went home at lunchtime to do an errand, that I decided to put on something different for our night out. But put on what? I didn't have anything different. A mental inventory of my suitcase came up with nothing but black.

Should I call Nora up again and ask her to meet me at some sexy store? She would definitely know the places to take me, and I was certain she'd be up for helping me to transform. I could just hear her, 'Let's go. Let's get you new clothes. Let's turn you into a sexy beast.'

No. I couldn't change my whole world in a day. Last night was enlightening enough – exciting enough for a year's worth of fantasies. Or more. I knew that Nora would be disappointed if she could follow my train of thoughts, but I tried not to be too hard on myself. Even more than engaging in an unexpected threesome, breaking up with Byron was enough of a shake-up for one week, wasn't it? I didn't have to respond by trying to recreate my entire demeanour, did I?

I gazed around my office. There was no clutter here, yet the shelves were filled with books. The walls were decorated with posters of shows I've worked on, the ones I've been most proud of. I have never considered myself even remotely artistic. I am a researcher, a chronicler of events. Now, I had a sudden urge to knock everything off the shelves. To create chaos from the order. Had Byron broken up with me because I was too old-fashioned? Too much like a school marm?

Why hadn't I seen the end coming?

I settled down lower in my chair, my eyes falling on a picture of Anthony in the recent in-house newsletter. He'd been given an award, and the photo showed him looking sheepish as some ancient patron of the arts handed over the statuette. Looking at him made me think once again of the kiss we'd shared at Christmas. It wasn't by accident that the newsletter was opened to this page. I'd read the article several times, on the pretence of learning more about my co-workers, but really because I wanted to keep gazing at his photo.

His kiss had been delicious. His lips on mine had made me feel guilty for weeks afterwards – guilty in both a good and a bad way. I'd been left wanting more, wanting him to fulfil every dirty fantasy I'd ever had – and each time Byron and I had gotten together, I'd imagined Anthony in our bed instead of my beau.

Was I a hypocrite for being so incensed at Bryon? No. Because I'd squashed my fantasies. And, besides, I'd never called out the name of my dream lover, whereas Byron hadn't only said the name of his crush. He was actually doing her.

Like I might be doing Anthony.

The very thought made my nerve endings jangle with electricity. I looked at the photo again. Now, I had the chance to find out what he'd really be like. And the thoughts consumed me. I actually shut the door to my office and, for the first time in my life, truly gave into my fantasies at work. I envisioned Anthony coming to find me, having some question about the manuscript that he wanted to discuss in person. I saw him barging in, finding me with my legs up on my desk, my hand in my slacks, my body arched.

I had a damn good feeling that finding me in such a compromising position wouldn't shock him at all. In fact, I thought he might simply lock the door behind him and come towards me, ready for action. Would he take me against my desk or take my seat for himself and fuck me on the wheeled contraption?

My face felt so hot. I rubbed one hand over my cheeks, then down my body, caressing my breasts through the fabric of my plain black shirt. Nora might be able to slide into that not-so-private room of her club and make her fantasies come to life. But this sort of thing was much more unusual for me. Was it because I was so focused on my job? And was it because my job was so focused on objects that were hundreds of years old? I had always wanted to be doing what I do now. But I had never wanted to become an actual relic myself. A dinosaur.

I thought about Byron once more, and for the first time I understood him. He'd gone after adventure. Yes, he'd done it in an abhorrent way, but he'd gone, nonetheless. I'd never given much thought to our relationship, assuming that boring was what happened after years together. Assuming that if you wanted danger, you got Nora. If you wanted safety, you got Byron. And then he got Gwen. And I got . . .

What did I get?

Did I get Anthony?

Would I be that lucky?

I pictured Anthony and me in Nora's club, heading down to the Cinéma Vérité room. I visualised the two of us totally disregarding the camera, but knowing that the watching electronic eye was there the whole time, recording our every move. In my mind, Anthony stripped my dress off me, and I had on a pair of Valentine-red lace knickers and matching bra beneath. Like a dream, I stripped off Anthony's shirt, revealing his muscular chest. I mentally placed him behind me, flipping me so that my hands were flat on one of the mirrored walls. I had him slip my panties aside, rather than take them all the way off me, and then I felt him slam inside of me.

His hands held onto my waist, and he moved me to the most perfect rhythm. We could hear the music playing from the dance floor – music actually playing from the iTunes on my computer – and Anthony fucked me to that rhythm. INXS, 'Devil Inside'.

In real time, I slid one hand under the waistband of my slacks, touching myself as I continued to fantasise. How amazing it felt to be alone with Anthony, while knowing the whole time that we were on display, the same way that sexy trio had been on display the other night.

Did I need to bring another member into our party?

Should I mentally invite Nora to join?

Oh, no. Not for this. I could never compete if Nora were in the room. Even in my mind. Being with her and Dean the night before had taught me that. Not that we were competing for his affections, but when Nora's involved, she tends to take over. The way she had in the Cinéma Vérité room. This fantasy need only be about me and Anthony – about the way he would take me, pressed up against the mirror, about the thought that others were watching. Everyone was watching. What would the DJ play next? Not a song by Peaches. That was so much more Nora than me. Something sexy, though. Something seductive.

I wracked my mental iTunes library, searching for the right single to play in my head. Ah, Massive Attack. 'Karmacoma'.

This was Nora working on me. I wasn't imagining fucking to Sting or Dire Straits, but to the unbelievably seductive rhythm of Massive Attack. That was *all* Nora. She should be proud. In fact, I'm sure she would have been if I'd had any plans to confess this scenario to her – which I didn't.

I opened my eyes and called up this particular sexy song on the computer, purchasing the tune with a click. Then I leaned back again and continued to touch myself while I thought of Anthony. I had a feeling that he would have no fear, that if I were to walk down the hall right now and confess to my desires, he would fulfil each one. What was stopping me? Social propriety. That's what. It's what I would have said to Nora, and she would have rolled her great green eyes and given me an unhappy little frown. Nora doesn't care what other people think of her. Why should I?

Because I do. Can't help it. I reserve judgment to any art that comes my way, yet I cannot help but judge my own actions on a daily basis. Even in my own fantasies.

With a sigh, I closed my eyes again and dived further into my daydream.

We were there, in the room, naked together. Anthony's hands were on my wrists, holding them over my head. He spoke softly to me, whispering so low that I couldn't hear him right away, but when I did make out the words, I realised he was speaking Italian. A language of love. I could make out the phrases because Nora had taught them to me during our trip. 'I want to sleep with you.' 'Do you want to sleep with me?' 'I want to tie you up.'

She'd had so much fun teaching these risqué statements to me, because she'd known the whole time that I would never need them.

Now, I did. In this fantasy world, I needed to know every single word Anthony said.

'Please,' I told him, and in a heartbeat he had a pair of my nylons in one hand, and was binding my wrists with them. I could feel the silky stockings on my skin, knew somehow what it would be like to be tied up, even though I'd never played that way before. Anthony tied my wrists behind my back, and then pushed me forwards, sliding inside of me from behind.

I was so wet, crazy wet, so ready for him. He slid inside me, his voice low but his mouth pressed to my ear so I could hear him. 'I've wanted you for years,' he whispered, now speaking English. 'You knew it, too. You made me wait.'

This was why he taking me like this, with my body forced up against the cold chill of the mirror. He was punishing me for delaying this inevitable encounter, and I loved every second of it. My eyes focused on the camera, knowing that there were people dancing in the other room, dancing while they watched us fuck.

* * *

The phone rang as I came. I had to shake out of the last whispers of my fantasy, try to find reality somewhere in the electric beeping of the black telephone.

'Bad girl,' Anthony whispered when I picked up the line.

Oh, Christ. Did he know? Could he guess how bad? I felt as if he could see through the phone line and into my office, see through my body and into my mind. My voice didn't work at all.

'Didn't I tell you not to be late?'

No, he didn't know, he was just playing. I mumbled a quick apology, making up some nonsense excuse about working so hard on the angel show that I'd totally lost track of the time. As I spoke, I was not sure what I was saying or what I *should* be saying. My hand was still trapped inside my damp panties. I felt dizzy, not like myself at all.

He laughed. 'I'll let you slide this time, Eleanor, because I'm in a good mood. A really good mood. You're going to be, too, when you see what I have for you. You're not going to fucking believe it.'

My mind continued to play its naughty tricks on me.

What did he have for me? A hungry mouth, a dominant attitude, a steel-like rod waiting to be discovered under his neatly pressed khaki pants? A knowledge of what I wanted and needed, desired, deserved?

'I've got five pages done,' Anthony said. 'Meet you downstairs.'

Chapter Ten

'You like the Stones?'

I nodded.

'Old Stones or new Stones?'

'Any Stones,' I told him, honestly. This is the one true rock band that I've always liked, and I am a die-hard fan. I remember when 'Start Me Up' came out. My mom was horrified when the song played on the radio. 'Are they *still* around?' she demanded, aghast. 'I listened to them back when I was in college!' As if nobody her age should still be allowed to play. But I'm fairly sure that from the way they're still going – playing Super Bowl half-time shows – my own future kids will be fans, as well.

Anthony chose 'Sympathy for the Devil' from his NanoPod, and I instantly thought of how pleased Nora would be. The man might drive an antique car, a 1964 candy-apple-red Galaxie convertible, and he might listen to antique music – the song was released more than thirty years ago – but at least he was modern in his technology.

As downtown LA disappeared in a blur of concrete overpasses and sunset sky, I wondered where we were heading. It didn't actually matter to me. I knew that later in the evening, I'd have to hook up with Nora. She was beyond excited about the prospect of her new reality show. But I didn't have to think about Nora's show at the moment. Now, I could focus all of my attention – and all of my nervousness – on Anthony.

As we drove, I wondered if he could smell the scent of my arousal. I had rushed to the ladies' room after his phone call and washed my hands in the pink liquid soap before hurrying to meet him downstairs. My panties were still sopping wet, and it seemed obvious, at least to me, that my perfume was more of the deeply personal variety than the kind that normally comes in a pretty glass bottle.

If Anthony knew, if he could tell, he didn't let on. He simply pulled up in front of Osborne's Plastic World, parked the convertible Galaxie between two identical silver BMWs, and ushered me inside. I liked the way his car looked there, book-ended between those two boring status symbols. The blandness of the Beamers made his Galaxie stand out that much more. For a brief moment, I thought of Byron and his desire to own whatever model car every other lawyer in his firm owned, and that thought made me even more happy to be here with Anthony.

As soon as we walked down the few steps and into the bar, I sensed a difference come over him. The museum fell away and he was at ease, in his element. Not that he isn't relaxed at work. But in the museum, he's always so focused. The hostess, a sultry brunette with eyes so violet they had to be fake, gave him a warm smile, and I watched the interaction between the two of them. My own eyes narrowed, and I felt myself growing suspicious. What was this? Jealousy already? I forced myself to look away, taking in the rest of the environment.

Osborne's is a long cavernous restaurant off Vine that seems even longer due to a well-placed wall of mirrors. I'd been inside once before, for a poetry reading, and had marvelled at the multitude of mobiles hanging from the ceiling, odd plasticine creations that shine even in the dimmest of light. These are what make Osborne's a 'Plastic World'. The mobiles move and flutter above the heads of the diners, rustling gently, creating their own music by softly brushing against each other. I appreciated the creativity that went into the installation and wondered whether the owner, Jack Osborne, had ever been displayed at any other location. The mobiles, reminiscent of Alexander Calder – a visionary who felt that art need not be static – were delicate, ethereal creations. Just watching them calmed my mood. Isn't that what art is for?

Once our mink-haired hostess had us comfortably seated in a corner booth and we had ordered our drinks, Anthony handed me a slim Manila folder. He seemed prepared for my reaction. As soon as the folder touched my hand, a strange feeling came over me. I was desperate to read what he had translated. In fact, I was filled with the same urgency, the same yearning I'd had when I first saw the manuscript in the rubble of the pottery. Thoughts of how I'd spent the afternoon disappeared from my head. The guilt left me. Longing made me ache.

'I love this place,' Anthony said conversationally. 'I bought a few of the mobiles and hung them outside on my deck. Well, not deck, exactly. My fire escape.'

I smiled at him, only half-listening, wanting so badly to read.

'Go ahead,' he said magnanimously. 'I'll order us dinner and you can read.'

The place was so dark that I had to steal several candles from other vacant tables in order to make out the typewritten words. The votives were each housed in multicoloured, shot-glass-sized holders. Within moments, I had created a semicircle of tiny candles that beamed a rainbow of light on our table. I pulled out my reading glasses and put them on, but I still had to squint. Moving closer to the papers, I refocused my eyes, squinted harder, and read:

She bent over, offering me herself from behind, lifting her loose garments so that I could more clearly see the secret pleasures, those wondrous pleasures, hidden therein. It was as if she were made of cream, so pale, so sweet that my mouth began to water. I took a step closer, bending to taste her and, as soon as my lips met her swollen sex, she seemed nearly to swoon, falling forwards onto the floor, her hands bracing her body, her hips still arched. This was not a real fainting episode. The move was ingenious, intending on giving me yet better access to the dulcet sweetness that I so truly craved.

I pressed my mouth to her font and drank, licking, lapping, until she cried out. Over and over, she cried out, her body shaking uncontrollably. It was as if she were possessed by a spirit, one that desperately wanted freedom. But I knew this was not the case. If she were possessed, it was by passion. If she were filled with another being, it was the Goddess Aphrodite herself.

What the hell was this? I stared up at Anthony, shocked

'Is it too dark to read?' he asked me kindly.

That wasn't the problem, and he must have known that. I searched for the words to explain what I was feeling, finally managing to whisper, 'You're messing with me.' He was, wasn't he? He *had* to be. There was no way that this was the real manuscript. Undoubtedly, he had given me these pages just to tease me. The real pages must still be in his car, or at work. But why would he do something like that? I didn't have the answer to that, but I repeated, dumbly, 'You're playing with me, aren't you, Anthony?'

'What do you mean?' he asked, eyes wide with false innocence.

'You're –' what? What was he? 'You're *fucking* with me.' I sounded a lot like Nora when I said that.

Now he laughed and, when I gazed into his eyes, I saw a wicked gleam there. He'd definitely expected my reaction, and he was obviously enjoying every moment of our interaction.

'I'm not,' he said softly. 'I'm not fucking with you at all.' Unsaid were words that I heard in my head: I'm not fucking with you, but I'd like to be.

He looked at the page in my hand. 'Oh, wait a second,

I think you started from the middle.' Like *that* was the problem. The middle of smut was still smut. With a flourish, he took the crisp white pages from me and reshuffled, then handed them back to me.

I stared hard at him for a moment, wanting him to explain.

'Go on, Eleanor. It's fascinating.'

'It's . . .' I wished for the right words. 'It's pornography.'

'Just read.'

Right then, the waitress sidled up to our table with our wine and Anthony looked over at me. 'I come here all the time. May I choose for us? I promise you'll love every bite.' He sounded totally different than he had moments before, solicitous, caring about what I wanted. Feeling absolutely confused, I nodded and, without consulting me any further, Anthony began to order.

I returned to reading. The piece was *more* sexual, not less. In fact, I don't think I'd ever read anything quite so dirty in my life. Yes, I've devoured the classic erotica, mostly at Nora's suggestion. Colette. Anaïs Nin. Anonymous. But this went beyond those vintage stories. Oh, well, *The Pearl* was pretty filthy – you know those Victorians and all their hidden deep-seated desires. And *The Story of O* did leave me speechless. So maybe this tale wasn't precisely dirtier than those – maybe I found this tale so scandalous because it was the last thing I'd expected to read this evening.

'Go on,' Anthony encouraged.

I started to stammer, wanting to ask him more questions, but he silenced me with a headshake, pushing a glass of white wine towards me and then nodding enthusiastically. 'I can't wait until you finish reading so we can talk about it.'

I took a sip of the wine and then looked back at the pages. I wished I were alone, some place where I could have curled up under a blanket and lost myself in the story. I felt incredibly naked with Anthony there, even though he wasn't staring at me. He seemed to be checking something on his cellphone now. An email? A text message? I didn't know.

'Read, Eleanor,' he said without looking up. 'Then we'll talk.'

'All right,' I told him, taking yet another sip. The wine relaxed me. The mobiles, slipping softly against one another overhead, soothed me. Still, I had an intensely difficult time focusing on the words on the page, because all I could think of was that Anthony was playing a trick on me.

But why would he do that?

I thought I knew the sort of man Anthony was. From our few times working together, I'd discovered his unbelievable focus, his biting sense of humour. I also knew, if I cared to believe the gossip, that he possessed a fairly large ego, that he'd blown up several times at our administrators over different policies he didn't agree with. I tried to think of all the information I had ever read on Anthony. But I drew a blank.

Helplessly, I went back to the papers in my hand, a world-class blush colouring my cheeks. This entire experience was new to me. I've never read erotica with someone watching me. It's always been something I've done alone, in the bed or in the tub. Byron and I never shared in this sort of activity together. The thought of confessing that I sometimes 'used' printed matter to get off was inconceivable to me. I wondered how Byron and I had ever gotten to that point of total inability to communicate. Weren't couples supposed to share everything – did he share everything with Gwen?

More importantly to this particular situation, I've never read erotica that has been translated for me by someone else, someone dark eyed and dreamy like Anthony. I'm sure very few people have had such an opportunity.

'Is it too dim to read here? We could go into the bar. Or I could steal you a few more candles.'

I looked down the long room. The bar was through a

door at the far end from where we'd entered, and it was even darker than the room we were in. Besides, I didn't want him to see how deeply I was blushing. More light was not necessarily a good thing at this point.

'I'm fine,' I said, shuffling the papers again, trying to find what I'd read before.

I spread her out on the rug, wanting to take her this way. I wanted to take her many ways, but this would be the first. She was wet and ready, and I was as hard as a sapling, my member twitching expectantly as if that rod of flesh knew the myriad of pleasures that were in store for it.

I looked down at the girl.

She was a beautiful sprite, so lively, so willing. I had been assured that this was her first time, that those secret pleasures between her supple thighs had been given to no man before. No man before now. But I found this difficult to believe once I was inside of her, for she moved with a knowledge, moved with an assurance that belied her innocence.

How she knew to draw me forwards, I cannot say. But if she truly were a virgin to this sort of activity with the men of our town, then she must have been taught by an educated female, because her position was not that of a novice.

I plunged inside of her, where she was dripping wet and ready, and she cried out fiercely, so obviously hungry for me, hungry for more. I wouldn't hurry. It had been a long time since I was with someone so delightful. I made it my business to go slow. She did not want slow. She pushed back on me, trying to take from me what I was not ready to give. I responded with a firm slap to her hindquarters, and this brought the most delicious response yet. She moaned and squeezed down on me, but she did not still her passion. If anything, that mild sting of pain made her more excited than she'd been before.

When I pushed in all the way, she gasped, and when

I let my hand find the great black ropes of her hair, tugging and making her bend her back like a bow, she moaned sweetly. Sweetly but loudly. Loud enough so that others from the adjoining room must have heard her, for when I looked up, I saw that we had won ourselves an audience.

There was the sound of enthusiastic voices and the stamping of feet, so many eyes watching, hoping that we would continue. And we did. There was no choice, no way that we could think of stopping.

But now I did stop. I couldn't help myself. I was more turned on than I'd been this afternoon, when I'd stroked myself to climax in the privacy of my office, watched only by the eyes of the angels on my resource books. The visions I'd teased myself with seemed remarkably tame in comparison to this ancient erotica. I realised that as I'd been reading, I'd automatically put myself in the girl's role and cast Anthony in that of the male's. Isn't this always the case with X-rated reads? One wants to star in the show.

'Hungry?' Anthony asked, bringing me around again to the present time. Our appetisers had magically arrived. Had the plate been there for a long time? I didn't know. I wasn't interested in the slightest. Instead, I took another sip of my wine and looked over at my dining partner. He appeared to be fully at ease, watching me intently as he ate.

'Where are they?' I asked, unable to contain my queries any longer. The pages shook in my hands as I moved from one to the next, and I shifted my hips against the booth, a longing building inside of me.

'I'm thinking it's a house of prostitution. That's what seems most likely to me.'

'But what *is* it?' I murmured, my voice trembling. 'I mean, what are the papers, themselves?'

'It's a diary,' he said matter-of-factly. 'Don't you think?

I mean, that's what I determined when I was working on it.'

I shook my head and shrugged at the same time. I didn't know what to think.

'Keep on,' he said, 'it gets better and better.'

'By "better" you mean –'

'Just keep reading, Eleanor.'

Oh, how I liked the way he said my name. Helplessly, I returned to the story.

The crowd was wild for our lust, and I gave them exactly what they wanted. Taking her. Plunging into her. My girl was like a wild steed, tossing back her gorgeous black hair, nearly whinnying with pleasure as I pushed forwards. Because she had responded so well the first time, I let my hand meet her rear cheeks again, and again, and, each time, she let loose with such a vibrant, powerful moan, that I almost could not stave off my own impending bliss. Her skin, previously so white as to appear nearly translucent, now took on a robust red glow. The colour of wine. The colour of fire. I paused to admire how hot these cheeks were, touching her softly where only moments before my hand had met with a resounding smack.

She did not seem to crave this tender touch. She gazed over her shoulder at me, a wildness to her eyes, and shook her head once. Yes, they said she was a virgin. This I had been told by the mistress of the house. But the look in her eyes was a look no virgin knows to give. This was an experienced maiden, one who wanted from me. Wanted. It was I who was the innocent in this game. She possessed all the power. Those eyes held me captive, told me what to do. Again, my hand met her lovely rump, and, again, she let loose that moaning sound of pleasure.

The crowd taunted me, calling out instructions, words of so-called wisdom that I did not need to hear. They were in a frenzy, as was she. With no more strength left within my body, I pushed hard into her, sealing our two selves together. One of my hands slipped beneath the lean underside of this goddess in the flesh. I rubbed my fingertips between the split of her lower lips, and she met my pleasure with me, holding tightly to me, draining me of every last drop with the squeezing motions of her inner muscles.

Our audience applauded. They had been well entertained. When I turned to look, I saw the couples pairing off again, clients and customers disappearing into darkened corners, leaving for other rooms, where they might re-enact the scene that they had just witnessed. I could have left, too, gone off to drink or to bed. I could have found myself a new maiden and started afresh. Someone called out to me to try again for a second round, and another voice joined the first.

But then, I needed to move. I could not give them all. Because there were things that she and I needed to do alone. In private.

Although I won the displeasure of those that remained of the crowd, I did not care. I lifted her into my arms and carried her down the hall. I need not have concerned myself too greatly. Within moments others had taken our place at the foreground, wooing the crowd with the wild wantonness of their actions.

I carried my nymph down the hall, to the last room, the one furthest from the festivities. I set her down on the bed, and admired her. She pulled her dress entirely off and, for a moment, I simply stared, lost in the beauty of her, the wonder of her body. I had been inside of her only moments before, but now, I took the time to truly drink in her loveliness. She played shy as I watched her. She ducked her head against her arm and refused to meet my gaze. Coy thing, she need not have tried to play that game. I knew her. As if I'd been her lover for years rather than hours. I knew her.

'It doesn't read like a diary,' I said, stopping when Anthony offered a bite to eat from his own plate. Our main courses had arrived while I'd been reading. I swallowed, then continued, 'I mean, not like any I've seen from this era.'

'That's what I assumed it is. Except that you're right. I don't think it's an average diary, because there appears to be more than one person's handwriting on the pages.' He took the papers from me again and then showed me photocopies of the originals, pointing to what he meant. 'It's as if multiple people shared the story, adding their own notes or comments as the passages continued. Perhaps the pages were passed from one person to the next, with each one adding his or her own versions, or favourite stories, or sexiest dreams.'

'And this is how it starts? With the man doing this virgin . . .' Fucking her, I thought. Spanking her.

'That was the first part I could make out. The top of that paper has entirely disintegrated. When I touched it, the edges just crumbled away in my hands. I don't know if this was the first page, anyway. This could have been part of a much larger body of work. We'll just never know. And I must admit that I filled in some of the spaces when I couldn't quite understand the words. I told you that I'm a bit rusty with this.'

He spoke as if he translated pornography on a daily basis. But even though I'm not totally naïve when it comes to this sort of thing, I couldn't wrap my mind around the subject matter. As I said, I've seen porn before – aside from the few erotic books I own, Byron subscribed to *Penthouse* and *Playboy*. And I've viewed an assortment of risqué artwork. Every once in awhile a piece turns up that surprises even the most jaded of art historians. People have been writing, drawing and sculpting naked bodies for aeons. We're all animals at heart, aren't we? Obsessed with what brings us pleasure. But this was different.

'What were you expecting?' he asked. I tried to hide my feelings by taking yet another sip of my chilled white wine. I was surprised to find that I'd drained the glass.

I wasn't sure how to answer him. I'd assumed the

papers would be part of some story, like *The Iliad* or *The Odyssey*. Or perhaps a play. Or maybe a political history. As the papers had been sealed within a pot, I'd also considered that perhaps they held important information, notes from a spy, maybe. The fact that this was basically porn left me flabbergasted.

'Really?' he queried me. 'What did you think?'

'I don't know,' I told him honestly.

'Just because it's about sex doesn't mean that the work isn't important. People will still want to read it. Really, they'll want to do much more than that. I can absolutely see a movie being made about this discovery. Everyone is interested when you throw a little sex into the mix.'

I knew that he was right. There always is more of a buzz when a museum features a sexually themed show. Recently, the San Francisco Museum of Modern Art had displayed photographs taken of porn stars on location. Larry Sultan's photographic exhibit called 'The Valley' featured coloured photographs of actual pornographers taken in the suburban homes of a San Fernando Valley neighbourhood. The show had caused some consternation, and Byron had gotten on his soapbox about what was and wasn't art. But regardless of his feelings, I knew that the exhibition had been a huge success.

If this manuscript were translated by Anthony and published as an example of some of the first printed erotica, it would definitely be huge. There would be magazine articles and photo shoots – Anthony and I standing side by side. 'I gave her the first pages to read at dinner,' he would say. 'You should have seen the look on her face. She was definitely surprised.' And then I would laugh and say, 'Nothing about art surprises me.' We'd make an excellent team, a perfect media darling couple.

But suddenly I remembered how wet I'd been today, fantasising about Anthony. Had he somehow guessed that from the way I'd handled myself in his office? Had he remembered our holiday kiss, as well? That moment was so clearly embedded in my own mind. Was there the slightest chance that he fantasised about it, as well. Here was the big fear I found myself circling: Was there a chance that he'd made up this stuff in order to turn me on?

'Do you want to read the rest now?' he asked.

I felt my cheeks go from simply bright pink to a dark crimson. If I said yes, would he know that I was envisioning him in the scenario? If I said no, would he think that I was some sort of prude? If he did, he'd be right. I *was* some sort of a prude.

'I'll bet Nora would like it.' He smiled at me.

I looked at him, shocked. 'You know Nora?'

'We met at the Christmas party.'

I nodded. It didn't surprise me that he remembered her. Nora had been unforgettable that night, as usual. She'd gone as a naughty Christmas angel in an outfit that actually sported wings on the back, made of tinsel and lace.

'And, of course, I know *of* her. You can't live in LA without seeing Nora spread out on her Pink Fedora billboard over Sunset Boulevard. So, yes, I do know who she is.'

I wondered if there was a deeper meaning to his statement. Had he *been* with her? I didn't think so. Nora would definitely have told me. At least, I thought she would. To hide from these thoughts, I returned to reading the manuscript, and Anthony entertained himself by staring at me, as if attempting to read the hue of my cheeks. Did my blush have a code, like the hankie code, or the one with Nora's hats? If so, I hoped Anthony wouldn't be able to break it.

Bright pink = mildly aroused.

Fuchsia = ready for action.

Scarlet = let's go to the ladies' room and get it on.

'Why don't you finish reading?' Anthony continued. 'Like I said, I only got through the five pages. There's plenty more to keep me busy.'

I nodded at him, lost once again in the words on the page.

Those flowing black ringlets were gathered off her face with a golden ribbon. I untied the ribbon and she immediately held out her arms in front of her, her wrists together, one atop the other. I understood what she wanted from the longing look in her deep green eyes, and I could not ignore the fantasies I could read there.

She wanted me to tie her up.

How could I resist such a decadent – if silent – request?

'It's bondage,' I whispered. I said the word as softly as I could, even though we were in the very rear of the restaurant, far from any other tables.

'Oh, good. You've gotten to my favourite part,' Anthony replied matter-of-factly. He put one hand out, gently touching my arm closest to him, and I trembled at his touch. His fingertips traced along the line of veins on the inside of my wrist. I closed my eyes for a moment, and his hand encircled my wrist. Oh, God, I thought. I'm going to burst into flames. He's going to touch me, and I will ignite.

To hide my emotions, I pulled my hand away and thrust myself back into the pages.

Once her wrists were bound, I found that I could not stop myself. I reached for her flowing garments and shredded them. She watched, her eyes wide, but not in fear. She gazed at me with an expression as cool as the first day of winter. For a moment, I was lost once again in her eyes, but then I pulled free. She would have bound me up with her look alone. She would have taken all of my power away if I had not concentrated on the business in front of me.

I felt her eyes watching as I tied the fabric around

her ankles. I used the next piece of fabric to blindfold her, and now I knew she could not see. But she would see. In the chamber of her mind, she would see everything.

For a moment, I came as close as I possibly could to her without actually touching her. I used my breath on her naked skin, blowing puffs of air over her nude body. She shuddered at the sensation, and I felt as if I could actually see her body asking me for more. There was a visible yearning to her, as if her skin could speak, her hair could talk, her sex could beg. She wanted more.

Now, I gave her more.

With my mouth alone, I touched her. I did not use my hands, my fingers. I was not bound as she was, but I did bind myself. I refused to stroke her skin, to touch her hair. Kissing was the only method I employed and, in moments, she was moaning, sighing sweetly as the wind.

I could hear her longing in my head, as if she were speaking from within my very soul. I could hear each thing that she craved, and I made sure that I honoured every one of her silent requests.

This was not my first time to behave in such a manner. I have always enjoyed binding a girl when I make love to her. Did this young sprite know of my past? I could not ask her, for in truth, I did not want to know. Instead, I told myself that we were two of the same, made for each other. Matching one another in our desires. She, wanting to be my captive. I, desiring to be her master.

The kisses I gave her seemed to illuminate her being from within. Her body moved against mine, and I saw with the rocking of her hips that she was ready for me, that she needed me.

She needed me as I needed her.

It was time for me to stop these childish games. These kissing games. I drew back my own robes, revealing the hardness there. With a deep breath, I moved forwards, giving her all that she required.

I didn't say anything else for a moment, my mind consumed immediately by an image of Anthony tying me up. Would he truly be into something like that? Byron hadn't been. At least, not with me. Perhaps, with Gwen. I didn't know for sure whether or not he liked this sort of sexplay. It simply wasn't something that had ever come up as a possibility between us.

'What are you thinking?' Anthony asked when he saw that I was no longer reading.

What was I thinking?

I couldn't tell him that I'd just been wondering about my ex and his new love. But that image didn't remain in the front of my mind. The thoughts were almost too complicated for me to unravel. From the way Anthony was staring at me, focused intently on my expression, he seemed genuinely interested. Once again, I wondered whether this could possibly be some sort of test he'd created. Maybe the text had been mundane: laundry lists, grocery items, everyday nonsense that wasn't special at all other than the fact that it was three thousand years old. But would Anthony be the type to engineer that sort of scam? I knew there were practical jokesters in our midst. Was he one of them?

'Come on, Eleanor. What are you thinking?'

'I can't believe this is real.' That was a fact, although it sounded rather lame to say. Sure, it was real. I had the papers right in front of me. But that's not exactly what I meant, and Anthony understood.

'Of course, I was surprised, as well, but you must have read about the hedonism of the time.'

'What do you mean?'

'There was wildness in some of the ancient fertility festivals, with everyone whipping each other with tied birch branches. I've read about the decadent parties way back when, parties that would have given Hollywood parties a run for their money.'

I nodded, still feeling sceptical. 'You think it's about a prostitute?'

He shrugged. 'There were words I didn't know: *hetairai*, *deikteriades*. I looked them up and learned that they were levels of prostitutes, which helped immensely. I've skimmed ahead, and I think I understand the gist of the story.'

'There's a story? It's not just . . . you know . . .'

He grinned. 'Well, there's definitely more sex. But I think there's more to it than that. From what I can tell, most of the entries seem to be about this girl who was brought to the house of a famous madam. The girl's father had been told prior to her birth that she was destined to be an important person in society. He had assumed she'd be born a male, and when she wasn't, he simply waited until she was of age, and then – I don't know – dropped her off at this whorehouse. But they weren't exactly whorehouses. There wasn't quite the stigma. These women were learned, and they served the goddesses: Aphrodite, Athena, Hera.'

I listened without truly hearing his words. Yes, he talked a good game. But what if he *had* written this up just for me? Was that really a problem? I was indescribably turned on by the images I'd read. Could I admit that to Anthony? I tried a trick I've learned from Nora. I turned his questions back on himself.

'What do *you* think of it all?' I countered, twirling one strand of hair around my finger nervously while I waited for his response.

'Unexpected,' he admitted, 'but sexy.' Another pause. 'Like you.'

If Nora hadn't called right then, I don't know what I would have done. Turned beet red, perhaps. Choked on the new glass of Chardonnay the waitress had just brought. Run for the ladies' room to regain my sense of control.

Instead, I was quite literally saved by the bell – the tinkling bell of my cell phone – and I quickly rummaged through my simple black leather purse to find the little ringing device. Anthony watched with bemusement as I pulled item after item out of my handbag. I'm organised, yes, but I rarely use my cellphone, so it occasionally disappears beneath the detritus of my purse. It looked as if I'd done an archaeological dig of my own by the time I found the little silver device and checked the number. On the table were a gold compact, my one and only lipstick, a silk handkerchief, a pen and notebook, my black leather wallet – Anthony began toying with the items while I looked at the LED display on the phone.

If it were Byron, I would not have answered, but when I saw the caller was Nora, I said, 'This will just be a second,' and brought the phone to my ear.

'Where are you?' Nora asked.

'Osborne's.'

'Why aren't you here yet?'

'What do you mean?'

'They're already starting getting ready for tonight's casting, Eli. There are all sorts of people here. I thought you'd definitely come. I need you.'

I hesitated for a moment. My mind had been so consumed by my own existence for the past 24 hours that I'd forgotten the constant drama that surrounds Nora.

'What for?' I asked.

'What do you mean, what for? Because I need you.' Rarely, have I ever heard Nora sound that stressed. Excited? Definitely. Enthusiastic? Of course. But she manages her stress in such an amazing Zen-like way that I am in constant awe of her. Now, her voice was cracking and she sounded desperate.

Still, I hesitated for another beat. I didn't know what to do. It would be rude for me to tear out of the restaurant right now. 'Can I bring Anthony?'

'Bring whomever you want,' she said, 'just get the hell over here.'

* * *

Anthony was charmed by the idea. 'A reality show? At Nora's club?'

I nodded, watching as he easily manoeuvred his gigantic convertible through the light evening traffic. As soon as I'd explained the situation, he'd paid the bill – even though I was the one who'd promised him dinner – and herded me into the car.

'And what does the winner get?'

'Nora lost her best bartender last year. The winner gets to take Vlad's place.'

'I'm assuming that means more than simply pouring drinks for starving starlets.'

'Well, Vlad moved on to his own talk show this season on the Bijoux Network, so the position can definitely be a step up. He is also the spokesman for a new pineapple-infused vodka, and I think Nora mentioned that there is a menswear line courting him.'

'From a bartender to talk-show host?' Anthony appeared incredulous.

'You know the skills bartenders have to have. They listen, they have good memories, they never forget a tip or the face that goes with it.'

Anthony grinned. 'You sound like you know something about the business.'

I shook my head. 'Only through Nora. I'm awful at remembering names and faces.'

'But you're insanely good about remembering dates of artwork.'

'Art's easy for me. People are difficult. I'm so impressed with the staff at Nora's club. I can't even remember what alcohol goes into which drink. I rarely stay up late unless I'm working on a tough project. Flat out, I'd never be able to work at a club.'

We had arrived and the bouncer made eye contact with me and waved us in.

He knows me by now. Anthony seemed impressed, but as soon as we entered the club, I heard a shriek that could only be Nora.

Chapter Eleven

'Who the fuck let them in?'

I stared at Nora, confusion coursing through me. At first, I thought that she meant me and Anthony. But how could she? That would have made no sense at all. She'd invited us here, demanded that we come – and besides that, we're best friends. Then I realised that she wasn't looking at me. She was staring over my shoulder, her face contorted with rage. I haven't seen Nora look that displeased too many times in my life. Thankfully, I've never been the one on the receiving end of her anger.

When I looked over my shoulder, I felt as if my heart had stopped.

There on the huge movie screen behind the dance floor were Byron and Gwen, larger than life, locked in a clinch right out of a triple-X movie. Gwen's glistening mane of wheat-blonde hair fell loose past her shoulders – her noticeably *bare* shoulders. She looked as if she'd been dipped in cinnamon, her skin uniformly bronze.

When did this woman have the time to get her hair blown out, get her brows arched, her teeth whitened? How did she manage to maintain a high-powered law career and still look as flawlessly sexy if she'd walked right off the cover of *Maxim*?

And what in God's name did she see in Byron?

That was answered quickly enough. She saw a willing, able man who would follow her anywhere she chose to drag him. Sure, there are many wandering souls searching for leaders in Los Angeles, but maybe not as many as gullible as Byron. He had an expression on his face that made me think he would trail after her like a puppy, any place she named. And right now, that location was the Cinéma Vérité room.

While I – and two hundred of my closest strangers – watched, Gwen slid her lanky body along Byron's, slowly, seductively moving to the beat. Was she wearing anything at all? The camera captured her naked back, her hair falling down nearly to her waist.

'Who the fuck –' Nora continued, on an absolute rampage. I watched briefly as she stalked towards the front doors of the club, and then I realised that I was gripping into Anthony's hand so hard that my nails must have left marks in his skin. I released him and tried my best to apologise, but he shook his head. I wanted to tell him what was going on. I wanted to explain. He didn't seem to need to hear the words. Instead, he led me to the bar and ordered us each a drink.

'My ex –' I started.

'I recognised him already,' he said simply. 'He showed up sporadically at ARTSI events, right? I have to admit, I never really understood what you saw in him. I tried to talk with him one time about a Jackson Pollack piece we had on loan, and he had this theory that if he could do it himself –'

'I know –' I couldn't hide the grin, just talking with Anthony was making me feel better '– then it wasn't art.'

Anthony nodded.

'And you know,' I continued, 'Nora's my best friend, and she owns the club.'

He toasted me, forcing the drink into my hand. 'Don't worry,' he said. 'You really don't have to explain.'

Maybe not, but I couldn't stop looking over my shoulder, staring at the movie screen, mesmerised. Gwen had undone Byron's belt buckle with her teeth. The woman literally had no shame. Just like Nora had no fear. I watched now as the door to the not-so-private room burst open and there stood Nora, bolstered by her two largest bouncers. She'd gone outside to get the men as back-up support, and the two bodybuilders looked like a pair of Herculean bookends standing on either side of the nymphet that is Nora.

The motion on the dance floor came to a stop as we all watched in unison as the drama unfolded. I'd never seen anything like this in Nora's club before. Yes, things get rowdy every once in awhile. That's why Nora has bouncers in the first place. But I'd never seen her personally eject a customer while all eyes were upon her. I watched, my heart racing, as Byron and Gwen were escorted from the Cinéma Vérité room. When Gwen turned around, I saw that she had on a tiny little tank top, the slim spaghetti straps of which had been hidden by her hair. So she hadn't been naked – she'd just looked naked.

Once the two were off the camera, the movie screen was taken over by a video clip, a crisp black-and-white montage of screen sirens from yesteryear.

'Why'd he have to come here?' I murmured, more to myself than the man at my side.

'The Pink Fedora?' Anthony responded. 'It's the place to be – at least, it is according to the *LA Weekly*. The club of the hour.'

Nora appeared at the bar, looking breathless. Her cheeks were flushed, but that added to her beauty. I saw that she'd dyed her hair pink, and she was wearing a sheer fedora, one made of Lucite or some similar hard synthetic material. It wasn't glass, was it? I could just imagine Nora dressing like Cinderella, with a glass hat instead of a glass slipper. What would she leave behind at the stroke of midnight? Nothing. The club would only be getting started at that hour.

She gave Anthony a half-grin, Cheshire catlike, and then said, 'I'm sorry for the uproar.' I understood her smile. She wasn't sorry at all. Nora lives for scenes like this. If she felt bad in the slightest, it was because I was involved. She never likes to see me hurt.

'You're not sorry at all,' he said with a similar smile. He seemed to understand Nora very well, even if he didn't know her personally.

'You're right. That was the most fun I've had all week.'

'Why did they come here?' I asked Nora, unable to stop myself.

'You know why,' she said.

I shook my head. I didn't.

'Because you told him that she didn't really love him. He's trying to show you that you're wrong.'

'By having sex with her in front of a bunch of club kids?'

Now, she shrugged. 'I've never pretended to know what makes your ex tick,' she said, 'I'm just saying why I think he did that.'

Anthony leaned in. 'I hope you kept the tape.'

'Why would I do that?'

'Because I'm sure her bosses would appreciate a copy. You could send it right on to the law firm. I'll bet they have a strict policy about the management level fucking the underlings.'

'How did you know she was a lawyer?' I asked, surprised.

Anthony gave me another smile, but didn't respond.

Nora looked gleeful at the idea, but I said no. 'Look, I'm not out to get them. I just want him to go away.' I took a sip of my drink and then faced the dance floor.

Nora said, 'I'm glad you guys are here. The casting starts at midnight, and I'm going to need all the help I can get.'

'Is it an open call?' Anthony looked shocked.

Nora shook her head. 'No, way. We'd have people lined up around the block. But it's been wild nonetheless. That's why I missed Byron at first. We've been overwhelmed tonight.'

'What do people have to do to try out?' She shot me a look, and I said, 'I'm not kidding. I really want to know.' I didn't think that they'd have to fuck her, or put on an act of their own in the Cinéma Vérité room. But what might Nora have dreamed up for the competition? I could only wonder.

'Mix up a unique drink and serve it with sophistication.'

'That's it?'

'You'd be surprised at how hard it is,' she said. 'Think of the sexy drinks you know: Sex on the Beach, Blow Job, Fuzzy Navel ... Our bartenders have to make drinks like that without batting an eye. And sometimes the person ordering the luscious libation is extremely flirtatious, yet our bartenders have to handle the request in as professional a way as possible. Imagine you're a girl working bar and a movie star walks up and asks you to give him a Blow Job.'

Anthony started laughing. He looked around the room, then back at Nora. 'Nine out of ten of your staff would be on their knees behind the bar.'

'That's not so!' Nora said in mock outrage.

'Why?' he asked. 'What do you think?'

'A hundred per cent. We aim to please.' And even I couldn't tell whether or not she was kidding.

At midnight, all of the attractive hopefuls had lined up against the wall. There were several Bijoux Network studio execs sitting at the bar along with Nora, Travis, Anthony and myself. Although I'd told Anthony that he didn't have to stay, sure that I could get a ride home with Nora, he said he wouldn't miss the event – that this was pure excitement. I was surprised by his attitude. Sometimes, artsy folks, or 'ARTSI' folks can be a bit on the pompous side. Art has its merits, but this sort of event would rank so far below what my co-workers would consider entertainment, they wouldn't even acknowledge its existence. I knew that Byron would have wrinkled his nose at the concept of the reality show, even though he'd been caught in the reality room only hours before. But I had to think that was all Gwen's doing. Byron had never been one to engage in PDAs in the past. The thought of him willing to fuck for the camera was almost frightening.

But Anthony looked as if he was having a blast.

'You sure you're OK?' I asked him, just to check.

'Are you kidding? I'm thinking of trying out,' he told me with a wink.

We watched together as more than fifty different beautiful people took their turn behind the bar.

'Why did you hold the auditions so late?' I asked Nora in between two contestants. When I looked around the room, I saw that one hopeful had already fallen asleep, her hands folded under her head, her blonde hair hiding her face. My guess was that she had already eliminated herself.

'Because the club is open until two. I need people who are true night owls. We're not filming a faux show. The thing is going to take place right here. During real club hours.'

'Some of your contestants are going to blow it before they ever belly up to the bar,' I told her, pointing to the sleeping blonde, and now I saw that a second contestant had fallen asleep, as well. It was amazing to me that either girl could sleep with the music playing so loudly. In order for any one of us to have a conversation, we either had to yell, or move in close and speak directly into one another's ears.

'That simply makes the choosing process that much easier.'

'How many people did you start with?' Anthony asked.

'We whittled down the list from several thousand. People sent in videotapes and headshots from as far away as New Zealand. I got so much email on the first day of the call for contestants that our server went down.'

Next up was a young Swedish girl who explained that she would be making a Tantric Kiss, a drink created by a mixologist at Tantra in Miami. The drink consisted of orange blossom water, vodka, peach Schnapps, two different fruit juices and a flower for garnish. I knew from experience that Nora keeps several types of edible flowers in her refrigerator at all times. But this girl won the judges' eyes by flirting slightly as she plucked a flower from her own silver-blonde hair and dropped it into the drink.

'Not so hygienic,' Anthony said.

'Perhaps not, but sexy,' Nora replied. 'Sexy is very important.'

'It is,' Anthony agreed, and he set his hand on my thigh under the bar. I knew that Nora couldn't see him, but I felt myself freeze. As soon as his hand touched me, I remembered the manuscript he'd translated. I wished that I'd thought to tie my hair up with a ribbon, something golden that Anthony could remove and use to bind my own wrists ...

'Who's next?' I asked quickly, to cover my nerves.

'You thirsty?' Nora asked. She was teasing me. I'd been the one to try several of the concoctions so far. Nora had chosen me to ask for the drinks, as I am not the average customer. She wanted to mix things up for the contestants. So far, I'd had to ask one bartender for A Piece of Ass, another for an Affair, and a third for a Slow Comfortable Screw. That one was my favourite.

Nora had put Anthony to work, as well, instructing him to ask for a Wet Dream, a drink called Wild Sex and another one called Party Girl. It was between that and a Dirty Girl Scout, and he said he felt too lecherous to order the last one. At this point, we were neck and neck, definitely drunk and getting drunker.

'I can't believe we're doing this,' I said as I lay back in one of Nora's booths. It was made of purple leopard-print vinyl, and it felt cool when I rested my cheek against the side.

'Getting plastered together?'

'Just all of it.'

'You mean it's an odd sort of way to spend a first date.'

I didn't respond right away. Nora had been right. This was a date. But it wasn't a date-date. I mean, it wasn't like any date I'd ever been on in the past. Perhaps that had been my problem. I've always been on the sort of dates you could find if you looked up first-date tips online: dinner and a movie, walk through a park, drive to the beach.

'I like it,' Anthony said, pulling my hand so that I moved back into an upright position. We sat there, side by side, watching as Nora spoke with the show's official casting director. They were honing down their favourites, deciding who they would ask to come back.

'The winner has a shot at creating his or her own drink,' Nora told us when she came to say the preliminary casting was complete. That we could all call it a night and go home.

'I'll bet I know what it's going to be called,' I said, but Anthony said it before I could: 'A Pink Fedora.'

Chapter Twelve

In my dreams, I attended the party described in the journal. But unlike the girl in the story, who had been blindfolded by her partner, I could see the different players, and they were all the co-stars in my life. Byron was there, in a mask with devil's horns. He and Gwen lay entwined on a shimmering white fur rug, and I watched as Byron lifted Gwen's sheer dress and pressed his face to her pussy. I could actually hear it as Byron's tongue plunged in and out, making Gwen arch and moan loudly, gripping my ex-boyfriend's shoulders as he came.

Across the room, Nora and Dean were entwined, smoothing golden oil on each other's naked skin. Nora's hair was as short as always, but in this vision, she did not sport a multicoloured look. Instead, her hair was its true midnight black, and decorated with tiny purple wild flowers. Dean's long dark locks shone in the light. His tattoos seemed to be living artwork, moving on his skin. I watched as he fucked Nora, watched as Travis came and joined them, turning Nora into an intricate sexual sandwich, and although I felt a twinge within me, I wasn't jealous. I was waiting. I knew that my lover was coming soon, and I held myself in check, preparing for his entrance.

But where was he?

I could smell the fragrant fruit trees just outside, the wafting scents of citrus and the still-blossoming honey-suckle, the flowers drooping heavily on the vine. Then I heard a voice call my name. I turned to the doorway, and there stood Anthony. As he strode forwards, all of the other partiers faded away. It was just the two of us, together.

'What are you thinking?' he whispered, as he had asked me at dinner. This time, I didn't let him down. I told him everything. All of my fantasies. All of my secret dreams. And slowly, as I slept, Anthony made each one come true.

He tied me up, the knots so firm, I couldn't fight. I tested the bindings, pulling my wrists, but that only worked to tighten the knots even further. Then he put me over his lap and spanked me. His hand came down on my ass, hard, and I cried out and kicked my heels in the air. He took no pity on me. He slapped my ass harder still, and I felt my pussy respond, tightening, contracting.

Just like the girl in the story, I let him know what I wanted with my eyes on his. I looked over my shoulder at him, begging silently for him to strike harder, and then to fuck me even harder than that. Anthony had told me when I'd reached his favourite part. The bondage part. He'd let me know that he was willing. That he was ready. And in my dreams, I responded as I'd been unable to in real life.

In the middle of the night – well, much after the middle of the night, since we had not gotten home until four – I jerked myself awake. It felt as if I had been physically pulled from the dreams, wrenched from sleep. My body was wet with sweat. The place between my legs felt swollen and used. I could not think of another time that I had touched myself in my sleep. Byron would have told me if I had, would have teased me mercilessly if he had caught me.

I brought my fingers to my face, smelled them, catching the scent of my pleasure. I must have pushed my fingers into my pussy, must have rocked my hand in and out, thrusting in deep, curving the tips of my fingers to stroke the inner walls of my cunt. This was so unlike me. I assured myself that I was behaving oddly simply because I wasn't used to sleeping in a strange room hearing strange noises. I lied to myself. My mind was filled with images of the couple in the diary, of me and Anthony, of naked lovers putting on shows for a rowdy audience.

Everything whirled at fast speed behind my closed eyelids. Images dripping with sex, girls bound on tables while others dined on the feasts of their bodies. These visions kept me awake, my heart pounding in my chest, and though I willed myself to go back to sleep, my mind would not let me.

I took a deep breath, tried all of the tricks I do when I am occasionally plagued by insomnia. I closed my eyes and counted backwards from one hundred. First in English, then in French. I imagined myself tucked into a hammock, swinging back and forth between two palm trees, the sun beating down on me, the waves folding over to kiss the sand just below the woven hammock. I created a mental paradise where I relaxed naked under the sun. But every time I closed my eyes, I was consumed by thoughts of Anthony. By images of him. I could see him without his glasses on, at close range, leaning in to kiss me. I could feel the warmth of his body in the booth at the restaurant, sliding closer to me, his hands probing under the table, finding the edge of my skirt and pushing it up. Revealing me inch by inch, playing teasing games with his fingertips until he got to the ridge of my panties.

What would he do then? What did I want him to do?

My mind spelled it out. I was in the restaurant once again, and this time I answered his questions. He said, 'What are you thinking?' and I said, 'I want to be bad. I'm tired of being good all the time.'

'What do you mean, "bad"?'

A question someone at ARTSI would ask. *What does the picture mean to you? What does bad mean in your world?*

'More than anything, I want to be . . .' To be what? To be different. To push the boundaries. To break free. 'More than anything, I want not to be . . .' Not to be what? Boring? Simple? Dull?

This was a simple statement – maybe too simple – that I could not seem to complete. Where was my powerful vocabulary? Where were the ten-dollar words that win me Scrabble every time, that help me do the *New York Times* crossword puzzle faster than any of my friends can.

The only words I had power over were these: I want to be naughty, bad, wicked.

Perhaps those were all I needed, because he nodded, and his fingers pushed forwards, and there, where I was wet and hot and ready, he discovered my centre, plunged my core.

Why hadn't I given in tonight?

After the casting call, Anthony had asked me if I wanted to go back to his apartment with him. 'I know it's late,' he said, 'but I'm not tired. Do you want to come to my house? Do you want to see my trains?'

And I'd said no.

As if to punish me for my lack of excitement, sleep would not come for me. I climbed off of the sofa bed and walked to the window. It was after 6 a.m. If I'd gone to Anthony's, what would we be doing? Would we be asleep yet? Or would we be watching his valuable train set go around and around his bedroom?

Fuck the train, I thought to myself.

We'd be on the floor, or on the bed, or on his fire escape. Yes, the fire escape. Even though Byron and I had lived in an apartment with a balcony for three years, we'd never managed to make love outside. I had a strong desire to do just that, to fuck where people might see me. To fuck where the wind and air could flow over my naked body. I could visualise doing this with Anthony, his strong arms around my body, his head leaning in towards the back of my neck to lick me, to kiss me, to bite me and make me squirm. His hips pressing against my backside, thrusting, teasing. There'd been a promise in Anthony's eyes. I wanted to see exactly what that promise meant. And I mentally berated myself for not going home with him, for not being daring enough to explore the unknown.

Why did I have to process every situation?

Why couldn't I simply give myself up to a new experience?

I contemplated this, coming quickly to the answer: It's my nature. Research and report. Edit and revise. Work slowly, steadily, methodically. Don't rush through your work or you might get something wrong.

It's difficult to live spontaneously when you're always fact checking, when you're always questioning yourself, adding in the proper footnotes. Ibid. Ibid. Ibid. Besides, why try to live in the moment when you can live vicariously through your best friend's exploits? Isn't that easier than letting yourself be free enough to try something new, something that might possibly get you hurt? Yes, I'd been adventurous with Nora and Dean – but that was one time, one night of fantasy in a life of predictability.

But maybe with the right person, maybe with Anthony, I could give into new things without a fight. Because there were so many things to explore, and Anthony might be the perfect partner to join me in my quest for knowledge.

I climbed back into the sofa bed and pulled up the sumptuous lilac covers. The street noises faded, the honks and sounds of car engines melded together, became a lullaby that I heard but could no longer recognise. When I dreamed this time, it was about the Christmas party ten months before, the tiny strands of white lights glimmering about the room, the warmth from many bodies moving on the makeshift dance floor, the throbbing music of a jazz band hired to play for the evening.

Anthony had his strong arms around me under the mistletoe. My voice did not interfere, did not offer up the folklore behind this plant. I shut up with the facts for once. Anthony's dark curly hair hung loose and long to his shoulders, out of its normal ponytail. His suede jacket was deliciously soft to the touch. His lips on mine made me feel drunk, as if I had downed glass after glass of the champagne being served by dapper-looking actors in tuxes and tails.

I dreamed about the kiss.

For the rest of the night, I dreamed about the kiss. Every moment of it, every nuance. And since words are my life, words are my world, at 9 a.m., I woke up with two specific words in my head: warm lips.

'You're up early for a Saturday,' I observed as I walked into Nora's sunlit kitchen. As might be expected, her kitchen décor surpasses the eclectic to border on the insane. She has a collection of antique egg beaters, and they dangle from every square inch of the ceiling, making the room feel smaller than it actually is and somewhat menacing. The refrigerator is covered with silver chrome; her cabinets are painted glossy indigo; and in the centre of her slate kitchen floor is a chalk outline of a body, as if left by a police investigation.

'Not early,' she corrected me, 'I'm up *late*.'

'What do you mean?'

'I'm *still* up,' she said slowly, as if speaking to someone who wasn't fluent in her language.

I couldn't believe it. 'How can you do that?'

'Do what?' She wasn't paying me much attention, focused intently on the computer screen in front of her. She had her laptop set up on the sparkly gold Formica counter.

'How do you stay up all night and still seem so refreshed?'

'Travis and I fucked in the shower,' she answered, grinning, 'so I'm all nice and clean.'

She went back to staring at her computer.

'What are you doing?' I asked now, leaning over to pour myself a cup of coffee. 'Playing Solitaire?' This is Nora's favourite way to relax.

'You know I never play it on the computer.'

'That's right. You like the feel of the cards in your hands. It's the one place where you are anti-technology. So what *are* you doing?'

'Posting on my blog. I want to write about what happened last night. We cut down the number of contestants considerably, you know? And since all of the hopefuls submitted headshots, I'm putting scarlet Xs on the ones who are no longer in the running.' That seemed a bit cruel, but I didn't comment.

'Did the Tantric Sex girl make it?'

'What do you think?'

I was quiet for a moment. 'Yes, I think you kept her.'

'Mm-hmm,' she said. 'That flower trick was absolutely lovely. I know Anthony wouldn't have drank the thing, but it showed spark and spunk. You gotta love that.'

'Who else is in?'

'You wouldn't remember the names, I think, but the man who created your Slow Comfortable Screw got in. He's yummy.'

I poured myself a cup of coffee and took a sip. 'So's Anthony.'

'Then why are you sleeping on my sofa?'

'You told me not to fuck him on the first night.'

'I did not.' She sounded aghast. 'I asked you whether or not you wanted to.'

'I wanted to,' I said with a sigh.

'Then let me ask again: *Why are you sleeping on my sofa*?'

'I don't know. He translated the papers for me, and he made me all confused.'

'He did a bad job?'

'He did an excellent job,' I told her, 'but –'

'But what?'

I didn't know if I could confess the rest to her. What would Nora say if I told her I thought he might be playing a game with me? I found that I just couldn't do it. Not yet.

'But what?' Nora asked again, looking up from the

computer, giving me her total attention. On the screen behind her, I saw that she'd crossed out the faces of more than twenty contestants. I felt sad for those people. They had taken a risk and been shot down. I hesitated another moment, and then I chickened out.

'Maybe I'm too inexperienced for him,' I said. 'He's dated some of the top artists in the world. The really extreme avant-garde ones.'

'So? You're a total catch, Eleanor. You don't give yourself enough credit.'

'What if he wants someone who knows what they're doing?'

'You know what you're doing.'

I shook my head. 'I don't. Not really. What should I do? What would you do in my situation?'

She was quiet for a moment, and I could tell she had a difficult time envisioning herself in my situation. Nora is always in control. She always knows what she's doing. 'Come on,' she said, 'you're not a virgin –'

'But I'm not avant-garde, either.'

She hesitated for another moment. Then she said, 'You know what I'd do? I'd take the upper hand.'

'What do you mean?'

'I'd tell him that I had a surprise for him, and then I'd go into his office with a little bag of toys.'

'Toys?' I thought I knew what she meant, but I couldn't believe she'd think this would work for me.

'Go to one of the sex stores on Hollywood and buy yourself a pair of cuffs. Or better yet, take the ones from my dresser drawer. They're velvet-lined. Just wait until Dean wakes up.'

'I thought you said Travis . . .'

'I said I *showered* with Travis. Dean came over after.'

'Oh,' I said. 'After.' Like that made sense. But I guess it did. In Nora's world all things are possible.

'When are you going to announce the winners?' I asked after I'd showered. Showered alone, of course, not with

Dean, Travis, Anthony or any combination thereof. Mmm, but there was a thought. Had even Nora ever had three men at once?

'The Masquerade Ball.'

'On Halloween?'

She nodded. 'It's only a few days away. It seems like the perfect time to make such an important announcement. The press will be there, and we have a great band lined up.'

'Are you sure about your choices?'

She nodded. 'I always am, Eli. How about you? Are you sure about yours?'

I looked down at my hands rather than looking at her. No, I wasn't. What if I'd chosen to go home with Anthony the night before? Nora seemed to be reading my mind.

'Everything will work out,' she whispered, as if she were some sort of oracle, herself, as if she knew the future. I was not so sure.

I leaned back against the wall of her kitchen, dreading the weekend in front of me. I'd have to go back to the apartment, pack my belongings, find a storage facility. I'd have to face the drudge of reality. 'How do you know?' I asked Nora.

'Because it will. Good things are going to happen to us –' she smiled '– both of us. I can sense it.'

Chapter Thirteen

I had just taken my first sip of Columbian coffee on Monday morning when Anthony came to my office. Before he arrived, I had been sitting on my black swivel chair, thinking about going shopping with Nora. Shopping for things I'd never normally buy, never normally need. Suddenly 'normal' didn't appeal to me any more.

The weekend had been a downer. Confronting Byron had taken all of my energy. He'd broken up with Gwen after the scene at Nora's club – according to his story, anyway. My guess was that she'd dumped him. He hadn't fully believed that the two of us were over. It was as if he'd thought that now that he'd gotten Gwen out of his system, we could pick up where we'd left off.

Nora was flabbergasted when I'd told her. 'How could he think you'd take him back?'

'It wasn't like that,' I explained. 'He thought of it more like taking me back.'

'That doesn't make any sense.'

'He's always been like that, turning things around. He wanted to make me feel as if I'd been the one who drove him into Gwen's arms, but now that he'd seen the light, we could continue on our path.'

'I hope you told him about Dean.'

I bit down on my smile, and she beamed at me. But the revelation hadn't made moving out any easier. We'd had another knock-down fight, and I hadn't been able to collect the rest of my belongings.

Although I'd brought my favourite suits with me from the apartment, I was already nearly out of underwear. Nora had insisted that we were due for a visit to Kitten's

Top Drawer, even though it's a dangerous activity for her. Nora spends hundreds of dollars on lingerie because she often wears underwear as outerwear. I've gone shopping with her every so often, but I always wind up with the most tastefully quiet ensembles one might imagine. And always black. But now, my thoughts took me to a different place. I knew that with each rustle of satin, each bit of lace, I would picture performing a striptease for Anthony.

My mind was on panties, frilly pastels with dreamy decorative designs, as Anthony knocked and opened the door. As soon as I saw him, I took too big a sip of my coffee and burned my tongue, but he didn't seem to notice. Or didn't seem to care.

His arrival was unexpected, surprising me before the java had sparked the synapses in my brain. Just seeing him made me think about my dreams from Friday night. Truly, the first wet dream I'd ever had.

'I've been waiting for you,' he said. 'Didn't you get my messages?'

I shook my head. While Anthony stared at me, I lifted the handset of my office phone. It beeped repeatedly, indicating at least one message on my voicemail. Instead of listening, I hung up the phone and looked at Anthony, waiting for him to tell me whatever information he'd left on the machine.

Ignoring the chair, he sat on the edge of my desk, then looked around the office, taking it in. My office is down the hall from his tiny space, at the other end of the building. Mine is twice the size, painted a pale yellow, with framed prints of my favorite ARTSI posters and paintings on the walls. I decided early on that if I couldn't actually have an office with a window, at least I could create my own views.

Anthony was obviously wide awake, apparently one of those morning people I've read about. He exuded energy and, when he moved, I smelled fresh air, thought of him riding in his convertible to work, picking up the fragrance of the jacaranda trees that were currently dropping their purple blossoms everywhere in town. The streets near the museum were carpeted with the slippery petals.

'I spent all weekend doing research,' Anthony said. 'The journal contained words that I simply couldn't translate. I think I told you one or two of them in the papers on Friday night: *hetairai, deikteriades*. And I told you that after looking them up, I discovered that they were levels of prostitutes, which helped immensely. I grabbed one of those huge volumes on ancient Greece from the library. I couldn't find anything more modern than the nineteen-forties, and the text is disgustingly dense. But I did learn several things. I learned that the women in the top level, the *hetairai*, had peculiar methods of meeting up with their clients.'

He looked at me to see if I was paying attention. When I nodded, he continued. 'Every day, men who were interested in having a little fun would walk through the cemetery. On the headstones, a man would write the name of the prostitute he hoped to sleep with and he would list a monetary amount. The prostitutes would send their servants through the graveyard to read the offers –'

'Servants?' I interrupted.

'These weren't streetwalkers, you have to understand. They were powerful women who got a lot of money for what they offered. If the women were willing to accept the offer, they would write a proposed meeting time on the stones. If they weren't interested, they would let the man know on the headstone. This could cause embarrassment, since all in the town could read the rejection.'

He paused, then continued, 'I couldn't find much else about the prostitutes, except that there were most definitely orgies, just like the journal says. There was lesbianism, and there were dildoes.'

God, I couldn't believe we were having this discussion. At work. At barely nine in the morning.

'Did you get a chance to read the paper today?' he asked. He thrust one hand into his pocket, and pulled out a folded clipping.

'Not yet. I just got here.' I pulled my coffee cup closer, as if it were some sort of security blanket. Steam curled upwards from the porcelain mug.

'There's a piece reprinted from Reuters. It's tiny, just a filler on the back page. But it's the kind of thing I keep a look out for, the type of piece Janice is always posting on the bulletin board in the commissary. This time, the tagline of Athens caught my attention. Archaeologists have discovered what they believe to be a two-thousand-year-old dildo in a brothel in Athens. I think the museum should buy it and place it in the Greek room with your journal.'

'Why?'

'Well, it's absolutely amazing,' he said, now producing a stack of typewritten pages and placing them on the centre of my clean desk blotter. Looking at them, I realised that he must have spent all weekend working. The pages were single spaced. He was going to make me blind, even if he didn't mean to. 'You're going to go bonkers, totally crazy,' he said, still smiling.

'What do you mean?'

'Just like you said, it's pornography,' he told me. 'Plain and simple. I guess I had thought from skimming ahead that the rest of it might be more about the girl's life. That you would be able to use this information to create a picture of how women lived in Greece two thousand years ago. But there isn't much about daily life. It's all about fucking. If Colette had been hired to write ancient Greek smut for a dollar a page, she wouldn't have been able to do any better than this. I don't know if anyone could do better. The stuff is incredibly hot.'

I didn't know how to respond. Was he teasing me? Looking at Anthony, again refined with his hair pulled back and glasses in place, customary blue Oxford-cloth shirt over a white T-shirt and khaki pants, I could hardly believe we had been out together. That he'd let his hair down – literally and figuratively. That he had touched my hand and sent tantalising shivers through my body. But when he winked at me, the whole of Friday night came flooding back, the feelings of it, the force of it.

'You mean there's more – more of the bondage stuff?'

'It's *all* sex,' he said, grinning even broader, obviously enjoying himself, and apparently wanting to see what my reaction to the news would be. 'It's not a few teasing lines about how the girl was tied up and the soldier came to visit her, used her, released her –'

'The soldier?'

'The man. He's a soldier. Someone high up, though. Not a drone. And it seems that he and the girl wrote their experiences back and forth. There are simply pages of play-by-play, rough-and-ready action. The stuff is smut, but delicious smut. If we worked on it together, I'll bet it would be as big a seller as *The Sexual Life of Catherine M.* People who don't generally buy pornography would snap it up because it's old. And for some people, old is better. We'd be interviewed on NPR's *Fresh Air*. The *New York Times* would do a profile.' He sounded extremely happy.

'But you haven't finished, have you? There were so many pages.' I recalled the way the sheath of papers had looked when I'd found them in the rubble of the vase or urn. Broken fragments all around a pile of disintegrating papers.

'I only did a few more scenes,' he said, 'and when I was done, I felt as if I needed to take a cold shower. A series of cold showers. With ice cubes thrown in for good measure. Or maybe I should have just gotten in my car and come to see you at Nora's place. You would have let me in, wouldn't you?' He looked at me pointedly, and I returned the look, waiting. I didn't admit that I had been up Friday night, as well, thinking that I should get in my car and drive to see him. 'As it was,' he continued, 'I stood under the shower for ten minutes, then dried off outside on my fire escape. I'm probably going to get sick, and it will be all your fault.'

Fire escape, my mind whispered to me. He'd stood naked on his fire escape thinking about me. I liked that thought. Naked in his shower, the hot water pouring over his hotter body. No, the cold water. What water? My thoughts were a blur. I tried not to think of any of these images, which was a lot like trying not to think of white elephants, or pink elephants, or any other kind of elephants.

'I'm going to have to save the rest of it for later,' Anthony continued. 'I've got a few things that need working on if I want to keep my day job. Plus –' he winked at me once again, making me feel as if we shared something dark and dirty, which I suppose we had '– if I do more translating of that, I'm going to have to drag you off to some empty meeting room, tie you down, and give you what for.'

'What for?' I murmured.

'For making me wait.' There was a long pause.

'You mean on Friday night? Being late for dinner?' My voice was a whisper.

'I mean for making me wait all these months since last Christmas. Don't you know I've been thinking about you every day since the party? Couldn't you tell that?'

I shook my head. I was having a difficult time processing the fact that Anthony was speaking to me like this. 'How did you know that Gwen was a lawyer?' I asked suddenly.

For the first time ever, I saw Anthony blush. 'I read Byron's blog.'

Was I the only person on the planet who didn't read Byron's blog?

'I wanted to know more about him – I was trying to figure out what you saw in him.'

I stared at him, feeling shock work through my body. So I hadn't been the only one fantasising . . .

'Finding our own empty meeting room wouldn't be so bad, would it, Eleanor?'

I flushed even deeper. It felt as if my cheeks were positively neon. Nora would have been displeased. Nora says you should never blush in front of a guy you like because it lets him know what you're thinking. It gives your hand away. As you might guess, Nora is a very good poker player; she has the face down perfectly. She's even been on that show, *Celebrity Poker*, several times, and she's always walked away the winner, earning thousands of dollars for her favourite charity.

But Nora is who she is, and I am who I am, and I couldn't help it. Tie me down ... those words hit me with enough erotic images that I had to shake my head to clear them away.

'We wouldn't be doing anything but research, would we?' Anthony continued in his low crooning voice. 'Simply re-enacting a love scene that is over two thousand years old. You're the best researcher at ARTSI. Everyone says so. Don't you think you ought to try out this stuff yourself?'

He was teasing me. I knew it. And yet I couldn't respond. With Nora, I'm often able to shoot back quick witticisms. With Anthony, I felt as if nothing I ever said would make any sense. I was mute and shy as a virgin. Although not the virgin in the story. The faux virgin. She seemed as if she knew what she was doing. Anthony didn't appear to mind my silence, though. He simply added, 'Those Greeks could be fairly kinky. I have to say that I'm impressed.'

I gripped my cup and stared down into the dark liquid. I could see my reflection in the coffee. I looked untamed, and I quickly took a sip to erase the image

Anthony stared at me curiously. 'Was that too much to say after just one date? Have I totally horrified you?'

He kept reminding me that he thought it was a date, too, just like Nora did.

Was I the only one who had a need to keep insisting that it wasn't?

Anthony slapped his forehead in comic horror. 'Now, you'll never come over and see my trains, will you?' It was as if he had revealed himself to me, shown me who he was behind the serious façade. Now it was my turn, right? I've read enough romance novels. I know how the scenarios are supposed to unfold. Anthony was the hero, and I was the heroine – not Nora this time. Me. Why couldn't I simply open my mouth and say, 'The conference room at the end of this floor is empty. You've got your belt on. What are we waiting for? Tie me down just like you threatened. Take me as fiercely as the man in the story.'

But when I didn't reply, he said, 'Are you OK, Eleanor?'

'I'm fine,' I lied. 'Let me read these and I'll get back to you.'

'After your own cold shower,' Anthony said, apparently not offended at all that I hadn't matched his dare. 'I haven't revealed the big secret, the crème de la crème, as it were. I've saved it. I want you to discover it all for yourself.'

He nodded at me, and then left me alone in my office to gaze at the painting of an open window and wish that it were real.

My coffee was calling to me.

I picked it up and took another sip. I gazed at the wall in my room for so long that the coffee grew lukewarm, and I drank it as if it were a glass of water. I wanted to be awake when I read the pages. I wanted to have my wits about me. I didn't have them now. I had only images of Anthony grabbing me by the wrist and taking me down the hall to the conference room, leading me off like a naughty girl in need of her punishment, locking the door and spreading me out, face down on the long black table.

The table was commissioned by a local artist and is made of a huge slab of black glass. How cool that would feel beneath my naked skin. The mere thought of it made me wrap my arms around my body, protecting myself. From what? From my fantasies?

Anthony would work slowly, unbuckle his belt with easy motions, pull it free from the loops and then stand where I could see him, fingering the worn leather and watching me. Waiting for my reaction.

What *would* my reaction be? I wouldn't beg him to go easy on me, because I didn't want him to. I would close my eyes, lower my head and wait for fantasy to become reality. For a brief flicker of time, I considered rushing after him, taking hold of him and spinning him around, saying, 'Do it. What you just said. Do it. Every part of it. Do more! Do what the man did to the girl in those pages.' But if I couldn't say the words by myself, all alone with my thoughts, how could I say them to Anthony?

After several moments, I picked up the pages he'd left for me, started to read them, then stopped once again. I looked at the clock, then walked to the door of my office, and turned the lock, not in the mood to be disturbed.

At least, not until Nora called.

Chapter Fourteen

Over a late lunch at the Queen's Road café, I confessed everything to Nora. Confessed to her what I could not make myself reveal previously. I told her everything because I knew she would offer help, not judgment, guidance not glee. Well, maybe a little glee. This was Nora, after all. Nora, who has a room in her club called Slave to Love, filled with assorted bondage devices, all coloured hot pink, many trimmed with marabou. A whip is so much less threatening when made of pink leather. That's Nora's philosophy. Who's afraid of a pink ping-pong paddle? Not Nora. That's for sure.

'Anthony said he wanted to tie you down?' my best friend asked, her eyes shining brightly at the thought. She had on casual clothes today – casual for her – decked out in an all-white outfit that was splashed all over with colourful graffiti. It looked like actual graffiti, as if an artist had stood her up against an abandoned building, and sprayed both her and the wall behind her. I could make out parts of swear words in the shimmering blues, purples and oranges. Her hair was done in multicoloured streaks, to match the outfit, and she had a silver boom-box charm dangling on a heavy chain around her neck. I felt as dull as a female peacock sitting next to her.

If Anthony were to see the two of us sitting here together, which one of us would he choose?

'Just casually,' I explained, closing the door on the thought of competing with Nora. 'He simply tossed it out there.'

I shut my eyes as I remembered the way he'd spoken to me, and instantly saw myself captured, bound to a four-poster bed with Anthony standing above me, presiding over me. Or was a four-poster not the sort of thing he was thinking of? Did he mean something more along the lines of the story, with a hair ribbon around my wrists and my own torn clothing holding me in place?

'Tell me exactly what he said,' Nora insisted.

I opened my eyes and looked at her. She was practically salivating at the thought. This story could have been pulled from Nora's own life. Never had I been able to come to her with an X-rated tale like this one. Of course, if Nora had been the narrator, then the scene would already have taken place. She'd have been bound and cuffed, and would be describing the sensations in great detail to me, her willing audience of one.

'He said he'd have to tie me down and give me what for.' I took a deep breath. 'You know, for making him wait the other night. But he might have been kidding.' I was lying to her. 'No, I don't think he was kidding, actually.'

Nora looked directly at me, but rather than offer words of wisdom, she simply said, 'God, he's sexy, isn't he? I was so impressed on Friday, the way he handled seeing your ex up there with Gwen. Most men wouldn't have dealt with that situation nearly as well. They would have been jealous or angry or gotten all puffed up on testosterone. He simply seemed concerned about your feelings.'

'He didn't have to do anything, though. You did.'

She grinned, relishing the thought. 'It was perfect, tossing them out of the club, banning them for life. I've never had more fun. Byron just kept hissing at me that he'd always hated me, and Gwen looked a bit crestfallen that she couldn't come back.'

'Thanks for doing that,' I told her. 'You didn't have to.'

'Of course, I did. You're my best friend. I can't have your enemies at the club. But I can have your friends. Why don't you ask Anthony to come back? You two can make your own movie in our Cinéma Vérité room. I think you'd look stellar up on the screen – and you do, too, don't you? When you let your fantasies go that way. Admit it, Eli. You do.'

I half-nodded, not wanting to admit that she was right. This was a difficult concept for me to deal with myself, let alone to anyone else. But Nora knows me. She remembers the wide-eyed way I'd taken in the scenarios we'd witnessed at the underground clubs in Europe. She understands what those visions did to me, how they lingered. We haven't discussed my own fantasies all that often, but Nora doesn't need me to put them into words. That's why she's so good at running her clubs. She's almost magical that way. She knows what people want, what they crave.

'Don't be ashamed,' Nora said. 'You have to know how many people like that sort of thing. We'd never have a Cinéma Vérité room if people didn't want to show off for an audience, or a Slave to Love room if people didn't want to tie each other up. I think you should experience everything there is to try. If you like it, great. If you don't, that's fine, too. You just chalk it up to experience and move on. Be a trisexual.'

'A what?' I asked, unsure that I'd heard her correctly.

'A *try*-sexual. That means you should try everything at least once.'

'So you really like being –' I didn't know how to put this delicately '– being tied up? Or tied down?' I asked. I was having such a difficult time saying the words. I've always known the power of words, but in the past I thought I had more control over them than they had over me. I guess I was wrong.

'You know me,' she said, 'I like a lot of things. I like being bound. I like being spanked. I like switching and being the boss if I'm with the kind of lover who brings out that side in me, or completely submitting if I'm with a dominant partner. That's why I've been playing with both Dean and Travis lately. Dean is a dom, through and through, as you could tell the other night. Travis likes to give himself over to me. Best of both worlds, if you know what I mean.'

I noticed that the two upscale-looking women at the table to our left had stopped talking and were staring at Nora with expressions of half-interest and half-disgust. My best friend might have noticed, as well, but she quite obviously didn't care. Nora's like that. If you want to eavesdrop on her, that's fine, but you'd better not try to judge her. She won't take it. In fact, she'll become even louder, even more obscene in her descriptions.

'It sounds as if you have a guy who's ready to play,' Nora continued. 'I know I told you to consider not sleeping with him right away – or, at least, to make sure that you were really ready first – but once you do hit the sack, you should definitely take advantage of the situation. When are you getting together again?'

'Tomorrow night. He's going to give me the latest portion of the journal.' Anthony had left this message on my voicemail after our morning interaction.

'Where are you going?'

'His place.'

Nora's eyes widened appreciatively. 'No dinner and a movie. No dancing. Just wham bam.'

'He invited me. He's going to make me dinner while I read the final instalment of what he's done. He mentioned something about Italian food.'

'He cooks?'

I nodded. 'I guess.'

'The man has a killer accent, an unbelievable body, is a graduate from Oxford, can drink mixed drinks without getting sick, and he can cook?' Nora was incredulous, and apparently a little bit jealous.

'I haven't eaten his food,' I said, 'but he claims to be a whiz in the kitchen.'

'But you don't really care about that,' Nora teased. 'You only want to know if he's a whiz in the bedroom. And from the things he's offering you, it sounds as if he's definitely experienced.'

I felt flustered, and suddenly I had a need to confess the rest. 'I did this bad thing today,' I said. 'And actually, I did the same thing Friday, too.'

'Do tell,' Nora prompted, all ears.

'Not totally bad, I guess. Not evil, or anything, but not like me at all.'

Nora waited, interested and ready. Like I said, it's not often that I have stories for her. In general, she is the one with the audience. She seemed to enjoy our role reversal.

'I read the pages he gave me, and then I locked the door to my office, and . . .'

'At work?' Nora asked, understanding immediately, as I had known she would.

'At my desk.' I paused. After that, I'd hardly been able to do anything. I had sat in my chair, staring into space, until Nora had called and I'd gotten the idea to invite her out for lunch. 'What's happening to me?' I asked her now.

'My little girl's growing up,' Nora crowed in mock delight. 'She's turning into a real woman.'

'I'm turning into a real slut.'

'Perfect. I'm sure that's just what Anthony wants. Most intellectuals, at least the ones that I've had the pleasure of being with, prefer their women to be sluts in the bedroom.' Nora sighed. 'Although I have to tell you one thing. This is the most intricate method of foreplay I've ever heard of. He's translating ancient pornography for you and it's getting you off. I can hardly believe it.'

She'd just named my total fear. 'What if it's not true, Nora?' It horrified me to admit that I'd even had this worry, but if I couldn't ask Nora about it, I was out of luck. There was nobody else.

'Which part?'

'What if he's making this stuff up to entice me?'

'He's wooing you with ancient Greek pornography,'

she said with a sexy smile on her face. The thought of what he was doing quite clearly delighted her. 'I've heard a lot of come-ons in my time,' she said, 'but never something as intricate as this one.'

'But maybe,' I continued, 'he's making up modern pornography to try to get me into bed.' As soon as I said the words, I looked away. I felt as if I were being unfaithful in some way to Anthony, and I also felt brash for believing that he might do this. That I might be worthy of him taking the time to make up such a detailed fantasy.

'And it was kinky?'

I flushed. 'It was for me.'

'Tell me.'

I bent over my bag and pulled out the papers, then handed them over to her.

Nora took a moment to skim the first few, and then started to laugh. 'He wants to tie you up, Eli. Just like in the manuscript. He's said so. He's going to pop your cherry.'

'I'm not virgin.'

'To this stuff you are.'

I couldn't tell her she was wrong. Nora knows me too well. But maybe he did want to tie me up and maybe that had been his plan from the start. I cleared my throat and said, 'Maybe the journal is only a series of boring letters, or political rants, or tales of gods and mortals and the Oracle at Delphi. Or, what if it *is* a journal, but it was written by some chaste young virgin who's never had sex, who hates the thought of it and lives until old age without ever experiencing the sins of the flesh? What if Anthony's just concocting the whole thing to get me all hot and bothered?'

'Christ, are you suspicious,' Nora said, finally understanding. Then she paused, pondering it. 'That would be a totally elaborate thing to do. He'd have to research the fuck out of ancient Greece in order to fool you, wouldn't he? And you only just found the manuscript last week.

There's no way that he would have been able to do all that research in that short a time period, would he?'

'So far there haven't been too many facts woven through it. He could have gotten any of them from the profiles on our exhibits. Plus, the stuff today was way out there.'

'What do you mean?'

'We're getting into hot girl-girl sex. I mean, I know all about Sappho, but this stuff is on fire. It's X-rated.'

'Like?' Nora asked, wanting examples.

'Like naked bodies and sweat and suckling and licking, and contests about the prettiest body parts. You're right that Anthony said that he had done research on it, that he had found items in our library that back up the text. Still, I'm just not sure about some of this other stuff.' I didn't look at her as I said the last part. 'Come on, Nora. What do I do?' I was practically wailing now. 'What if he's just making it all up to get me into bed?'

'I don't believe he'd do that,' Nora said, finally. 'I like Anthony. I mean, I know I don't know him all that well, but he was a real trooper at the casting call. I liked the way he ordered that last drink, the Party Girl.' She considered the situation, for a moment. 'But if you're really unsure, why not take a page or two and have someone else translate it for you. Someone who you're sure doesn't have any sort of designs on you.' Nora hesitated. 'But not someone too straight, in case it *is* pornography. You don't want to shock anyone and have the person tell your bosses what you're really doing with your time. I mean, aren't you supposed to be working on an Angel show?'

I leaned back in my chair. 'Good idea. I'd never have thought of doing that. It's sneaky and underhanded.'

Nora beamed, happy with herself. She didn't take either of those words as insults.

'But I really have to know. I mean, Anthony's writing these things down that totally meld with my fantasies. Tie me up, tie me down, make love to me outside.'

Nora leaned forwards in her chair, as if ready to drink up every word I was saying. This was the type of conversation she lived for.

'If he's making it up to get me into bed, I need to know.' I took a deep breath. 'I actually need to know before tomorrow night.' I thought about it for a moment. 'That's just not going to be possible.'

'Postpone the dinner for another day, then,' Nora suggested, pleased with the idea. 'Whenever you make a potential bedmate wait, it drives the person extra wild. If Anthony is being a good little boy and translating the stuff honestly, he'll be totally out of his head with lust by the time you arrive for the date. If he's lying, then you'll be able to figure out a way to get back at him, like invite him to the Slave to Love room and put the cuffs on him. Plus, now you can still go shopping with me tomorrow night, like you promised.' Nora put on her pout, which made her look extra charming. Our waiter did a double take when he brought over the check, clearly captivated by Nora's pretty face.

I nodded. 'It's a plan. I'll photocopy a few pages and give them to Marcia. She's only average at ancient Greek. That's why I didn't use her in the first place.'

Nora gave me a look, then said sarcastically, 'Of course, that's why you didn't use Marcia.' She snorted, unable to help herself from jabbing at me. 'What a total lie, kiddo. You've wanted Anthony for three years. I've never waited that long for any man in my life.'

'Still, Marcia and Anthony had a rather publicised flirtation last spring,' I said, thinking out loud. 'She had a crush on him, and he didn't respond as she'd have liked. There were bad things said, but never to anyone's face. Gossip spread. Ever since then, there's been intense rivalry. If he found out I went to Marcia behind his back . . . I don't know what he'd do.'

'Don't let him find out obviously,' Nora said. 'Or don't do it. And let your mind get the better of you. Can you handle not knowing?'

I shook my head. I couldn't. I had to find out for real if Anthony was being honest with me. 'It doesn't matter how good Marcia is. She'll at least be able to tell me if it's sexual.'

'But be sure you really want to know,' Nora said softly. 'Maybe that's not the real issue.'

'I don't know what you mean.'

'Maybe you don't want Anthony to be a good guy. Maybe you don't think you deserve someone like him.'

'That's not true. Why are you saying that?'

'Sometimes, you think you're living vicariously through me, don't you?'

I was silent. Was I? Had I always been. I didn't have an answer for her.

'You're not,' she insisted, her green eyes bright in the blazing light. 'I'm the one living vicariously through you.'

'What are you talking about, Nora?'

'You're the one who's stable. You're the one always in a solid relationship. You're the one with the happily ever after.'

'And you're the one who read Byron's blog. You know that happy ever after doesn't exist.'

'It might. If you'd give Anthony an honest chance.'

ThePinkFedora.blogspot.com

Halloween is here at last – or almost here. Forget counting the weeks, we're now counting the days. In fact, it's nearly time to count the minutes. The Pink Fedora's annual Halloween Masquerade Ball begins at 10:00 on Halloween night. At midnight, we'll announce the contestants chosen for Bijoux Network's new You Can Leave Your Hat On *reality show. A show that will be filmed live in the Pink Fedora!*

Oh, you can guess how excited I am! Twelve gorgeous and lithesome bartenders-to-be will be signing up for the ride of their lives. Only one can win. Judges include myself, of course, and Vlad, our former beau of the bar. We will have two guest judges each week, as well, from top chefs to top models. You'll have to tune in to see who we've invited.

Even more exciting, we'll be passing out goodie bags to all of you tricksters featuring my brand-new fragrance: The Pink Fedora. Now, all of you lovelies can smell just like me! Soon, we'll be presenting a Black Fedora cologne, for the men. These scents join my cosmetic line of lipsticks, blushers and eye shadows, and are available on our website.

Remember to wear your sexiest, slinkiest, studliest costumes on Halloween, and anyone in a pink fedora gets a free drink on the house.

Kisses,

Nora

Quote for the Day: As Jimi Hendrix said, 'Knowing me, I'll probably get busted at my own funeral.'

P.S. Check out my latest Pink Fedora Mix on iTunes.com It's perfect for Halloween!

Chapter Fifteen

'It's sexual,' Marcia told me in a stage whisper. Her face was flaming. I am the queen of blushes, and I don't think I have ever seen anyone turn quite that vibrant a shade of crimson. Her cheeks reminded me of a piece of neon artwork I'd seen at MONA (the Museum of Neon Art) by Guy Marsden called *Crimson Cubed*. Marcia has hair the colour of an Irish setter's. Now, her cheeks were nearly as flaming as her hair. 'I mean –' she lowered her voice '– it's like pornography.' Lowering her voice even further, she said, 'It's absolutely the dirtiest thing I've ever read in my entire life.'

She had finished the translating quicker than I'd expected. I had already postponed the dinner with Anthony to the night before Halloween, giving me time to think about what might happen if the journal turned out to be false. I had played out several scenarios in my head. Yet somehow I hadn't prepared myself for the possibility that the journal was real, that the entries I'd been reading had been honestly translated, not new creations made just for me by Anthony. Because of this, I didn't exactly know what to say to Marcia. I was thrilled that Anthony wasn't lying to me, but now I had to deal with the fact that I'd had Marcia, one of our youngest members of the team, translate something that was intensely X-rated. Still, I found myself needing to know more. I needed to know if there was kinky sex, bondage and dominance, or if the story was simply about a prostitute fucking a soldier.

'Could you be more specific?' I asked, pushing my reading glasses on top of my head. When she didn't respond, I looked up at her. She was staring at me, her lips trembling. She obviously had never even said the words aloud I'd just had her translate. 'I mean, could you tell me this: is there a submissive and a dominant together in the pages I gave you? Is the girl tied to a bed?'

She nodded. Then, finding her voice, she whispered, 'What is it? Where did you get this?' She hesitated. 'Is it some sort of joke, Eleanor?'

'Why do you ask that?'

'I mean, it's ancient Greek. But the stuff is so dirty ... It's like something the *Harvard Lampoon* might try to pull. I remember there was this guy in my Latin class who used to do stuff like this for the tests. We were supposed to write something original in Latin, and he would create these scenarios that seemed plucked from modern soap operas. Our teacher was horrified. That's what this reminds me of, except it's far dirtier. But is it real?'

'Yeah, it's real,' I assured her, and she took a step closer to me.

'Well, it's completely wild. I was blushing so badly when I translated it, I was sure someone would catch on to me. I mean, it was clear that I wasn't working on something boring.' Now she looked around my office, closed the door, then came back to the desk and leaned over it. 'Do you have any other pages? Do you have more for me to do after this? Do you, Eleanor?' In her voice, hushed but somewhat desperate sounding, I had the distinct feeling that I had done something horrible. 'Do you, please?'

'Nothing else,' I said. 'Not yet. I'm still digging through some papers, though, so I'll let you know.'

She continued to stare at me longingly, but when I didn't saying anything else, she opened the door and fled from the office. Had she thought I was coming on to her? Had I done to her what I'd feared Anthony had done to me? Seduced her with pornography literally thousands of years old and made her want something from me that I wasn't prepared to give. I'd heard that she had had a crush on Anthony – but that was just office gossip. Maybe she was gay, or bi like Nora.

I probably should have worried a little more about what I'd done, but I didn't linger on it for too long. Instead, I started to fantasise again immediately after Marcia had left my office. I almost couldn't wait to touch myself, sinking into my chair, sliding my pants down to get them out of the way. It was becoming a routine for me now. Fuck off at work, literally and figuratively. The visions appeared quickly even before I shut my eyes. It was like coming into a movie that had already started – sitting in a darkened theatre, heart beating too fast as the picture rolled on the screen before me.

One of the best things about fantasies is how they change. You can find something you enjoy, something that titillates you, and then you can mould it, work with it, add and subtract characters. Change the setting, the time of day, the entire scenario. Blondes become brunettes in an instant, no trip to the salon necessary. Bedrooms become outdoor gardens. Sweet and tender romping becomes bondage and dominance, blindfolds and cuffs.

This time, I pictured myself back in Nora's club, after hours. I saw myself in the Cinéma Vérité room, all alone. The room is small and mirrored, so that it has the illusion of being filled with whomever stands inside of it. Music was playing, not by Peaches this time, which is much more Nora's speed than mine. No, I was listening to the Stones – 'Under My Thumb', one of my favourite songs.

In this fantasy, I started to move, my body sexy – except that I was still clad in work clothes. But that wasn't right. Why would I have on a suit to go to Nora's club? For an instant, I saw myself in the outfit Nora had worn at Queen's Road, covered in graffiti from head to toe. But that wasn't anything I'd ever wear, couldn't feel comfortable in a piece of clothing that looked as if it belonged on a wall rather than on my body.

In rapid succession, I envisioned myself in a wide range of outfits: one covered in pictures from the Cirque du Soleil, one made of all turquoise leather. This was an outfit I'd seen in Nora's closet, dyed leather but not butter soft or faded. Hard and crisp like people who ride motorcycles wear. Not me.

I could be naked – *there* was an idea – but once I envisioned myself without any clothes on, I was confronted by all those similar images of my naked body reflected and re-reflected. In an instant, my fantasy self looked more uncomfortable than ever. I needed clothes. Sexy clothes. Something I would actually wear.

Even in my fantasies, my mental closet was filled with black.

For inspiration, I thought of my favourite outfits of Nora's. Nora's closets (yes, plural, closets!) are filled with her fantastic wardrobe. She has the best high heels, the most decadent coats, boots that range from ankle length to thigh high. Maybe, at least in my fantasy, I could dress like Nora.

I tried to imagine myself in a pink fedora, and even my fantasy self started laughing. How crazy was this? What did I do when I was with Byron? My mind had been on autopilot during our Thursday night sex sessions. I'd thought of the people down below on the beach, the ones who might see us. But I'd never really delved much more than that.

Yes, I'd touched myself occasionally, especially in the shower, but mostly I'd thought about Anthony's Christmas kiss – and, again, the people who were watching.

Now, I pictured Anthony standing in the centre of the club, watching the movie screen that showed all of my transformations. Then I imagined hearing him walk down the hall towards me.

Waiting for Anthony to join me. I sketched out this illusion in great detail.

What to wear? What to wear?

Suddenly inspired, I dressed myself in an outfit I'd seen at a fetish store on Santa Monica Boulevard in West Hollywood – one called Don't You Want To? I'd never been inside the store, but the daring ensemble had caught my eye and I'd stood before the window, staring at it. Now, I visualised myself wearing the merry widow made of intensely shiny red and black vinyl, the red fishnet thigh highs and dangerously high red heels. Something about the surface of the vinyl made me think decadent thoughts. I wondered what would happen when the outfit got wet. I wondered what would happen when I got wet inside it. Would the costume stretch over me as I moved, as I bent in it, as I made love? If I stood out in the rain with a lover, would the water glide off the plastic coating, bead up and run to the hem like silver tears?

I pictured myself with my light-brown hair up, curls falling around my face. My mental self wore more make-up than I ever wear, as if I'd used the cosmetics I'd seen at Nora's. The eyelash curler and mascara. The liquid liner. That dark-red lipstick of Nora's that she likes so much – Tainted Love – a robust red like the inside of a velvety rose.

I felt uncomfortable, waiting. This was my fantasy, why couldn't I speed things up? The answer was obvious. I could, but I didn't truly want to. I wanted it to go slowly, like the climax had for the woman in the journal. I wanted to feel myself grow more and more aroused from just thinking about my lover – the soldier – knowing he was on his way to join me.

The door in my daydream was closed instead of open, and there was a knock. Anthony didn't barge in.

'Yes?' I called out. No response. Then the door opened slowly, and there he stood. His hair was down. He had on a white T-shirt and faded jeans. Anthony's body is intensely strong. He looked amazing like that and, for an instant, I wanted to tear his clothes off him, to skip to the good part, but instead I forced myself to go slowly. I watched as he looked me up and down. My heart raced, wanting to see his response, hoping that he would appreciate my outfit. Finally, he smiled.

'Naughty girl,' Anthony said. 'You know that everyone can see you out there. Everyone on the dance floor is watching you. Watching you dance. Watching you touch yourself. Watching you dress and undress. Everyone is watching ... Such a slut.' He shook his head, as if he couldn't believe it. 'Do you know what happens to bad girls like yourself, Eleanor?'

I wanted to speak but couldn't. No words would come out.

'They get spanked.' This was a surprise. I hadn't known I was going to go there. Perhaps what Nora had said at lunch the other day had affected me. She's always been open with me about her likes and dislikes. And, truly, I can't remember any of her sexual dislikes. She enjoys the whole world of sex. The whole intense range of possibilities.

Could I?

The way he said the word 'spanked' made me want to come. Immediately. Right there. No touching. No nothing. I shuddered, in my fantasy and in reality. I wanted to hear him say that word again. I wanted to know exactly what that word meant. I wanted to learn the definition with my mind and with my body, memorise it like I had memorised definitions of words for the SATs before high school.

'Here?' I whispered.

'Here,' he said, but suddenly 'here' wasn't here, wasn't at the Pink Fedora. We were in a new room, a room I'd never even seen before – Anthony's room.

Anthony came to the edge of the bed and sat down at my side. Gently, he pulled me until I was draped over his knees. In this outfit, I was exposed to him, my ass covered only by the two slim ribbons of garters. Anthony rested one hand on my naked skin and then said, 'You have been a bad girl, haven't you, Eleanor?'

And now, since it was a fantasy, Anthony suddenly had a wooden-backed hairbrush in his hand. He set it against my naked skin so that I could feel the smooth shiny surface, cold against me.

'Haven't you, Eleanor?'

I sighed, but didn't answer.

'I asked you a question.' His voice made me weak.

'Yes,' I said, 'yes, I have.' Had I? Masturbating in my office. Giving Marcia the pages to retranslate as a test. Just *having* this fantasy seemed bad, seemed naughty, seemed reason enough for Anthony to spank me. In fantasies, you rarely need more than that. In *my* fantasies, at least, I can do with much less than that.

'Are you ready for your spanking?'

I didn't want to answer, but I did, my voice hushed. Hoarse. Not my voice at all. Someone else's voice. Some naughty young girl who had done all these bad things and who needed to atone for her sins, who needed to be punished for them. 'Yes, Anthony.'

'I'm going to give you ten. You count them for me. Count them out loud. Even if you think you can't. Even if you're crying. Otherwise, I'll have to start again, Eleanor. Right back at the very beginning. But maybe that's what you want.'

I came before I'd counted to two.

Then I sat at my desk for a long time, wondering what I was doing, what had come over me. Who was I? I turned and caught a glimpse of my reflection in the glass frame of one of my prints. Seeing the heated, haunted look to my face, I realised that I hardly recognised myself at all.

Chapter Sixteen

Nora needed me. That's what she said on my cellphone voicemail.

'I need you, Eleanor. I know you've got a lot going on, but I need you.'

I called her back at the end of the day to find out what was going on. That was the first time I'd checked my messages because I was avoiding the ones from Byron. She answered immediately.

'The perfume launch,' she said. 'The company has decided to coincide the new perfume with the announcement of the winners for *You Can Leave Your Hat On*. I knew it before, but I didn't really put it together.'

'Aren't you pleased?'

'Sure, it's great. But I don't have anything to wear!'

I had to laugh. I'd spent the afternoon, or at least part of it, fantasising about Nora's clothes. Her claiming that she had nothing to wear would be like me stating that I didn't have any books to read. The concept didn't compute.

'I don't,' she wailed, as if reading my mind. 'I can't wear something I've been photographed in before.'

'That shouldn't be a problem for you. You never wear the same thing twice.'

'Yes, but I can't even wear different items I've put together before. This has to be entirely unique.'

'Well, why don't you wear the same outfit you had on for the advertising shoot they did for the perfume. I'm sure they'll have the ad spread up, right? Then you'll look just like you did on the shoot.'

There was silence.

'Come on, Nora. What did you wear for that? You didn't tell me.'

'A pink fedora.'

'And?'

Again, there was a silence on the phone.

'Oh, my God. Were you naked?'

'It's tastefully done. Don't worry. It was great, though. Do you remember that gorgeous spread of Kate Moss? I think it was in *Vogue*. She was totally naked on this furlike rug. I don't know whether it was real fur, or not, and the caption said that she was wearing Dona Karan's Cashmere body lotion. *That's* what the fashion spread was for. As if you could smell the scent of her.'

'So your ad campaign is like that?'

'No. It's totally different. No rug. And I'm not sprawled out, showing off my ass. But all I have on is the hat. You'll understand when you see it.'

I couldn't help but smile. 'I can see why you don't want to wear that.'

'Stop teasing me. You have to help me, Eli. We have to go shopping!'

Shopping with Nora is an experience in itself. Being her consultant is always a wild ride. Nora doesn't shop like a normal person, as might be expected.

With a phone call, she made sure that several of her favourite stores would stay open for her. These were places in Hollywood that she tended to drop a fortune in whenever she visited. The shopkeepers were more than happy to help her out in her time of need.

We had plans to visit a leather store, a vintage shop and a place that made jewellery from the chrome bumpers of antique cars.

'We need to get something for you, too,' Nora insisted. 'You'll be at my side all night, so you're going to appear in the pictures, as well.'

'I can't afford any of this,' I told her at the first store, looking around in awe.

'Don't worry. This trip is on me.'

'Nora –'

'You remember when I was poor and you helped me out?'

'I bought you coffees.'

She made a little tutting sound with her tongue against her teeth. 'You made sure I had enough to eat. You ordered large and split half. I remember it all. I kept careful notes.'

'You're crazy,' I told her, as I always did when she brought up stuff like this. In school, Nora was on a work scholarship. She put in time at the coffee house and in the library to balance her tuition. She bought all her clothes vintage and splurged on music and hair dye. And she's right. I made sure she ate well. I did it without a thought, and without expecting repayment. Nora would have done the same for me if our situations had been reversed.

'I'm buying,' she said now. 'My treat.'

It's not that I don't have money. I can afford my clothing budget and gas for my Prius and dinners out. But I can't drop money on frivolous items the way Nora can. That's why I continued to shake my head as she reached for outfit after outfit for me.

'You're the one we're shopping for.'

'But you need something, too. Something sexy to wear to my Halloween bash.'

I took a deep breath. As much as I love Nora, I am not the type of person who goes to her wild Halloween parties. This year, she insisted I make an exception as I was without Byron and it was a bigger event than normal with the release of her perfume and announcement of the reality show contestants.

'Do you have any idea of what you want to wear?' I asked her. We'd been around the store several times now.

'I'm torn. I'm thinking Naughty Nurse Nora or Naughty Nymphet Nora.' She still names each outfit. It's part of her charm.

'And for me?'

'Something wild,' she decided. 'Something wicked and wanton.'

'You know me,' I told her. 'I'm none of those things.'

'Yes, but this is Halloween. You should let yourself go.'

'*You're* not dressing different from usual,' I countered.

'What? You want me to go like a librarian? Or a translator. Someone shy and bookish like you?'

I gazed at her in mock outrage. 'I am not bookish!'

'If you were any more bookish you'd be an actual book.'

'All right,' I said. 'Here's the deal. You be me, and I'll be you.'

'What do you mean?'

'You dress like me, and I'll dress in any outfit you choose.'

'Are you serious?'

'Dead serious.'

She got a gleeful look on her face. 'Fine. But for the reveal at midnight, I need to change into an actual costume.'

I hesitated for a moment, and then put out my hand. Nora shook before I could change my mind, sealing the deal. Sealing my fate.

When we'd both chosen (and Nora had paid for) too many items – we drove down the street to Dinnah's Diner for a late supper. Nora had decided to wear one of her new outfits to dinner. She had on a purple velvet catsuit that fitted her body like a second skin. The catsuit actually had a tail, which she curled around her lap and stroked in an absent-minded manner. While we were in the dressing room, she'd used gel that she carries in her purse at all times to spike her hair in the front, so that she almost looked as if she'd sprouted kitten ears. The truth is, she looked amazing, and she knew it.

'What do you call this one?' I asked as I watched her

add a dramatic cat eye using liquid liner when we were stopped at a traffic light.

'I don't just name them off the top of my head,' she said, sounding insulted. 'It'll come to me when I take the picture.'

'Still Polaroid? Or have you updated to digital?'

'No, Polaroid. This is all about my art.' She shot me a smug smile. 'Someday, it'll all be chronicled in a coffee-table book. And you know I'm right, too.'

I didn't say anything. Knowing Nora, she was definitely speaking the truth.

At the restaurant I started to ask her about the Halloween party, but my phone rang. Nora said, 'Anthony,' at the same time as I said, 'Byron.'

Unfortunately, I was right.

'Does he still want to get back with you?' she asked.

'Not since I told him about Dean,' I said. 'But the funny thing is, he doesn't actually believe me. He thinks I've made up that story as a way to punish him for his indiscretion with Gwen, and he keeps texting me to say that I need therapy before we can consider resuming our relationship.'

'Like you're actually going to do that.'

I shrugged. Being away from Byron for a few days had made things clearer in my mind. Whenever we'd fought in the past, I'd always ended up feeling crazy. Now, I saw that he was the one putting those thoughts into my mind. I was grateful that Nora had brought me into bed with her and Dean – it showed me what I was missing in my life. Even if I might not choose a threesome again in the future, I also wasn't going to choose the routine of being with Byron.

'Are you all set for the party?' I asked Nora as I tucked my phone away.

'Of course. We've been ready for weeks. We have all sorts of exciting new ways to dazzle the customers.

Amazing decorations. Dancers wearing nothing but strategically placed silver stars. We have a fortune-teller with a crystal ball and tarot-card readers and a tattoo artist is going to be doing fake tattoos in the Body Graffiti room.

'And you're really going to let me dress you?'

'That's the deal.'

I thought about it. 'You know, people aren't going to understand what's going on if I actually dress you up to look like me.'

'That's not really the point. The point is for *you* to look like *me*. I'll fade into the background.'

I couldn't believe I'd gotten myself into this. 'I'm not going to fool anyone, Nora.'

'Not with your hair like that,' she agreed. 'We'll cut it.'

'No way.'

'Then you'll wear a wig. That won't be too hard for people to handle. On Halloween, anything goes.'

'But what are you going to put me in?'

'Something suitable,' she promised. 'Don't you worry.'

I looked at her, and she smiled at me. At least the concept took my mind off my dinner with Anthony. But in spite of her words, I couldn't help myself. Worrying is something I do best.

Chapter Seventeen

On the night before Halloween, Anthony answered the door to his apartment holding a wooden spoon and wearing a white chef's apron. The apron didn't make him appear overly feminine or silly, simply serious about what he was doing. I realised that this was how he always looked, whether he was in the middle of translating an ancient work or parking his Harley sportster in front of the museum. Anthony's Harley is black with crimson flames bursting on the sides. The first time I saw the bike was in a write-up about him in ARTSI's in-house magazine. I'd thought it was a prop for the photo shoot until I saw him drive up on it one morning.

I'd never have imagined that the sight of Anthony in an apron would be more arousing than the vision of him on his motorcycle, but I was wrong. Every day, I found myself learning how multifaceted this man was. He appeared at ease holding court at ARTSI functions, in his element on a Harley and at home with cooking gear. He'd had no trouble hanging out at the Pink Fedora, and seemed to be fine with coming on to me in my office at work. Was there ever a place where this man's confidence didn't shine through? He was the masculine equivalent of Nora. Perhaps, I'd been searching for him ever since I first met my best friend. I didn't want to analyse that thought too closely, unsure of how I'd feel if I were right, so I focused instead on what Anthony was wearing.

Underneath the apron, he had on a pair of faded jeans and a black T-shirt. From the words that showed above the top of the apron I could tell that the T-shirt was from

Sturgis, the infamous motorcycle rally that takes place each year in South Dakota. I know a bit about motorcycles since viewing 'The Art of the Motorcycle' exhibition at the Guggenheim in the late 90s, which had featured about one hundred of the most important bikes in the history of motorcycle production.

I appreciate when a curator can look beyond the norm to find art. There is definite art in a Harley, or a Triumph, or an Indian Chief. I wondered whether Anthony went to that motorcycle show, and I instantly pictured myself on the back of his Harley. The vision made me smile. There was Anthony in his jeans and T-shirt and me in my over-buttoned suit. I was going to have to broaden my wardrobe if I continued to hang out with him, something Nora had been begging me to do for years. But no matter how broad I made my wardrobe, I'd never have the creativity to name my looks.

'The pages are on the table,' Anthony told me, all seriousness. I realised suddenly that he hadn't smiled once since I'd arrived. 'I'm finishing up dinner in the kitchen. You can read the latest instalment while I cook.'

There was no talk about showing me around. No tour of his home. He sounded absolutely businesslike. I felt my heart start to race.

He knows, I thought. He knows.

I watched him head back into the kitchen, and then I looked down at the pages he'd left for me on his coffee table. I had the mental awareness to realise that the table was made of a surfboard. Not just any surfboard. A lemon-yellow board with a big chunk taken out of one side, as if gnawed on by a shark. I wanted to ask him about the unique piece, but he had already disappeared into the next room.

Feeling antsy, I sat on his sofa and looked around the room. The walls were done in varying shades of blue – from deep indigo to pale turquoise. It was like sitting inside of a wave. The fabric on the sofa looked almost as if it had been tie-dyed, also in blue. The candles burning on the coffee table were housed in abalone shells. Nora would appreciate this room, I thought. Anthony had decorated it not to look like a beach house, but to look like the beach itself.

I glanced through the pages. Again, he had typed them single spaced. Next to the pages was a wooden-handled ping-pong paddle, black side up. I turned towards the kitchen, thinking of asking Anthony what the paddle was for, but a stirring at the pit of my stomach made me keep quiet.

I knew why it was there.

If I asked, it would be an admission that I knew. I couldn't do that, couldn't make myself do it. Instead, I forced myself to focus on the pages. As had happened before, once I'd started to read the words, I was pulled in, free-falling into a world that had existed thousands of years before. This segment of the journal was written by the girl.

His name is Marcus. He told me this only after several hours had passed. Passed in the most delightful of ways, with us, the two of us, embarking upon the most decadent of activities. I had never truly understood the ways of the flesh. I had images in my mind, of course, images that were lent to me by our artists, by the painters and sculptors who have their way with the human body every day in the work. I had played kissing games with Alita, the kitchen maid at home, touching and fondling and caressing in that almost juvenile way. None of my fantasies – or realities – came close to the actual act.

When he was finished with me, when the night was ending and the sky opened up pink and blue, he lay down at my side.

'Untie me?' I asked. 'Please untie me?'

He shook his head. 'You have felt tremendous pleasure tonight,' he whispered, 'but I am not through with you. It is my desire to introduce you to pain. Pain that clarifies your mind and makes the pleasure that much more immense. I can assure you one thing: you will truly understand me afterwards.'

I listened to him and instantly pictures flooded my eyes. Pictures of fertility festivals in which girls suffered the spectacle of public flagellation in hopes that it would help them to bare a strong and sturdy child. My own mother had taken it upon herself to be treated in this way before she gave birth to me. I recalled stories of orgies attended only by the most beautiful girls in the village, so-called banquets hosted by hetairai, *just like Danae, the owner of this house, private parties that women went to alone, and that were whispered about for months afterwards. Girls with girls with girls. Head to tail, body pressed to body, the sheer curtains of their clothing thrown away, their naked forms together on the grass. Outdoors, always outdoors, where the goddess could witness and take delight in the festivities.*

In my head, I saw paintings: Tsuguharu Foujita *Five Nudes* from 1923, the milky-white skin of the models. The luminous quality of the women. Paintings flowed through my mind – Picasso's *Les Demoiselles d'Avignon.* These visions accompanied the text for me. Art and words, together. I went back to reading:

While my thoughts were filled with such decadent episodes, Marcus reached for the knife again, using it this time to cut through my bindings. I stayed still and silent, and I let him manoeuvre my body, roll me over until my face was against the mattress, before he bound me again, tighter this time, my wrists over my head, my ankles stretched out wide.

'Are you ready for me, Elena?'

The fear swept me in a way that I had never imagined, and I could not find my voice to answer, although with all my heart I wanted to say 'yes'.

'Are you ready for me? You have already seen that I know how to treat you with the ultimate kindness. Trust me now to prepare you for the rigours of your future

life. After me, there will be others, in the nights, there will be women for you to engage with. But every day, every evening after they have left you, there will only be me. Are you ready, Elena?'

Did I say yes? Did I speak at all? I do not know. I cannot tell. All I know is that he was right. He spoke the truth: his words opened a door to a new world. His body on mine had pushed me over a brink and into a sea that I'd never known existed. Now his belt against my naked skin revitalised me. He coiled it, swung it, let the leather lightly hit my thighs. It stung, but did not hurt.

'Are you ready, Elena?'

Was I ready? If so, I could not make myself speak.

He brought the belt back up, doubled the leather in his hand, again let it fall on my skin, a little harder this time, giving me a taste of what truly sensual pain might be like.

'Elena, are you ready?'

The third time, he hit me hard, as I had somehow known he would, and I gasped for air and buried my face in the bedding, trying to find a way to deal with the burning sensation. I searched for a hiding place, but there was none. I was exposed. I had nowhere to go. The only thing for me to do was surrender.

'Eleanor, are you ready?'

Anthony was standing at the side of the sofa, and he stared pointedly from me to the paddle to me again. His gaze was as hard as steel when he met my eyes. His mouth was set into an expression I couldn't immediately decipher. A look I didn't really want to decode.

'Are you?' he asked in a tone of voice that was not unkind, but firm nevertheless. Instead of looking at him, I looked down at the floor – he had a sand-coloured rug beneath the surfboard table. I tried to lose myself in the golden strands.

'Eleanor.'

I wasn't sure how I should answer. If I said 'yes', what

exactly was I admitting to being ready for? Anthony has an aptitude for confusing me, rather seems to enjoy this fact. Knowing this, I remained silent. It was my best bet.

'I made pasta primavera.'

I breathed in, smelling the spices, oregano, fresh basil. I could definitely say 'yes' to that. I was ready to eat. Agreeing to dinner couldn't get me into any trouble, could it? But then Anthony suddenly moved around the sofa, coming to sit by my side. Without a word, he handed me two additional pages, creased from being kept in his back pocket. The pages were typed just as neatly as the others, but the names had been changed: Elena was now Eleanor; Marcus was Anthony. The scenario unfolded entirely in the modern day, modern time. In the very room in which I was sitting.

I read the words describing the room – the cool ocean walls, the surfboard table, the ping-pong paddle there, waiting. Waiting for what? I knew exactly what. Waiting to meet my hindquarters, to make them as red as the crimson side of that two-toned paddle. I read the first sentence of dialogue while Anthony watched me. I understood the meaning. These words meant one thing. They meant only this: he knew about Marcia.

'Why didn't you trust me?'
'I had to be sure.'
'You should already have been sure.'

I felt the touch of his fingertips on my bare shoulder as he watched me read. I was aware of how close he sat by me on the sofa, his knees brushing against mine. Subtly. Casually. As if the heat between us didn't exist. But when I looked up, looked straight at him, I saw his eyes had gone darker than I'd ever seen them. They were no longer green. They were black.

'Are you ready, Eleanor?'

Answering was torture. Like the girl in the story, in the ancient memoirs, I could not make my lips work.

Could not make my voice come out, at first, and when it did I sounded unnatural, not like my voice at all. 'Ready?' I whispered, my fingers twisting together in my lap. I couldn't still them. They gave away my nervousness. But Anthony didn't seem to mind. He motioned for me to read on, smiling at me in that soft way of his. As if he understood. As if he knew everything I'd ever wanted. As if he knew things that I did not realise about myself.

'I'm sorry.'

'Don't say that. I don't need to hear the word.'

'But I am.'

'Not yet. You will be.'

'I had to know for a fact. I had to see the words on paper, translated by somebody else.'

'Behind my back. I know that Serina told you a lot about me. Did she leave out the part about my honour?'

I met his eyes again, feeling my heart jump into my throat. It hadn't been about honour. Couldn't he understand that? I had to know if he were playing with me. I wanted to tell him this. But I couldn't speak.

'Read,' he insisted. I gave him my most pleading look, then went back to the page.

I shook my head. No, of course not. That had been the first thing Serina had said.

'If you want to be with me, you'll need to play by my rules.'

'Your rules?'

'My world is made up of rules. Power and rules. At least, in the bedroom. When you're good, you'll be rewarded. When you're bad, you're going to be punished. When you've been very good, your reward might be punishment.'

I looked up and saw him smile. Whose world had I fallen into? Nora's? The club kids who go to the Pink Fedora?

This wasn't my world. I didn't belong here at all. My world is all about research and studying. My quiet world is about learning everything I possibly can about a situation before taking the first step forwards.

Anthony said nothing. He simply looked at me, and I could tell that he was waiting for me to behave as he wanted me to, act the part of the naughty schoolgirl, caught cheating on a test. If I could do as he asked, would everything be forgiven? But before contemplating that, *could* I even do what he wanted me to? Was I capable of behaving in this manner?

His black shirt revealed his strong arms. When he moved to grab the paddle, I could see the lines of his muscles, and I wanted to lean forwards, to run my tongue along that naked flesh, to kiss and lick everywhere, ripping through the T-shirt, revealing the tender skin, the golden-hued flesh that would make me whole if I felt it. Just my fingertips on it, running up and down, would make me complete.

But Anthony didn't want to start like that. He wanted to start with me over his lap, his paddle slamming against my upturned ass. He wanted to start where all my fears hid, instead of working in slowly, as I always want to do. He wanted to start at the top, which, in this case, was my bottom.

I watched as Anthony played with the paddle between his hands, motioning with a nod for me to read the rest of what was written on the page. The flagellation scene. What had I started? Here was my world crumbling around me. Words were letting me down again, making me shake and tremble.

'Keep reading,' Anthony insisted.

And I read on to find my heroine, the sweet girl in the story, poised on the brink of endurance. I read of her being tied face down, ass bared and ready, to Anthony's four-poster bed. I knew that when I reached the end, when I reached the point in which the girl in the story and the man in the story came together, it would be my cue to strip my clothes off, to bend over Anthony's lap and take the punishment he was poised to mete out.

I deserved the punishment, didn't I? I'd cheated, I'd gone behind his back. If I'd been up front with him, if I'd at least told him what I was doing – getting a second opinion, as it were – I could have explained myself ahead of time to ward off exactly this type of scenario.

I read further. Read exactly what it was Anthony planned to do to me, my body, my naked ass. Read on to find out what would happen afterwards, when tears ran down my face – tears of embarrassment more than of pain – and he stood me up before his bedroom mirror and had me stare at my reddened ass cheeks, had me take in the look visibly, as if I were some work of art and he the commissioned artist.

He played with the paddle in his hand. He slapped it against his palm, slapped it hard enough to make a solid jarring sound, a noise that made me jump. There was a second page to his story that I hadn't yet finished reading. I found it difficult to concentrate with the steady rhythm of his paddle smacking against the naked skin of his hand. I had a hard time making my mind dance around the words that spoke brightly to me from the paper: exposed, spanked, punished, then having all the guilt erased with more pleasure than I'd ever known.

That was the final promise in the last line of the page. Explain myself. Explain and apologise for my cheating heart, and then experience a lifetime of pleasure in one single night.

I wanted what was on those pages. Desperately, I wanted what was in the journal. Tie me down. Cut my clothes loose with a knife. Turn me loose inside and out. Your touch could set me free; it could. I know it. Make me burn for not trusting you, for not believing in you. Then wash it all away with pleasures that I have never possessed, never let myself experience outside the privacy of my mind.

Anthony didn't speak. He was playing me, playing

with me. That's all there was to it. He was tormenting me because he liked to do so, because he could. He knew exactly what he was doing. He had known all along.

Maybe I didn't need to say anything. *There* was a happy thought. Maybe I didn't need to explain myself. Perhaps, I could get by with just staring into his eyes and *thinking* about what needed to be said. Nora says that soulmates, *true* soulmates, don't need to talk. That's what she says, although she also admits she's never found a true soulmate, just a true 'fuck mate'. If Anthony and I were actually meant for each other, we wouldn't have to discuss the past because it didn't matter. All that mattered was that he knew.

The paddle hit the palm of his palm. Once. Hard. Then again.

From his expression, I learned even more about him. I learned that he was patient, that he could wait and that he was cruel. The way his eyes picked up the flame of the candles on the coffee table. The golden glow of fire in his eyes told me secrets, made me promises.

'Read it again at Nora's,' Anthony said suddenly, not mentioning dinner. Not explaining. Without changing his expression from one of patience and understanding, he set the paddle down on the table – red side up this time – picked up my coat, and helped me slide into it. While I watched in stunned silence, he scooped up the rest of the translated pages, shuffled them together and handed them to me. I felt numb. Confused.

'You're not ready yet,' he said as we walked outside, as he led me towards my own car. He didn't sound angry. As I replayed the words in my head, I realised that he didn't sound anything except resigned. If this were Byron speaking, he'd have been furious. I had to get used to this new way of talking, of thinking.

My head felt heavy, as if it were filled with sand. I felt trapped, moving in slow motion, unable to defend myself, unsure what I needed to defend.

I wanted to argue. I wanted to disagree emphatically,

shake my head and stamp my feet. Throw a tantrum right there in the middle of the street, so that he would be forced to deal with me. I knew somehow what Anthony would do if I pitched a fit. He would throw me over his shoulder and carry me back into the apartment. He would treat me like a bratty child. But he was right. If I *were* truly ready, I'd have done what his story told me to do. I would have followed each step precisely, fully giving myself over to him. Anthony had spelled everything out for me.

What the fuck was I waiting for?

I let him walk me to my car. I had parked across from his building, and when we got to my siren-red Prius, he leaned against the side of the car and looked at me. Looked me over, the way a lover would, up and down my body, in the most sexual way I'd every imagined. He had an expression on his face as if he were adding up a long list of numbers – numbers of ways we could fuck, numbers of ways he could take me. There was total silence as he gazed at me. Nora would have been bold. She would have copped the same attitude, returning his stare without flinching.

I'm not Nora. I wanted to run and hide.

With his arms folded across his chest, he continued to take me in. As if he were measuring me for future fittings. Then he nodded his silent approval and moved aside so that I could unlock the passenger door.

For one wild moment, I thought he would climb into the car, thought he might let me drive him home with me. Home. I had no home. Back to Nora's house, then. But that wasn't a sane person's thought. Where would he and I go for privacy? What if Nora walked in on us? Would she join us as I'd joined her and Dean? What would Anthony say if I told him about that night?

I thought about the things we might do together. And then I thought maybe he would go to Nora's club with me, that we would christen the Cinéma Vérité room for ourselves. Or perhaps venture down the hall to the black-walled Slave to Love. Clearly, that was more Anthony's speed. I could just picture him putting the fuchsia cuffs on me, positioning me exactly as he wanted me, taking charge.

But no, he stepped away and watched as I took off my coat and put it inside, put my purse on the floor, then he stepped back and closed the passenger door for me. It was the move, somehow, of a gentleman. Chivalrous.

Aside from everything else, he had manners.

Anthony smiled at me, his head cocked, as I walked to the other side of the car and unlocked the driver's side door. I thought he'd say something. I thought he'd *have* to say something. But he didn't. He watched me get in. He let me drive away, into a darkened city without him.

Because he knew.

Chapter Eighteen

'People don't fucking behave like that.'

Anger coloured Nora's normally pale cheeks a dusky rose. Nora always gets upset for me when she thinks someone is doing me wrong. It's great to have a friend who is so intensely loyal, but I couldn't bask in this outrage. For once, I didn't agree with her. 'Come on, Eli,' she insisted. 'People don't invite you to dinner and then give you the silent treatment. Not people who like you.'

'You're wrong. Anthony does like me.' No, *like* wasn't the right word. It wasn't that he *liked* me. It was that he *wanted* me. But on his terms. This was his way of testing me, the way I'd gone to Marcia behind his back to test him. Nora shook her head fiercely, looking as if she were going to launch into a counter-argument, but I continued, 'He felt that I'd challenged his integrity.'

'You mean his ego. His huge ginormous inflated ego. You don't need another man like that, do you? Not after Byron. What you need is someone who *adores* you. Check out the line-up of my new male bartenders. They're all young, all gorgeous. Any one of them would bend over backwards to please you. In fact, one of them is a practitioner of that really difficult type of yoga. He did this thing on the bar earlier that shocked us all, bending backwards in order to deliver the drink. He would definitely be a man to consider. He could probably blow himself if you asked him to.'

'Why would I ask him to do that?'

'I mean, just to show you how flexible he is.'

'He'd bend over to please *you*,' I corrected her. 'I have

no say as to how long these contestants stay or go. There's no reason for these hopefuls to try to please me.'

'There is while you're dressed like that.'

It was Halloween. Finally, Halloween. And I'd given in to Nora's begging and dressed how she wanted me.

'I'm not going to fuck someone just because he thinks I could help his career.'

'You're not?'

'Is that why you're with Travis ... or Dean?'

'I can't help either of them.'

'Not true. You can help anyone you want to help, Nora.'

'I don't need to help either of them,' she insisted. 'That's not why they're with me.'

'So why do you think I'd want to be with someone for the same reason?'

'I didn't,' she said lamely. 'I just meant, since you are decked out like that, you might want to take advantage of the costume. Live it up a little bit.'

I knew what she was saying. In Nora's world, a fuck session would fix everything. My mood. My frame of mind. It would make all my problems with Anthony disappear like pixie dust. This was how she'd helped me deal with the first night of breaking up with Byron. But this time, I didn't want to hide from my problems. I wanted to confront them. Somehow, being dressed up like Nora helped me with this attitude. I felt strong and empowered. Nora, meanwhile, looked only a bit like me. She had on a wig to cover her short hair, and she was wearing a black suit, but it was so tight-fitting it could have been made of that shiny spray-on vinyl. She had on a pair of reading glasses with clear lenses, and she held a book under her arm, a great big book like one that I would read, except this one was *The Joy of Sex*. 'I'm a professor of sexology,' she'd told me earlier when I'd asked for an explanation for taking a few liberties with the outfit I'd suggested.

I'd let her trick me out exactly how she wanted to. I

was dressed as Little Red Riding Hood. The sexiest Little Red Riding Hood in the world.

Now, I shook my head 'no', when a wolf came up and growled at me about my goodies, 'not interested' was the look I gave him.

'How did he find out, anyway?' Nora asked.

This was the first I'd told her about what had happened the previous night. I'd needed to process the situation myself. But when Nora had asked where Anthony was, I'd broken down and told her.

She waved to the bartender nearest our table, and we each ordered a Flirtini.

'Come on, how? Did Marcia tell him?'

I shrugged. It wasn't important. What I did wouldn't have been less wrong if he hadn't found out. What *was* important was something I didn't even think I could say aloud to Nora. So how was I ever going to be able to say it to Anthony?

'Normal people just don't act like that,' Nora insisted again, which was an odd statement for her, as she doesn't put much stock into 'normal' anything. 'They don't pick a fight with you and then nicely walk you to your car, stare at you the way you said. Look at you longingly. They don't stay quiet like that, waiting for you to make amends. Waiting for you to do what they want. How did he let you know he'd found out about Marcia? In some fucked-up story? What a stupid fucking thing to fight about.'

'It didn't feel like a fight,' I said softly. My cape was cumbersome, and I pulled it off and set it next to me at the bar. Beneath, I had on little tight red dress, something that I would never have felt comfortable in if Nora hadn't been right next to me. She'd picked the form-fitting scarlet dress for me to wear, and high-heeled red Mary Jane shoes. I had a hat on, too, of course, a fedora that was more shocking pink than actually red, making me the hippest Little Red Riding Hood of all time.

* * *

Nora lasted as long as she could in the suit. Even a tight suit like this one made her feel ill at ease. At midnight, when she had to announce the contestants for her new show, she hurried off to change into her real costume. Now, her bright-pink panties were clearly visible through the sheer white nurse's uniform. She'd gone with Nora the Naughty Nurse after all.

Aside from our little bet, why was I dressed up like this? I longed for my comfortable uniform, my black slacks, cashmere sweater, sensible black shoes. Why was I even here?

That was simple. Nora had insisted that I come to the party. There were too many things going on, she said. The announcement at midnight of the winners. The launching of the perfume. Besides, I'd promised. She needed to have at least one person nearby who she could trust. One person who she knew didn't want anything from her. That person was me.

And I did honestly feel a bit special for the fact that Nora had shrugged off all of her admirers in order to talk with me. There were photographers who wanted to take her picture in a line with all the up-and-coming bartenders. There were fans who wanted her to sign their bodies with lipsticks and ballpoint pens. There were investors who hoped to woo her into agreeing to another deal with them. Nora had eyes and ears only for me, loyal beyond loyal.

'It was a fight,' she insisted again. She'd just come back after changing her outfit, but clearly she wasn't ready to change the conversation. 'He pushed you, challenged you. And when you wouldn't explain yourself, he stopped talking. Aggressive behaviour. Then passive aggressive.'

'But it didn't feel like a fight,' I said again, trying to sound insistent. 'I liked being next to him on the sofa. I was turned on watching him play with the paddle. I didn't feel angry. Just intimidated. I didn't know what to do.'

More than that, really, I chided myself. Be honest now,

Eleanor. It was much more than that. I knew exactly what to do, and, as usual, I had fled. When was I going to stop running away from the things I wanted? When was I going to silence the frightened voice inside my head and go after the experiences I truly desired. Like being draped over Anthony's knees, his hands on the waistband of my panties, pulling them down my thighs. His fingertips playing over my naked skin before bringing the paddle down hard. I'd liked the sound it made when he'd simply slapped it against the palm of his hand. I got wet simply from imagining the sound it might make when it hit my ass.

I shut my eyes tight, but the image didn't leave. It was so easy for me to imagine Anthony doing things to me. Tying me up. Spanking me. Fucking me.

So why was that so hard to admit to him?

Worse things are said aloud every single day. I thought of Byron and his admission that he didn't love me. I thought of his insistence that I was the one who needed psychiatric help. That I had somehow driven him into the willing arms of Gwen. Byron able to say those hurtful things, without having the decency even to blush. This wasn't something evil or harmful or even all that shocking.

Then why couldn't I even say it to Nora. Why couldn't I look at her, turn rose red if I had to, and say, 'I can get wet simply by looking up the word "spank" in a dictionary. Of reading that word aloud. Sometimes, when nobody's nearby, I look up that term in Wikipedia. And I lied before. I do read blogs. It's just that I mostly read spanking blogs. Late at night. When nobody's up. Or in my office, when people think I'm focused on some new research assignment.'

But this was the kind of thing I ought to have been telling Anthony. Here he was, giving me the opportunity to experience a fantasy that I'd only ... well, fantasised about, and I'd fled like a frightened mouse.

'Next time, you leave,' Nora insisted. 'Case closed.'

'That's what I did this time,' I told her emphatically. 'Next time, I won't.'

Next time, if Anthony agreed to give me a chance at a next time, I'd suggest the activities myself.

The band started up again with a punk version of 'Monster Mash'. Nora, unable to politely keep an Elvis impersonator at bay any longer, asked him if he really wanted a rectal examination right there, in front of God and everyone, and the man scurried away from us with a hurt expression on his face.

In the time it took for Nora to lose the geek, I got control of my voice. Made it say the words that most wanted to escape. Words are my friends. Words can set you free. 'That's what I did this time,' I repeated. 'I won't fail myself again.'

As I spoke the words, I saw Byron enter the club, despite the fact that he'd been banned. He was in costume which he probably hoped would allow him to go unnoticed, but I recognised him immediately. Every year that we've been together, he's dressed as a woman on Halloween. This is a way for him to let his alter ego out, a way for him to get in touch with his feminine side. That's what he's always claimed. I think he just finds it kinky to put on ladies' lingerie.

He didn't look good enough to pass as a woman, but he'd managed to pass by Nora's bouncers. When she turned and saw him, I felt her stiffen.

'No,' I said. 'Let me.'

'Are you kidding? I can get Travis to help.'

I shook my head, and then started to walk towards Byron. He was Gwen-less, which backed up what Nora had told me about reading his blog. That I'd been right. Gwen had only really been interested in the excitement of having an illicit liaison.

'You look amazing,' he said when he saw me.

'Yeah? You think?'

'You look different,' he said next, 'not just the outfit. Something else.'

I felt different, but I wasn't going to tell him why.

'I knew you were going to be here, and you weren't taking my phone calls, so, I thought . . .'

'What do you want, Byron?'

He shrugged, and in that shrug I saw that he wanted to erase what had happened, without having to say so himself. Everything that had happened. The break-up and the fights. For an instant, I thought about going to one of Nora's private rooms, of fucking Byron and calling out Anthony's name at the climax. But he just wasn't worth it.

'I want you,' he said finally, when he saw I wasn't going to make things any easier for him. 'Eleanor, I want what we had.'

And as he said the words, I understood something that had eluded me. What we'd had was gone. Or maybe we hadn't ever really had it.

Nora was glaring at Byron from the bar. She looked as if she would like to eject him without any help from Travis. But I didn't need her help. All I needed was to shake my head at Byron and turn away. Like he enjoyed saying on his blog: Case Closed.

Chapter Nineteen

Upstairs in the office at Nora's club, I read the manuscript again. I focused hard on the words – trying not to think of Anthony. Trying only to think of the ancient lovers, dead now for thousands of years. The music throbbed from down below, but I lost myself in the journal.

The pages explained the rest. The pages gave me more history, more romance, than I would have guessed. Marcus continued to make love to Elena. All night long, he made love to her with his fingers, his tongue and his cock, and with the finely crafted handle of the knife he had used to cut away Elena's clothing. In the privacy of the bedroom, the two took more pleasure from each other than I could have fantasised about, than I could have created in my very active imagination.

After, wrapped up tight in each other's arms, Marcus said, 'You will have an important spot in this house. Danae is lucky to have been given the rights to you. Through the years, you will bring much money to the temple, but you will do more than that.'

Elena waited, silent, wondering.

'You know the power that *hetairai* have over the men in this community. How the words of one woman have caused wars, have ended reigns of power. Danae is too well known to be of much use to us. But as I have infiltrated the ranks of the soldiers, you will infiltrate the bedroom of the captains, you will bed those highest ranking officials. The child of your womb will be our future king.'

Elena realised that her father was wrong. The Oracle was right. If Marcus spoke the truth, and Elena trusted him implicitly, then Elena would give birth one day to the king of their people. Her child would grow up to rule all. The journal said:

> *I turned over and wrapped myself in Marcus' arms. I wanted nothing else but to serve Aphrodite as she and Danae would have me serve. No, I lied. I wanted something else. I wanted to serve Marcus, as well, side by side to give him everything he needed, everything he wanted, every fantasy that played itself out in his mind.*

This is what *I* wanted, too. This is what I wanted to do for Anthony.

> *Marcus said, 'The party is over tonight. The festivities are finished and all of the guests have left. The only thing that remains is for you to be presented to the rest of the girls.'*
>
> *'I met them,' I said, confused.*
>
> *'You met them, yes,' he agreed, 'but you were not presented to them. You were brought into the house, rushed into it to prepare for tonight. This morning –' and he indicated with a look skywards that it was morning, '– you will be presented to them as a sister.'*
>
> *He cut me loose of my bindings, finally, and had me sit on the edge of the bed. While I watched, he called out to the hall, and a young handmaiden came rushing in to help us. Marcus instructed her with his wishes, speaking softly to her, pointing and indicating what it was that she was to do. Without a word, she came to the bed, and she used cosmetics to adorn me, painting my face. I watched with the help of a polished silver mirror. I had been told that I was pretty. All my life, people have spoken of my beauty. But now, with the help of these added powders, the girl transformed me into a woman, a creature who would rival the goddesses with her beauty.*
>
> *'Your lips are more luscious than Danae's,' Marcus said softly. 'Look at yourself. Look at your beauty.'*

I stared at that other person, the vision in the mirror. I gazed upon her in awe, as mesmerised as Narcissus was by his own captivating reflection. Then I shook my head, not wanting to look any further.

My eyelids were gilded, my lips slicked with colour as dark as the ripest berries. She decorated my hair with a glittery powder, then wove it through with fresh flowers. When she was finished, she dressed me in another transparent toga, and then Marcus led me from the room, down the hallway to the large living area.

No trace of the party remained, except for my new-found sisters, all curled up asleep on the various beds and sofas. At Marcus' approach, the women awoke, stared up at us, gawked at me.

'Like Danae,' Marcus said softly, 'you have the ability to transform. Only a little preparation and you take on the body and the spirit of the goddess.'

My sisters did not move from their positions, eyes wide, mouths slack. Marcus said, 'Show respect,' and they bowed their heads before me. What could I do? I walked among them, touching them lightly, letting them feel my acceptance of the honour they bestowed upon me. And then, moving back into the safety of Marcus' shadow, I waited for his next command.

He remained silent.

'What do you want from me?' I whispered.

'Nothing but to observe your beauty.'

I stayed still, as still as I could, while he stared at me, his eyes filled with the same wonderment of the women in Danae's household. Danae, herself, curled up on one of the sofas with several other girls nestled close around her, simply looked at me and smiled.

'You will make Aphrodite proud,' Marcus said. 'You will make all of us proud.'

I lowered my head, as my new sisters had done, and sighed. I could ask nothing else. Even my father, had he been present, could have expected nothing more. The Oracle came true in an instant and my fate, my destiny, was sealed.

Chapter Twenty

The party went on and on. I thought, hoped really, that Anthony might show up, surprising me as Byron had. That he might suddenly appear when Nora was passing out the bright-pink hats indicating which contestants would be invited to join the reality show. If he had come, he would have seen two girls collapsing in hysterical sobs when they did not make the cut. He would have seen one future bartender kiss Nora fully on the lips and another do that bending over the bar trick that Nora had talked so eloquently about.

But he didn't.

I waited as long as I could, before feeling the muscles in my body start to tighten. Anticipation made me tense all over. The possibility of being let down was almost too much to bear. I drove the bouncer crazy, asking repeatedly whether Anthony had arrived. 'No, honey,' he said. 'I promise to let you know when your man shows up.' *If* he shows up, I thought, but didn't say. I didn't want to hear the words aloud.

Finally, I gave Nora a hug and told her I had to go.

'You're not staying? You *have* to stay.'

'No.' I shook my head. 'I have to go.'

She gave me a look that let me know she understood.

Before heading towards Anthony's apartment, I changed my clothing. It was crazy to do this, but I no longer felt as if I was operating on a completely sane level. Besides, where had acting normal ever gotten me? Wasn't it time for me to break out of my box? I stood in the fancy bathroom at the Pink Fedora and looked myself over. I wasn't in costume any longer, but I might as well have been. A man walked in and gave me the once over, his head nodding in approval – Nora's bathrooms are unisex as might be expected.

I slipped out of the room before he could say a word.

I arrived at Anthony's apartment later, wearing only my lightest nightgown, one that reminded me of the togas described in the story. It was a sheer, silvery floor-length number, made of expensive silk. I wore it under my black cashmere coat, which I took off outside of his building, shivering in the cool night air while waiting for him to let me in. I prayed to God that he would let me in, that he wouldn't leave me out there in the cold. What would I do if he refused to speak to me? I couldn't go back to the club, back to Nora's house ...

The buzzer sounded and I gratefully made my way up to his apartment floor.

He opened the door quickly and, at first, he didn't say a word, simply stared. I wondered what he was thinking until he motioned for me to follow him down the hall to his bedroom. The patter of our footsteps on the polished wooden floor sounded so loud to me. I felt as if we'd already been down this path together, and that we were replaying that experience in slow motion. Every movement seemed heightened. Every action seemed choreographed.

I'd never been to his room before, but I didn't focus too seriously on the surroundings, other than taking note of the raised circular track, the model trains in place at the starting line. After that, I focused on his four-poster bed. It was unmade and, when I put out my hand, I felt warmth at the edge of the bed sheet. I pictured him in bed, and then visualised myself under the covers, naked, alone. I didn't need him for this first fantasy; I only needed his heat. Needed to wrap myself in the sheets that smelled of his body, needed to put my head in the indents on his pillow, mould myself into the shadow that he had left behind.

But normal people don't do things like that, do they? Normal people don't strip off their clothes and climb into their date's bed. I still had some little desire to be normal, even if it didn't make sense any more.

I sat on the edge of the bed while he stood in front of me, and now his fingers moved to lift my nightgown, pull it up to my shoulders, and his lips followed the trail of his hands. He revealed more and more pale skin, and his fingers moved all the way up my ribs to my small breasts. My body trembled as he touched me. He was being so gentle. Too gentle. What was this? What did I want from him?

Anthony pushed me back on the bed, slid the nightgown over my head and off me. He straddled me, looked down at me. 'Good girls are rewarded,' he said. 'Did you know that?'

When I shook my head, he said, 'Liar,' and I instantly blushed. Was I lying? I didn't know. Confusion beat through me, and I wished I could find my voice and explain. Wished I could confess to him everything I'd wanted from the start, from that very first kiss, from long before his lips had met mine.

He put his hands forwards and into my hair. His fingertips stroked my hair away from my face, then tangled in the strands of caramel softness pulled free.

'Don't be silent,' he said. 'Talk to me.'

'I'm sorry.'

'But don't say that.'

'I don't know what else to say. I'm sorry. I'm sorry that I didn't trust you. I'm sorry that I went behind your back. I'm –'

'Don't say that,' he said again. 'It's not what I want to hear.'

'Then what?' I asked. I could feel how hard he was against me, and how much I was desperate to feel him inside of me.

He said, 'Good girls are rewarded, and bad girls are punished.'

And now I did understand. He didn't want me to tell him I was sorry. He wanted me to tell him what I needed.

'Punish me,' I said, my voice faltering, dying down to a whisper.

'How?'

Oh, God, he was going to make me say everything. He was going to make me ask. I wanted to hide my face in his sheets. I wanted to flee – but not really. Because I understood now that fleeing didn't get me what I wanted. And more than anything else, I wanted him to put me over his lap and spank me. Spank me and then fuck me.

'How, Eleanor?'

He knew. He was playing with me. He'd had that paddle out. He knew everything that I wanted. And *still* he was tormenting me by making me ask. But that was part of the whole scenario. I wasn't some blow-up doll, without a mind, without a heart. I had to take responsibility for my actions. I had to ask him for what I wanted.

I took a deep breath. One that I could feel in the very depth of my soul. 'Spank me,' I said, and then as if the act of confessing had opened some previously dammed floodgates, the pent-up words finally came out in a rush. 'Spank me, Anthony. Please, Anthony. Put me over your lap.' My voice trembled, but I didn't stop. I needed him to understand how much I wanted everything I was asking for. I would have gotten down on my knees and begged if that's what he required, but luckily, Anthony took pity on me.

As I was speaking, he began to make my fantasies come true. His hands were strong and warm and, in a flash, he had me upended over his sturdy lap. Even through the faded fabric of his old blue Levis, I could feel how hard he was beneath me, how much this encounter turned him on. We were the perfect pair in this situation. He wanted to give me everything I so desperately craved, and I wanted to take everything he had to give. Had I always known he would? Was that why I had avoided this for so long? Keeping a fantasy just that – a fantasy – made me never have to fully confront my true desires. But now everything was different. Anthony knew.

He understood.

For the first series of spanks, he simply used his hand on top of my panties. But even with his bare hand alone, he warmed my rear for me, the heavy sensation of his open palm against my satin knickers reverberating throughout my whole body. Over and over his hand connected with my panty-clad bottom. Over and over, I responded to the new sensation as if trained. My pussy became swimmingly wet, and I could not believe how turned on this sensual punishment was making me.

That's another lie.

I lived for every single smack of his hand against me. My heart seemed to beat at the same rhythm of his hand on my ass, and I could feel my juices pooling between my nether lips, the liquid of my sexual desire filling me. I knew that if he touched me there – just *touched* me – I would come. The orgasm would be sweet. I knew it.

But, greedy thing that I was, I wanted more.

'Please –' I begged, hoping that he wouldn't mind my requests. I had no idea how he would react to my speaking. Once he'd gotten me to ask for what I wanted, he might have been the type to expect to control every part of the encounter. I didn't know, yet I couldn't stop myself. 'Please, Anthony,' my tremulous voice begged, 'take my panties down.' I wriggled my hips as I spoke, letting him know with the urging of my body what I wanted as well as my words.

Don't deny me, I pleaded, silently. Give me what I need. I've waited so long. I've been such a good girl. Such a bad girl. I've been desperate . . .

'Why?' he asked, and his voice was so deliciously stern that I could hardly control myself.

'I want you to spank me bare. I want you to take down my panties.'

Once again, as I spoke, my wishes became reality. His fingertips didn't linger within the waistband of my panties. He had my knickers down my thighs so fast that the fabric almost whistled in the air. But then, for one agonising moment, he waited, and I could guess that he was admiring his handiwork. My behind must have been charmingly pink by now, blushing rosy all over, my rear cheeks far pinker than ever before.

Don't, I begged in my head. Don't stop. Don't wait.

I rocked my hips against his, and I could feel once more how hard he was. A burst of thankfulness ran through me. I needed to know that this scenario turned him on as much as it did me.

Then his fingertips traced over my rounded ass cheeks, and he seemed to be doing more than admiring me – but now inspecting me. Embarrassment flooded through me, and I turned my head into the crook of my arm. I could feel myself blushing harder than ever, and I guessed that my face was becoming as scarlet as my blooming rear cheeks.

How long would he make me wait before he continued?

That query was answered almost immediately. As if determined to outdo his work so far, his hand came up and then down, connecting ferociously with my naked bum. The spank was louder than ever, and the pain was instantaneous. Yet this was what I had dreamed of. This was what I required. His hand came down again on the other side, and then continued quickly, landing a medley of blows back and forth on my rapidly reddening rear.

He smacked my right cheek, then my left, then focused on the underside of my rear, the most tender part of the skin, the sweetest spot. I rocked on his lap as he spanked me, but not because I wanted to get away. Thoughts of escape were far from my mind. Redemption was the only thing I craved.

Anthony didn't say a word as he punished me. He was as intent on the act of spanking me as he was at any other task I'd ever witnessed him doing. Right now, I was his work. I was his focus. As I revelled in being the most important thing in his world, the pain echoed inside me.

I had asked for this!

That thought sounded loud in my mind, louder even than the smacks of his hand on my naked skin. I'd begged for this punishment. I deserved it.

I tried my best to stay still for him, but I failed. He had not told me to hold myself steady for him, and I was grateful for that because I thrashed across his lap, my legs kicking in the air. To make his job easier on himself, he scissored one leg over both of mine, and stilled me this way, keeping me in check as he continued my punishment.

I thought of the girl in the story. I thought of my fantasy of Anthony spanking me in the conference room. I realised that all I'd ever wanted was this – to be thrashed like this, by Anthony. How had he known? Way back at our Christmas party, when he'd kissed me, and then let his hand find my ass for a light little tap – how had he known? Was I that transparent? To the right lover, were all my desires visible?

The spanking went on until tears wet my face, and then suddenly, as if he knew my exact breaking point, Anthony was pulling me tightly into his arms and kissing me. Kissing away my tears. Kissing my wet cheeks, my full lips. I felt so exposed, my panties still twisted around one of my ankles, my bottom throbbing from his punishment. My hair a mess, strands in my face. My eyes wet.

But Anthony didn't seem to find me out of sorts at all. I understood how I'd been pushing my fantasies down, denying them. This is what I wanted. This is what I'd always wanted.

At the end of the kiss, Anthony bit hard into my bottom lip. I relished the way that felt, the spark of pain that made my clit twitch. When we parted, I tried to hide my smile, but I knew he saw it, knew it didn't matter any more. I sucked in my lip, feeling the indents from his teeth there, touching them as I traced over the marks with my tongue. Adoring them.

'That's your reward,' he said, and I heard the dark laughter in his low voice. 'That's the kind of reward very good girls get.'

I wanted to laugh, too, because everything suddenly felt so right. Nothing in my world was wrong. He was on me, with me, needing me, and it was right.

We did not re-enact the scene from the story. He didn't paint me up and stare at me. Instead, he fucked me in his bed. Not using anything but fingers and tongue, lips and cock. He made my upper thighs wet with the decadent sex of my arousal, and he teased me for it, slapped my thighs as they grew wetter still. When I came the first time, he went and got his paddle, and he used this on my naked ass, reddening it even more than it had been all night.

It was a vicious circle. The more he spanked or slapped or pinched me, the more excited I grew, and the more he punished me for the arousal. It was all a lesson.

'Good girls are rewarded,' Anthony whispered as he slid inside of me. 'Sometimes the reward will be pain.' His fingers sought out my nipples. Pinching them until I tossed back my head and cried. 'Sometimes the pain will make you come.'

He was right. I came. I came and came, my body shaking, my voice lost against his skin, biting into his shoulder as he took me. God, I came. Squeezing him over and over, aching with the feeling of being overwhelmed.

He taught me lessons. I learned from him. All night long, I learned.

* * *

After, it was just like the journal. Outside, dawn was breaking over a quiet city. Inside, we lazed in bed, both of us naked, my skin flushed all over from his love and his heat. Anthony looked at the clock on the bedside table and said the numbers out loud. It was almost five in the morning. The hours had passed so quickly, they'd blurred together.

'I still owe you dinner, you know.' His voice was light, his tone cavalier. I wasn't hungry. Wasn't anything but happy. 'But I guess it's really breakfast time now.'

I sighed, feeling as warm as a pool of melted butter. I didn't want to move at all. 'I'm not hungry,' I said.

Anthony began to kiss his way down my body once more. 'Breakfast,' he said softly, 'is in the eye of the beholder.'

'That's beauty,' I corrected him.

'Yes,' he agreed, looking down at me. 'That is definitely beauty.'

'I didn't mean it like that.'

'Don't blush,' he said, catching me almost on the brink. Blushing comes naturally to me. Like breathing. But I did my best to meet his gaze, to look straight into his eyes. 'Of course, you meant it. Beauty is in the eye of the beholder. And anyone who beheld this –' he gestured to include my entire body '– would agree that I have beauty before me.'

Without another word, he began to lick his way even lower, finding the split between my legs and starting to dine. Only moments before, I'd thought that I would never move again. Now, I stared up at his ceiling, feeling awash in a range of emotions. The way Anthony touched me was unique. His hands were so firm on my body, yet his tongue was gentle, making the tiniest little lapping motions over and over on my clit. I started to breathe faster, and Anthony raised his head. 'Don't worry,' he said, 'I'm not going to leave you wanting more. You trust me. And I'll make it happen.'

Trust him. That's all he wanted from me.

This time, when I looked down at him, I kept my eyes open. I focused on him, on his dark hair, his strong hands. I watched him work, and I let the climax come to me, rather than chase after it. Anthony was right.

He didn't let me down.

ThePinkFedora.blogspot.com

It's happening, and it's real.

Reality, that is. You Can Leave Your Hat On, *each Saturday night on the Bijoux Network.*

The show has started, the contestants are at the gate. We'll be whittling them down, one by one, until only the best remains. And that lucky someone will be King or Queen of the bar at the Pink Fedora. Watch us at 10:00 if you're a homebody. Or come see for yourselves if you live in La-La Land. We are waiting for you to order your drinks and place your votes. Do you want an Angel Kiss or a Denmark Orgasm? Are you longing for a Kiss in the Dark or a Long Hot Night?

Sexy drinks aside, let's focus on the sexy bartenders!

Are you dreaming of Dameron or are you routing for Roan? Does Bella make you want to beg or does Bowen make you want to bend over?

You tell us.

And I'll tell you – I'm caught in a conundrum myself. I don't do relationships – most people know that about me. No judgment to you happily settled couples, but the grim badge of monogamy is simply not my thing. Yet, I've recently been bouncing back and forth between two handsome hunks: Travis and Dean. Dean and Travis. They each know about the other and so far, there has been no explosions. No jealousy. No guilt.

But I'm having my own personal, private reality show. One contestant has to go.

Follow along with me, and I'll tell you all my secrets.

Kisses,

Nora

Quote for the Day: As Axl Rose said, 'It's not easy to be in a one-on-one relationship if the other person is not going to allow me to be with other people.'

Chapter Twenty-One

'So what happened with Anthony?'

I shrugged. 'Nothing important.'

Nora's enormous emerald eyes bored into mine. She knows when I'm lying to her. But I wasn't lying now. I was teasing. There's a difference. Yet because I was dying to tell her everything, I couldn't hold out very long. I found myself the first to laugh, and I started speaking in a rush, wanting to tell her everything at once, and starting at the end rather than the beginning – 'Well, nothing except that we're going to Greece on Thursday. ARTSI will pay for the journey. We're supposed to research to see if the journal can be backed up, if we can find other corroborating writings to lend it more credibility.'

'You're going where, Eli?'

'To Greece. Athens, specifically. I wish I had the funds to take the Orient Express all throughout Europe with him, because we are both due to have a few weeks' vacation. But money's tight right now. So . . .'

Nora squinted her eyes at me, and I could tell that she was trying to figure out if I was joking with her. Traditionally, she's been the jokester of our duo. Still, after silently regarding me for several moments, Nora seemed to realise that I wasn't kidding.

'I know this is all happening fast. But it's not what you think. We're going to the dig where my Aunt Rose found that pot. I want to know more about the lovers who wrote the manuscript. I need to know more. I don't know why, but I do. Anthony is going with me because he can translate ancient Greek. And he has vacation time, and he just wants to.'

While I watched, Nora stood up from her desk and came to sit at my side on the sofa. She had a pack of cards in one hand and began to deal out a game of Solitaire, her favorite way to calm her nerves. Nora is as poker-faced as they come, and she cheats even when she plays herself, but I like to watch her fingers dance over the cards.

She didn't have anything to say for several minutes, which was unusual for her. Or maybe she had too much to say, but she didn't know where to start. Finally, she asked, 'Did the Little Red Riding Hood costume make that big a hit?'

I burst out laughing. 'Something like that. I thought you'd approve, you know. You're always telling me that I'm going to grow dusty and old from sitting inside the museum. That I'll grow crooked from bending over my computer typing all day. Now, I'm doing something exciting, for once. Something you'd do.'

Nora looked up at me again and she shot me a half-smile. 'That's it. That's the problem. If you start doing the things that I would do, what am I going to do?' She sounded as if she were only partly kidding.

'What do you mean?'

'Will I become you?'

I shook my head. That didn't even seem possible. Nora could hardly stand dressing like me for a few hours. She'd never fall into the sort of rut I'd found myself in. 'We'll do the things together,' I said. 'Except, not this thing. This thing I'm going to do on my own ... with Anthony.'

Nora's cards found the correct places as if of their own accord. Red queens on black kings. Black jacks on red queens. I watched as she uncovered the ace of hearts and moved it to the top row above the rest of the cards. She said, 'I probably ought to tell you that it's too soon. That you're on the rebound, but I somehow don't think you are.' I watched the ten of diamonds find a spot on the jack of clubs. 'Besides, I've never been the one to tell you what to do. You've always done a good job of that yourself.'

'Not such a good job,' I told her. 'Look where I was for the past four years.'

'You didn't think you had a choice. Or, rather, you thought you'd made the best choice possible.'

I shrugged. I didn't know. Why had I stayed so long with Byron? Had I decided that dreams were only for dreaming?

I stared from the cards to Nora again as she took a deep breath. 'Fuck it, Eli. It's great. Go to Greece and have an amazing time. Bring me back a souvenir. A Greek sailor or something.'

She set down the deck, stuck with her hand, and I picked up the stack and flipped through the cards for her. Nora watched as I drew the jack of spades. She seemed to be waiting for me to tell her more, to tell her something else. 'Before I pack, I have to ask you a question,' I said. Nora looked at me expectantly. 'Have you decided?'

'Decided?'

'About Dean or Travis.'

'You've been reading my blog!' She looked exceptionally thrilled.

I grinned at her. 'All right, so I do read it sometimes. Insomnia, you know.' I winked at her, fully aware I was echoing her own statement. 'And I'm curious. Are you going for a dom like Dean? Or is Travis more your speed? I know you're writing to please your fans, but have you decided?'

She nodded, still focused on the cards.

'Which one?'

'Which one what?'

'Nora –'

She laughed, pleased with herself. 'You know me, Eli. I can never choose just one. But we're working it out. Dean on weekdays, Travis on the weekends. Seems like a good plan for now.'

She stood suddenly and walked to the blood-red file cabinet in the corner of her office. I watched as she opened a drawer in the middle and rifled through the contents. Even from where I sat, I could see that her files were the opposite of mine – chaos has always controlled Nora's world – but I held my tongue. After several moments, she seemed to have found what she was looking for, and she brought a folder to the table and set it on top of the cards

'I was winning,' I told her.

'You're right. You're winning big time.'

'What do you mean? What is this?'

Nora didn't answer right away. She just ran her fingers down the list of names and dollar figures. When she got to my own name, I looked up at her. 'I don't understand.'

'You're a partner.'

'In what?'

'The clubs.'

'How is that possible?'

'I always told you I'd pay you back.'

'For what? Coffee?'

'Everything. Over the years at school, you paid for me so often. I wouldn't have eaten nearly as well without your help. I might not have eaten at all. I thought hair dye was more important than food.'

I shrugged. I've always been of the mentality that if I could help out a friend, I would. I knew Nora used to keep track of those expenses in her little notebook, but I never gave that much thought.

'But what's it mean?'

'You're a silent partner. You own a tenth of the empire. There's an account in Switzerland with your name on it. Why not take the Orient Express, Eli? You deserve it.'

'Why didn't you tell me before?'

'I was saving it for a rainy day. Or a sunny day. For the right day to share it with you. And I didn't want you to have to share it with Byron.'

'Oh, my God,' I said when I looked back down at the

numbers, when I understood what they meant. I felt tears in my eyes, but when I glanced up at Nora, she was looking down at the floor. I couldn't figure out what was bothering her.

'Nora –'

'It's nothing,' she said, but I didn't believe her.

'Come on, Nora. What's wrong? Everything's going well now. Your show. Your club. Your perfume. Your men.'

'You don't really need me any more,' she said softly.

'I always need you,' I told her. It was the truth. 'Always. I couldn't have come this far without you. Couldn't have transformed this much. Couldn't have gone after Anthony.'

'You'd have done it, Eleanor. You would have – with or without me.'

Now, I shook my head. 'Nora,' I said, 'you're my best friend. There is no without you.'

Chapter Twenty-Two

'Come here,' Anthony whispered.

'Where?' I was in bed, wrapped in his blankets, feeling as if I'd never move again.

'Here,' he said, and he grasped my hand, and I followed, followed him outside where he made yet another one of my fantasies come true. The air was cold and clear, and even though we were in the heart of Los Angeles, home to ten million people, it felt as if we had the whole city to ourselves.

On the fire escape, Anthony took me from behind. He had me put my hands on the chilled iron railing, had me stare out at the lights of the city, twinkling like a fairy city before us. Yes, the situation felt similar to that in my daydreams. But this was better because it was real. Anthony lined his body up with mine, not fucking me, not kissing me, just letting me feel his warmth against my skin. I couldn't have asked for a better sensation. Being so close to Anthony made me more aroused than anything I'd thought of – or nearly anything. Just his body pressed to mine. Because his body told me stories, made me promises:

If you trust yourself, then everything you want will come true. If you let yourself go and stop playing games, then I can make magic with you.

I thought for one quick flash of fucking Byron – our weekly routine, with everything in its place. U2 playing on the stereo during my weeks to choose. Some pompous jazzy combo playing if the choice of music selection was his. Who chooses Dave Brubeck as a background for sex?

With Anthony, there was no melody at all but the

sound of the traffic below. Distant and hollow. No routine, because all of this was uncharted territory. Yet, even though we were new to one another, I could sense his queries.

Did I trust him?

Would I give myself over to him?

I would. I agreed. My silence was all he needed. No questions, no preparation, no guessing what was to come. Anthony ran his hands along my arms and his touch sent a shiver through me. He cradled my breasts in his hands as gently as if he were holding two ripe pieces of fruit, then brushed my nipples with his thumbs. His touch created a yearning inside me. I could picture a fire in my mind, flames of orange and gold licking up and down beneath my skin. Still, I kept my tongue, didn't beg, didn't tell him what I wanted. This was Anthony's time to teach me, and I played the good pupil and remained silent.

Anthony worked his fingertips down my sides to my waist, and gripped me here. He held me steady, and then he slowly brought his cock against me. So slowly. Slipped it between my thighs and pressed forwards, teasing me with just the tip. This was delicious, dreamy, and the languidness made me realise what I'd missed for so long with Byron. We had equality, I suppose: you come first this week, I'll come first next. We were diligent score keepers, focused on our rights. We had the give and take of a modern relationship.

Screw give and take, I thought now.

Anthony pressed forwards, agonisingly slowly. My body accepted him, pulled on him, but he would not be rushed. 'Wait, baby,' he said when he felt me pushing my hips back against him. If I'd been in charge, the whole thing would have been over in minutes. In seconds. A flash of white-hot light and we'd be at the finish. Anthony wasn't interested in a big bang. He slid a bit deeper inside of me, and now he used his hands to split apart my nether lips. Cold air rushed over me, and I felt my heart throb.

'Oh, God,' I murmured, lowering my chin towards my chest, forcing myself to trust him. To let this scene unfold at his pace. I wanted to rush. I wanted to scream. Anthony had his own plans.

He thrust the slightest bit forwards, and I would have collapsed if he had not been holding me steady. He fucked me in slow motion, at his speed, his rhythm. I could not force him to go faster. I could not make him do anything at all. I had to abide by his wishes, play by his rules. My thoughts spiralled out of control, as if making up for the slow quality of this lovemaking session.

Sometimes what's important is not equality. Sometimes who goes first doesn't matter in the slightest. I realised with a sudden unexpected clarity that what I wanted most was to be taken, and Anthony took me.

Would there ever be something that he could do that I wouldn't like?

I didn't think so. I couldn't imagine.

Epilogue

On the train to Athens, Anthony spoke perfect Greek with the conductor. When he caught me giving him a quizzical stare, he shrugged, embarrassed. I wasn't accustomed to this gesture from him, but I recognised it as one of my own. Anthony looked as if he'd been caught doing something he wasn't supposed to.

'You're good,' I said. 'Why would you tell me you're not? Modesty aside, you really are excellent at speaking Greek.'

'Ancient Greek is different from modern Greek.'

I continued to stare at him. 'Come clean,' I said. 'I know you're teasing me, I can tell when you are, now. But I don't know why. What aren't you telling me?'

Anthony leaned in towards me and said, 'Can you keep a secret?'

I nodded.

'I'm Greek.'

I continued to stare at him, baffled.

'Half-Greek, really, on my mother's side. My father was English and my parents split when I was young. I spoke only Greek until I was in my early teens. Then I went to school in London and learned English there. Hence,' he said grandly, 'the accent.'

I was in shock. 'But why on earth wouldn't you tell me that? Why would you pretend it was so difficult for you to do the translation? You made me trade you things, made me dare you, when you could have done the whole thing in your sleep.'

'Ancient Greek really is different from modern Greek,' he insisted. 'Plus, if I told you I could do it all in an evening, I wouldn't have had the chance to really get to know you.'

I let his words sink in for a few seconds before responding. 'So you knew from the start? You made it seem as if you were working so hard at deciphering the pages. But you knew.'

He hesitated. 'Would I be on a train with you right now going to Athens? It would have just been a job. You would have dropped off the manuscript. I would have typed it up neatly. Then you would have gone on your merry way.'

'The pages would have still been porn.'

'But you might not have discussed them with me. You might have looked at me as if I were simply a helper. An assistant. You might have spent hours pondering the pages with Nora, rather than with me.'

I considered what he said, and decided he was right. 'Still,' I said, 'it wasn't entirely honest, Anthony. After all that –' I hesitated '– that trauma over me going behind your back. What do you have to say for yourself?'

'You thought I was lying to you, so you went behind my back to check up on me. I simply left out a bit of information that I didn't think was necessary to our relationship. And it was worth it, right? You'd never have seen my model train set, or ridden on my Harley. Or anything . . .' He let the sentence remain, unfinished, between us, and I instantly visualised Anthony behind me on the fire escape, the cold night air on our naked skin. I blushed, no great surprise there, then said, 'You never know. Nora believes it was fate that made me break that urn, fate that led me to your office with those tattered pieces of paper. That if it hadn't happened in that way, we would have ended up here due to some other circumstances.'

'Nora,' Anthony said slowly, 'is your very best friend in the world. I know this. And I've kept my mouth shut about everything you've said so far that she's told you. But now I must tell you exactly what I think. Best friend, or not, Nora is also a little bit crazy. And I mean that in the nicest possible way.'

I looked at him.

Anthony clarified. 'I believe that we had one chance, or, really, I had one chance to get you to notice me. And it worked.'

'You'd already gotten my attention,' I reminded him, 'at the Christmas party, under the mistletoe, with your –'

Anthony silenced me with a kiss, as warm and deep as it had been on that night, but now that I knew what a kiss like this could lead to, this one meant even more.

When we parted, Anthony looked at his watch. 'Twelve more hours,' he said sadly. 'How am I ever going to make it for that long?' He caressed my face gently, stroked my hair and then smiled broadly. He has an impish look when he smiles like that. 'And how are *you* going to wait that long?'

'Who said we had to?' I asked, not even believing myself as I uttered the words. Was I really going to be daring? Why not? The dark-haired conductor strolled by us, and Anthony flagged him down, requesting a blanket and two pillows. I leaned back in my seat and closed my eyes as Anthony covered us both with the soft grey-and-white-striped blanket. He didn't do anything else, at first. I didn't make a move either. I knew that Anthony would set the pace.

I was right.

Anthony reclined his seat to match mine. His hand slid beneath the blanket and found my fingers. He squeezed my hand once, then let it go and allowed his fingers to continue wandering. I was wearing a dress that buttoned from neck to hemline. Anthony deftly undid three buttons in the centre of the dress, and I sighed. He pressed his lips to my ear and murmured, 'I've never done it on a train, with all my love of engines.'

'Now?' I asked, suggesting it.

Anthony's fingers slid into the opening of my pale-yellow dress – quite a change from my staid black suits

– and then moved downwards, searching out the waistband of my panties. I was wearing a pair purchased with Nora on our latest lingerie escapade. For once, I had gone to the racks of colour, shunning the black I've worn my whole life. These ones were white satin and rode low on my hips. Anthony pushed them down even further, feeling skin he had shaved bare himself, parting the lips of my pussy very gently and then stroking between my lips with his third finger. Wetness enveloped his finger and he pushed it in further, slipped it in until I sighed and leaned my head back.

'Tell me how it feels,' he whispered to me. 'Tell me what you're thinking.'

Once again, as they had so often in the past few weeks, words failed me. But this time the lack of mental ability was a good thing. This time, the failure to find the right word came because of the happiness in my chest, making it difficult for me to speak, making my breath start to come in a rush from only the tiniest touch of Anthony's fingers.

'Tell me what you're thinking,' he said again.

Even with my eyes closed, I knew he was watching the change come over me. He had said that he liked to see it happen. That witnessing my arousal was more intense than any other foreplay he'd ever experienced. As his fingers moved in and out slowly, I could sense that he would take his time.

That was fine with me.

We had all the time in the world.